Between Shadows and Light

LEAH OMAR

PEMBERLEY PRESS

Between Shadows and Light
©2024 Leah Omar

All rights reserved. This is a work of fiction. All characters, organizations, and events are either a part of the author's imagination or used fictitiously.

No part of this publication may be reproduced, distributed, or transmitted in any form or by any means, including photocopying, recording, or other electronic or mechanical methods, without prior written permission of the publisher, except in the case of brief quotations embodied in critical reviews and certain other noncommercial uses permitted by copyright law.

Published by: Pemberley Press
Edited by: Cindy Hale Editing Services
Paperback ISBN: 979-8-89546-502-8
eBook ISBN: 979-8-89546-503-5

Book Cover Design and Interior Formatting by 100Covers.

Table of Contents

Chapter One 1

Chapter Two 9

Chapter Three. 13

Chapter Four 23

Chapter Five. 29

Chapter Six 37

Chapter Seven. 45

Chapter Eight.. 55

Chapter Nine 65

Chapter Ten 71

Chapter Eleven.. 83

Chapter Twelve.. 89

Chapter Thirteen 99

Chapter Fourteen.. 107

Chapter Fifteen.. 117

Chapter Sixteen.. 123

Chapter Seventeen 131

Chapter Eighteen.. 137

Chapter Nineteen 147

Chapter	Page
Chapter Twenty	155
Chapter Twenty-One	163
Chapter Twenty-Two	173
Chapter Twenty-Three	181
Chapter Twenty-Four	193
Chapter Twenty-Five	207
Chapter Twenty-Six	215
Chapter Twenty-Seven	227
Chapter Twenty-Eight	237
Chapter Twenty-Nine	245
Chapter Thirty	253
Chapter Thirty-One	261
Chapter Thirty-Two	269
Chapter Thirty-Three	277
Chapter Thirty-Four	285
Chapter Thirty-Five	295
Chapter Thirty-Six	305
Chapter Thirty-Seven	315
Chapter Thirty-Eight	325
Epilogue	337
About the Author	347

To my mom:

Thank you for suggesting I write this book all those years ago, and for the work you've done your entire life, caring for those who are often unseen. You've touched their lives. You've touched mine.

Chapter One

For a nursing home where everyone's come to die, there isn't a dull moment.

"You know you can't leave, Joe." I gently place my hand on his shoulder and pull him away from the door.

Joe initially resists my touch but then turns and steps back.

"It's like a prison in here," he says. "Look outside, Birdie. There isn't a cloud in the sky. The sun is shining. And I'm stuck in here where it smells like death and dirty Depends."

I suppress a smile and guide Joe into one of the lobby chairs where many of the other residents are. An old episode of *Gunsmoke* plays on the big television, but most of the people are slouched over, asleep in their wheelchairs.

"It's nothing like a prison here," I say. "You get to take the bus every day. I bet they don't let you do that in prison."

"There are still too many rules," he says, folding his arms over his chest.

"You're right." I place a pillow beside him to prop him up. "But the rules are there to keep you and the other residents safe. The bus will be here at eleven and will take you anywhere in town that your heart desires."

"You're lucky you're cute," Joe says, turning toward the television. "Because your bossiness is getting on my nerves."

"You're lucky you're cute too, Joe," I say. "Because you trying to escape is getting on my nerves."

Joe tries to cover his mouth to suppress his laugh, but it comes out anyway. I can't help but smile this time. Joe and I have had a daily argument since the day I started at the nursing home about two months ago. He's had a challenging time adjusting to the rules and hates more than anything that there is a code to get out of the building.

"I'll be back at eleven to get you all on the bus," I say. "But until then, watch some *Gunsmoke*."

"I've seen every episode. At least a hundred times," Joe says as I walk away. "It's all that's ever playing in this damn lobby."

I go back to finishing my morning rounds. I pop into Marilyn's room, but she's sound asleep, her television blaring in the corner. I hit the off button and check on her.

Ever since being put on new meds, she's slept a lot. Her family usually pops in for their daily visit around noon.

After checking on Marilyn, I continue down the hallway, past the bird sanctuary, the library, and on to the largest rooms where some of our married residents reside.

"Hey there, Sunny." I knock lightly on his already open door. He turns to me and smiles.

"Well, Birdie. You're a sight for sore eyes."

His eyes shine with the grin that extends across his face. He pivots his blue chair to face me.

"Is Sis already at her morning therapy?"

Sunny nods. "You just missed her."

I sit in the chair next to him, needing to give my feet a rest. Sunny's wife goes to cognitive stimulation therapy twice a day for her Alzheimer's, which is part of the memory care programming at the nursing home. Sunny needs this break from Sis as much as she needs the extra care.

"Who's meeting you for lunch today?"

After working here for only two months, I know the family and friends of the residents almost as well as I know the residents themselves. Sunny is one of the more popular people in the nursing home. He doesn't need to be here. He's sharp, and although his body moves slower than it probably once did, he's in great shape overall. He's here only because Sis needs to be, and he doesn't want to be without her.

"Walt's already been by for coffee," Sunny says. "Camilla is bringing the kids over for lunch."

"Oh, good," I say. "It's been too long since I've held Signe and Asher."

"You're welcome to have lunch with us." Sunny pushes himself out of the chair. "Camilla always brings something fresh and homemade."

"I appreciate that." I also get up. "But if I have lunch with you, all of the other residents will know you're my favorite, and we can't have that."

Sunny holds his stomach as he laughs. "And here I thought everyone already knew."

The truth is, I like all of the residents at the Wheaton Nursing Home equally and have a unique relationship with each one. Sunny, though, is someone special. He reminds me of my own grandpa back in South Dakota, who passed away when I was a teenager. The residents are what make me eager and excited to come to work every day.

"I'll check in on you and Sis later." I pause at the door. "And enjoy those grandbabies of yours."

"You know I will." Sunny lifts his hand to wave.

At eleven, I make sure everyone who wants to take the bus is safely on. It stops at a few sights in town, and the residents who are still mobile have an opportunity to pick up snacks for their rooms, supplies they're running short on, or just a chance to get out and remember what life felt like before they were in a nursing home. The staff takes turns chaperoning the bus around town, and next week is my shift.

The door to my mom's office is open so I peek inside, but she's not there. She's the reason I moved to Wheaton and work at the nursing home. Her mom was moved here for their specialty in memory care when I was young. When she found out that the nursing home was on the verge of closing, she stepped in as the administrator. She's only been here for a little less than a year but has been working hard to turn this place around. When I desperately wanted out of being a travel nurse, she suggested that I come work for her.

The lunch crowd starts filing past me, so I turn to walk with them to the cafeteria. The food around here isn't great, but my mom is trying to improve that too.

"Is your family here?" I say to Marilyn as she moves past me with her walker.

"They should be, Ms. Birdie." Marilyn is a Southern belle and only ever addresses me formally.

I help everyone get situated at their tables. I laugh to myself that everyone here ends up in the same places almost every day, much like a high school lunchroom. Even in their old age, they have their cliques. There's the group of men who play cards. The bingo group. The knitting ladies, and then there is always the table of the non-verbal residents.

Many of their families join them for lunch too, and I always find my way to Abigail, who has never had a visitor in the two months I've worked here.

"Hey, Birdie." I stop walking and turn to Sunny.

Camilla smiles and waves, her son, Asher, on her lap and daughter, Signe, in a chair next to Sunny. Next to her is a man I've never seen before.

"I'd like you to meet my grandson," Sunny says, gesturing toward the man. "This is—"

"You must be Robby," I say. "Camilla's brother. I hear you recently got married. Congrats."

"No, this is—"

"Liam." The man narrows his brow, studying me.

"My oldest grandson." Sunny places his hand around Liam's back and smiles. "He's visiting from New York City."

"For how long, Uncle Liam?" Signe turns her attention to him, and he grabs her and puts her on his lap.

"It's really nice to meet you," I say, and he only nods in acknowledgment.

"Birdie is my favorite nurse in this place." Sunny grins at me.

"Well," I say, biting the corner of my bottom lip as I step back from the table. "I hope you enjoy your visit to Wheaton, and Camilla, it was great to see you."

"You as well." Camilla warmly smiles at me, but I glance at Liam, who continues to stare at me, expressionless.

How can that man be a relative of one of the nicest men I've ever met? He was rude and dismissive and looked at me like he was too good to share the same space with me. I turn and glance over my shoulder, and Liam continues to watch me as I walk away toward Abigail.

"Hi, Abigail," I say, gripping the back of the chair next to her. "Do you mind if I sit and join you for lunch today?"

Her smile is from ear to ear. "Oh, I'd love that, Birdie. Thank you."

She picks at her food, and I open my brown paper bag and put my peanut-butter-and-jelly sandwich on the table.

"I don't think I've ever asked you." I turn toward Abigail. "But do you have a family? I've never seen them here visiting."

Abigail pushes her potatoes around on her plate. "I have two daughters. One lives in Minneapolis, and the other lives in Davenport, Iowa."

"Do they visit you here?" I press on.

"Oh, no." Abigail shakes her head. "We haven't spoken in several years. My grandkids are all grown, and I haven't seen them in ages either."

"I'm really sorry to hear that," I say. "It must be hard."

Abigail closes her eyes. "It is, but we all have to live with our decisions, I suppose."

I open my mouth to respond, but Camilla approaches our table with Asher on her hip, his head heavy on her shoulder.

"Hey, Birdie." Camilla smiles. "We're having Asher's second birthday party this Saturday. It's from two to four at our place on the lake. It will be pure chaos, but we'll have a lot of food and beverages for the adults, and Jake and I would love for you to come. I mean, if you don't already have other plans."

"I'm free," I say. "That sounds fun."

Camilla laughs. "Well, I don't know if I would classify a second birthday party as fun, but I'm so happy you can come. Give me your number, and I'll text you the address."

I hand Camilla my phone, and we exchange numbers. She texts me the address. I've made no effort to get to know anyone outside of this professional setting since arriving here. I'm not sure how long I'll stay, but my mom seems to love it and I want to be near her.

"Don't bring a gift," Camilla says. "Seriously. Asher has more toys than he knows what to do with."

"Thanks for the invite," I say.

"See you Saturday," Camilla says. "Now it's time to get my boy down for his nap, or he's going to disturb the peace here." Camilla chuckles as she walks away.

Abigail places her hand on mine when I turn my attention back to her. "Good for you, Birdie," she says. "Get out there. Meet people. The lonely life isn't meant for everyone and certainly not for you."

"Well," I say, taking a bite of my sandwich. "It isn't meant for you either."

Chapter Two

My mom works much longer hours than I do, so I often find myself at the house alone. When I moved to Wheaton two months ago, my mom had just moved into this house after living in an apartment when she first arrived in town. The house is over a hundred years old and much bigger than needed for two people, but my mom got a great deal on it—probably because it's directly next to the town cemetery. I plan to fix up what I can and leave it better than when I found it.

"Hey, Birdie," my mom calls from downstairs. "Are you up?"

"I've been up for hours," I call back. I pull my shirt over my head and go down the creaky, winding stairs to find my mom standing in the entryway.

"You're back earlier than I expected." I glance at my watch, and it's only one in the afternoon. Usually, on Saturdays, my mom doesn't walk through the door until at least dinnertime.

My mom's face lights up when she sees me. "You look nice. Are you going somewhere?"

It's been rare since living in Wheaton to wear anything besides scrubs. But today, I put on actual clothes.

"You know Sunny and Sis's granddaughter, Camilla?"

My mom nods.

"Well, she invited me to her son's birthday party. He's turning two."

Her smile grows even wider. "That's so great, Birdie. I want you to meet people. You're too young to be cooped up in this house hanging out with me."

"You could try to meet people too," I say. "You're also too young to have no life whatsoever."

My mom laughs and walks into the kitchen, and I follow her.

"I need to get the nursing home stabilized before I can pull back on some of the hours."

She's been my only constant my entire life.

My mom had me when she was eighteen. She and my dad were high school sweethearts, and she gave birth to me the summer after their senior year. They got married the month before I was born and lived on my grandparents' farm in South Dakota. My dad left us for good when I was one. He stayed in the same small town throughout my life, so he was always around but never in the role of a dad. I was raised by my mom and grandparents, and my relationship with my sperm donor, as I sometimes call him, has been complicated my entire life.

"Where's the birthday party?" My mom turns to me as she pulls takeout from the fridge and sticks her fork in the stir fry.

"It's at her and Jake's place on the lake."

"Oh, fun," my mom says. "You haven't gotten out to the lake yet. It's beautiful—probably the best part of this town."

"I figured I should at least try to get to know people while I'm here." I grab my mom's fork and wrap a noodle around it.

The best thing about being a traveling nurse is that I never had to invest in any relationships. I'd come for a three-to-nine-month assignment and then be on to the next town or city. My mom and I have that in common. She usually only sticks around until a nursing home is healthy enough to run itself. She likes fixing things, much like me. But sticking around hasn't been our strong point.

"I agree." My mom puts the lid back on the takeout. "And I really like it here. Who knows? Maybe I'll stay."

"I'll believe that when I see it."

"Oh, Birdie girl." My mom comes around the island, puts her hands on my shoulders, and inspects my outfit. "I can't remember the last time I bought a house when I moved to a new town to run a nursing home. I'm getting too old to keep moving from one place to another. Wheaton is showing real promise."

I check the time again, not wanting to be one of the first to arrive. "The party only goes until four. Do you want to go out tonight and grab a pizza?"

"Oh, honey," my mom says. "As much as I'd love that, after I go for a run, I'm headed back to the nursing home. We had two folks call in sick today, and we're short-staffed. I'll be back late."

"I won't wait up." I grab my car keys and phone and kiss her cheek. "Love you, Mom."

"Love you, Birdie girl."

Chapter Three

I glance at the address on my phone to make sure I'm at the right place. This house is massive. Several cars are parked outside. I grab the card for Asher sitting on the passenger seat, inhale sharply, and step out of the car.

Getting to know people seemed like a great idea, but now that I'm here, I find myself oddly nervous. I could use friends in my life. My two closest ones are from nursing school, but as the years have gone by, we talk less and less. It doesn't help that they live in the same city, and I don't. If I plan to stay in Wheaton, at least for a while, it would be good to know people outside of the nursing home.

The door to their home is closed, but I can hear many voices inside. I knock once, then walk in. There are at least ten kids, ranging from babies to about five years old, all playing and making a lot of noise.

"Birdie!" Camilla rushes to me with Asher on her hip and gives me a quick side hug. "I'm so happy you came. As expected, it's total chaos. Please, help yourself to food, and we have tons of beer and wine in the fridge."

"Happy Birthday, Asher." I smile and hand Camilla the card. Asher kicks his feet, looking like he's about to explode with excitement.

"He's been a pill today," Camilla says, glancing at Asher. "Please, make yourself at home."

My worst nightmare is realized. The one person I know here, Camilla, is preoccupied with the party and taking care of an overstimulated toddler. I wander to the kitchen island, where several other adults are standing around talking. A striking woman with long auburn hair approaches me.

"You must be Birdie," she says, greeting me with a warm smile. "I'm Carrie. I've seen you from afar at the nursing home, but you've always been busy. I'm married to Dax, and I'm an old friend of Sis and Sunny's."

"That's why you look familiar," I say, shaking her hand. "It's so nice to meet you."

"My husband, Dax, is that guy over there in the corner," she says, pointing to a man talking to Liam. "He's Jake's brother."

"Ah, okay," I say.

"You're going to realize a lot of us in this small town are related." Carrie laughs, and when Dax meets her eyes, she waves him over. Liam glances at me and then walks over to talk to Jake, who is handing a bowl of fruit to Signe.

"Dax," Carrie says, "this is Birdie. She's new to town and works at the nursing home."

"You're the famous Birdie," Dax says, extending his arms and giving me a hug. "Sunny has gone on about how fabulous you are. We're all so happy for the positive addition to the nursing home."

"Does Sunny know everyone?" I say, laughing.

Dax smiles. "Actually, yes. My grandparents were best friends with Sunny and Sis. We grew up with the Bergland family. Liam was my best summer friend growing up. Have you met him?"

"Yes," I say, glancing in Liam's direction. "A few days ago."

"Those two boys there"—Dax points to two dark-haired kids playing with trucks on the floor—"are our twins, Charlie and James. And that big girl over there is our pre-teen, Kylie."

One of the boys hits the other on the head, and both Carrie and Dax rush in their direction.

"I'll catch up with you soon," Carrie says, looking at me over her shoulder. "It was so great to meet you."

I stand by myself, wishing I could disappear. I put some food on my plate so it at least looks like I'm doing something instead of awkwardly watching everyone else converse.

"Aren't kid birthday parties the worst?" someone says, leaning in next to me. I turn to face him, and he puts out his hand. "Malik."

"Birdie," I say. "I barely know anyone here, if that isn't already clear."

"This town is small." He laughs. "It's obvious you're an outsider. Do you want a quick rundown?"

I shrug. "Yeah, sure."

"Okay." He points to Camilla and Jake. "You know them. But did you know their families were best friends growing up? Camilla and her brother Robby grew up all over the world. Camilla came back for a summer a few years ago, got reacquainted with Jake, and never left."

"Wow." I nod, popping an M&M in my mouth. "Good to know."

"I mean, he's gorgeous, right? I get it." Malik points.

"Dax is Jake's younger brother," he continues. "He grew up with Carrie, who is my best friend and coincidentally used to work part-time with Sunny and Sis before they moved to a nursing home. She owns a fabulous bed-and-breakfast down the lake. She meant to live in it but met Dax, and oops, moved in with him. The place is very popular."

"And they have Kylie and the twins?"

Malik nods. "His first wife died when Kylie was young, and Carrie is her bonus mom."

"That there is Liam," Malik says. "He's the oldest of the Bergland grandkids of Sunny and Sis. I haven't gotten to know him well, but he's staying at the cottage, which is another property not far from here, and he doesn't seem thrilled about it."

"This is all fascinating," I say.

The door opens, and Sunny and Sis walk in with two people. Malik points.

"And that's Robby and his wife Jenna. Robby is Camilla's brother, and Jenna is Jake and Dax's baby sister. Now you've been introduced to our very incestuous town."

I laugh. I like Malik.

"Well," I say, "I feel like I should have been writing this all down. I'll never keep it straight."

"I've got you, Birdie." Malik grabs my hand and walks me over to Sunny and Sis.

The rest of the party goes by quickly, and when I check the time, it's well after four, even though a lot of people are still here. Once Sunny and Sis arrive, I don't have to talk to anyone else, as the three of us keep each other company. My biggest takeaway from the party is that both the Bergland and Abram families have very good genes.

I get to my car, and when I try to start it, it's completely dead. No purring. Nothing. I try again, and there's an odd clicking noise, but it doesn't turn over. It's the first car I've ever had, and I got it shortly after getting my license. It's a beater and should have been tossed aside years ago, but I couldn't afford a better one, especially on my current salary.

"Perfect," I murmur under my breath and rest my head on the steering wheel.

I glance up, and Liam is standing in front of my car, each hand carrying a bag full of garbage. He throws them in the can and walks to the driver's side door. I get out.

"My car won't start."

"I can see that." He puts his hands on his hips. "Do you have jumper cables?"

"No," I say.

Liam raises an eyebrow. "You drive a car from the early two thousands and don't have jumper cables?"

He pops open the trunk of the car next to mine. He positions it so our engines are facing each other. He connects the cables to both batteries and tells me to start my engine.

Still, there's nothing. So I try again.

Liam turns off his car, and I get out again.

"It's not even turning over," Liam says. "There's no way your car is going to start. Probably ever."

"Okay." I nervously bite my pinky nail.

Liam rolls his eyes but nods toward his car. "Get in. I'll give you a ride."

His car is spotless on the inside and has that new car smell. He pulls out of the driveway, and we travel down the gravel road until we hit the highway. I glance in his direction, and his jaw is clenched, his hands squeezing the steering wheel.

"So," I say, attempting to break the awkward silence, "I heard you left New York to come here?"

He nods but doesn't say anything.

"Were you tired of the city life? Looking for something a little slower paced?"

Liam looks at me out of the corner of his eye. "No. I love it there. I am here very temporarily and counting the days until I can go back."

"You're not moving here? I thought Sunny—"

"No," Liam says, interrupting me. "I'm here until I can find a job there. I'm passing through."

We fall back into silence for several minutes. I stare out the window, looking at the farmland we pass, the corn starting to sprout up from the black dirt.

"What did you do before moving here?" Liam turns to face me. He looks uncomfortable trying to have a conversation.

"I was a travel nurse," I say. "Most recently in Denver."

Liam narrows his eyes. "The money must have been a lot better than what you're doing now. Why the change?"

I shake my head. "My mom is my only family, and I missed her. I hated being so far away."

Liam nods, his jaw still clenched. "Where do you live?"

"The big purple house by the cemetery."

Liam's eyes widen. "Sorry, what? You live in the Hurst haunted house?"

He takes a left turn at the end of Main Street.

"The what?" I say, fully turning to him.

"Everyone knows the Hurst haunted house. It's famous here. Anyone who ever lived there has experienced paranormal activity. It's well documented."

He pulls into my driveway, and my mom's car isn't here.

"Dead people don't scare me." I shrug.

"You aren't freaking out that you're about to go into a dark and haunted house?"

"Living people are much scarier and more unpredictable," I say.

"You're odd."

Liam removes his hands from the steering wheel. He hits the unlock button on his car.

"If you die tonight, I'll tell everyone I warned you."

"If I die tonight, someone at the party probably saw me leave with you, and you'll be the first suspect."

Liam unbuckles his seatbelt, leans across my body, and pushes my door open.

"Lovely," Liam says, unbuckling my seatbelt.

Our gazes meet as he hovers near me. His are a beautiful shade of deep blue, something I haven't noticed before. I brush that thought out of my head.

"Well, thanks for the ride, I guess." I dramatically step out of his car and slam the door.

"You may want to invest in a car made in this century, Birdie. Just saying."

He rolls his window back up and drives away.

Chapter Four

Family care planning days go one of two ways. All of my faith in humanity is restored, or it's completely destroyed. Sometimes, all those things can happen on the same day.

Once a month, I sit down with all of my patients and their families, and we discuss what's going well and what areas we could improve. First up for the day is Abigail, and it goes exactly like the other ones. We send the meeting notice to her power of attorney that we have on file, but no one ever calls in. It breaks my heart every time.

Abigail's mind is still very sharp, but she's wheelchair-bound, in liver failure, and receiving daily dialysis. She acts like it doesn't bother her when no one shows up or calls in, but she doesn't say anything about it. She and I discuss her plan, and I move on to my next patient, Marilyn.

Marilyn is also very sharp but has terminal brain cancer and has opted to stop treatment. She's not well enough to be moved home, so she's asked to die at the nursing home. Each month, her son, Tommy, and daughter, Tina, show up to the meeting, as well as her husband, George. They also visit her at the nursing home almost daily.

"I can't see out of my left eye," Marilyn says. "That change has been recent. But besides that, things have been going well."

Marilyn's son takes her hand and looks at me. "How much time do we have left with Mom?"

"It's hard to tell," I say. "But your mom is starting to lose some function, including her eyesight, and has been consuming less food recently, too."

"I'll go willingly when the good Lord wants to take me." She pats her son's hand. "And it won't do anyone any good sitting here crying about it."

It's going to be a sad day when Marilyn leaves us. She's the cheerleader here and goes into the residents' rooms when they're feeling sad and urges them to be social. The people who fare the worst are those that stay in their rooms and resist any human interaction.

Thirty minutes later, I move on to Sunny and Sis's monthly meeting with their family. Their sons, Rob and Larry, always dial in. Rob is sweet and thoughtful. He thinks carefully before asking a question. Larry is usually short and questions why we can't do more for his parents.

When I walk into their room, Liam is sitting in one of their blue chairs.

"Good morning, Sis." I squeeze her hand as she lies on her side. "Hey there, Sunny."

"Let's get Larry and Rob on the phone," Sunny says.

I glance at Liam. "And you consent to having Liam here today?"

Liam narrows his eyes at me and glares, and Sunny nods.

"He thought since he'll be here for a bit, that he'd like to hear what's going on with our care," Sunny says.

Rob and Larry prefer to video call, so I get them set up on my laptop so we can all see each other.

"Good morning, Rob. Larry. Thanks for joining today. I thought I would give a few updates, and then I'd love to hear any questions or concerns you may have."

I go through their current schedules. Sis is pulled into memory care activities every morning, seven days a week, for two hours. Sunny is going through daily workouts to keep his body strong. They are eating and sleeping well.

"Everything sounds great," Rob says. "Thanks for taking such good care of our parents."

Liam folds his hands together. "I actually have a couple of observations."

"Okay," I say, grabbing my notebook.

"Grandma Sis needs more than two hours of memory care a day. It's not enough currently. And sorry, Grandpa, but you seem bored. You need more stimulation."

I hold the pen up to my mouth. "Let me address your first point. Unfortunately, the Wheaton nursing home only has the capacity for two hours of memory care a day. We'd love to be able to offer more, but we don't have the funding or resources. Although that's something we'd very much like to change."

Liam tilts his head. "And about Grandpa?"

"Well." I turn to Sunny. "You don't need to be here. You, of course, know that. But we're also really happy you're here. Because you have such low needs, all I can recommend is that you continue partaking in the activities provided and try to get out more."

"Liam," I say, turning my attention toward him. "Now that you're here, you could help greatly with this. Pick up your grandpa when your grandma is in memory care."

He opens his mouth to say something but then snaps it shut.

"She's right," Larry says. "You don't have anything else going on there, Liam. Spend time with your grandparents and quit being so lazy."

Liam glances at the computer, and it occurs to me for the first time that Larry is his dad. A look passes between them. There's tension, and when Larry talks, Liam leans back in his chair and wilts.

"But, Liam," I continue, "you've been such a great presence since getting to town. I appreciate you raising this, because I too want to make sure your grandpa has enough to do. I'm always happy to sit down with you and brainstorm ideas."

He jerks his head in my direction, and his face softens.

After a morning of meetings, I get on with the rest of my day. I administer medications, monitor my patients, and schedule follow-ups with our traveling physician. All the residents under my care are either ailing physically or mentally. I often wonder what would be worse. Although I'd prefer to never have to end up in a nursing home, if I was going to lose something, I think I'd want it to be my mind. The people here who still have theirs struggle the most because they understand their physical limitations.

"Hey there, Birdie," my mom says, coming up behind me. "How'd the family meetings go?"

"The same as last month." I lower my voice. "Abigail's family didn't show up again. It makes me want to—"

"You don't know what's going on there," my mom interrupts. "Our residents lived full lives before ending up here. I have no doubt there was an opportunity for things to go wrong."

"I know." I release a breath. "But my heart breaks for her."

My mom reaches for my hand.

"Are you heading out soon?" I say.

"Oh, Birdie girl," my mom says. "I have hours left. I'm sorry."

"No big deal. I'll walk home."

My mom lets out a sigh. "We need to figure out your car situation. Your life can't be limited to this town."

"I'm working on it."

I close out my work for the day and hit the code to exit the building. The sun warms me the moment I'm outside. I close my eyes and breathe it in. Joe isn't wrong. The nursing home does have an odor to it that could be improved. It's always magnificent stepping outside and breathing in the summer air.

A voice interrupts my peace. Liam is sitting on the stone bench, in a heated conversation. I glance at my phone and walk past him, trying to mind my own business.

"Really, Dad? That's all you have to say?" Liam says into the phone.

He looks up just as I'm passing, and we lock eyes. I quickly glance down and keep walking.

Chapter Five

"I've been awful to you, Birdie," my mom says, tossing a pillow at me as I lie on the couch, scrolling through my phone. "Tonight, we're going out for pizza."

"Mom." I roll my eyes. "I'm tired. I've already taken my bra off. Let me get lost on social media in peace."

My mom grabs my feet and starts pulling me off the couch. I drop my phone and laugh as I fall off.

"I'm not taking no for an answer. I've been working eighty-hour weeks since begging you to come here. We're getting dressed, and we're having pizza."

"I must really love you to put a bra back on," I yell as I walk up the stairs.

"Don't put one on for me," my mom says, laughing. "I don't care what you wear."

"Gross," I say. I sit and stretch my arms up. "Give me fifteen minutes to get dressed and make myself presentable."

I throw on cutoff shorts and a tank top and look at myself in the mirror.

Thirty minutes later, my mom and I walk through the doors of the pool hall. I've heard about this place but haven't been here. Now that I think of it, I haven't been anywhere.

"There." My mom points. "Let's grab that table in the corner."

My mom didn't actually beg me to come to Wheaton. It was the other way around. I started getting so lonely on the road. She and I would have our daily calls and texts, but it started to get harder to be away from her. I also got so tired of living out of a suitcase. When my mom took over the nursing home administrator position in Wheaton and then let me know a few months later that one of their RNs retired, I jumped at the opportunity to come here.

"I think I like it here." My mom studies the menu. "Sure, the house needs some work, but it's got character."

"You mean the haunted house we live in?"

My mom swats my arm. "You know I don't believe in that stuff."

We order a drink and a pub pizza.

"Are you liking it here, Birdie?"

"The town is cute," I say. "And I'm in love with the residents. Who knows? I'm ready to give this place a try."

The ranch where I grew up is only an hour and a half away from here. But besides my sperm donor, I have no real connections there. My mom is my family, and although I didn't picture myself living at home at twenty-five, I don't hate the simplicity of life I have at the moment.

And my mom and I have always been best friends more than anything.

"Birdie." I turn when I hear my name. Carrie stands there, with Dax at her side. She pulls me into a hug. "I thought that was you."

"Hey, Carrie." I smile. "This is my mom, June. Mom, this is Carrie."

"Carrie," my mom says warmly. "It's so good to meet you."

"Dax," he says, stretching his hand out to shake my mom's. "I've seen you at the nursing home once or twice. I visit Sunny and Sis pretty regularly."

"Of course," my mom says. "They're lucky to have so many family and friends around that stop in to see them. Lately, I've been stuck in my office and barely get out."

"Liam is grabbing us drinks from the bar." Carrie points. "Do you mind if we join you?"

"Please," my mom says. She gets to her feet and pulls three chairs to our table.

Liam glances at me as he sets down drinks. He turns his attention to my mom.

"Hi, Mrs. . ."

"Please, call me June," my mom says.

Liam clears his throat. "It's nice to meet you, June. I'm Liam Bergland. Sunny and Sis are my grandparents."

"Liam." My mom smiles warmly at him. "Birdie and I adore them."

"All Grandpa Sunny does is talk about Birdie, so I know the feeling is mutual."

He pulls up a chair across from me. I study him as he takes a long sip of his drink. Objectively speaking, Liam is a handsome guy. He's tall and has a muscular build. His blond hair is swept to the side, and his dark blue eyes hold a lot in them.

"Yes," Liam says, and I realize I'm staring. "Can I help you?"

My face heats, and I force my gaze down toward the table. Carrie, Dax, and my mom are laughing next to us, which leaves me at the end of the table, Liam studying me in silence.

"Your mom looks our age," Liam says.

I shrug. "She was eighteen when she had me."

Liam narrows his eyes. "How old is she now?"

"Forty-three," I say.

"Wow." Liam leans back in his chair. "You have a mom that's only ten years older than me."

This is always someone's reaction when they meet my mom. She's never been like the others. She'd show up for school conferences fashionable and cute. But she worked hard to make sure we had a mother-daughter relationship.

It wasn't until I became an adult myself that she allowed us to shift into friendship too.

"Birdie's an odd name." I look up, and Liam is watching me, running his finger around the rim of his glass.

"Sorry," I say. "Was that a question or just an observation?"

Liam picks up his drink and then sets it down. "Where'd the name come from?"

"It's a nickname," I say. "My grandma gave it to me when I was a baby, and it stuck."

"What's your real name?"

I glance to the side where the three of them are still engaged in a conversation. I lean forward on my elbows.

"I only share that with my friends," I say.

Liam rolls his eyes. He leans forward too, our faces only inches apart.

"So, if your mom had you when she was eighteen, that makes you twenty-five." Liam's gaze shifts toward her, and then back at me.

"Good math skills," I say. "You should find a job in finance."

His jaw ticks. "That is what I do."

"Figures." I press my lips together.

I find Liam impossible to read. I don't expect him to open up to me, but the wall he has up both puzzles and intrigues me. It's familiar too. I can be very closed off as well.

"I'm going to grab another round of drinks. Can I get you anything?" Liam says, shooting up from the table.

"I'd love another gin and tonic," my mom says, elbowing me in my side.

"Nothing for me, thanks," I say.

"I'm good too," Carrie says.

Dax holds up an almost empty beer. "I'll have another one of these."

Liam nods and walks to the bar.

"I was just telling Carrie and Dax about the ranch you grew up on in South Dakota," my mom says. "It was beautiful but I'm an only child and would never be a rancher, so after my parents passed, it made the most sense to sell it."

"Do you still have family there?" Carrie asks, directing her question toward me.

"My sperm donor still lives there," I say. "At least I think he does."

Liam approaches just as the words are out of my mouth, and he puts the drinks down and suppresses his laugh with a cough.

"I haven't seen him in years," I add.

"Liam told me you bought the Hurst haunted house. Any action?"

My mom laughs. "Not yet, but the house is too big for just me and Birdie, so if some spirits want to hang out, I welcome it."

Carrie sighs but then turns to Dax. "We should probably go pick up Kylie and the boys. It's getting late."

Dax nods. "Yeah, I suppose we should. It was really great to meet you, June. And to see you again, Birdie."

"Yes," my mom says. "Be sure to stop by and say hi the next time you're at the nursing home."

"We will," Carrie says, smiling.

"Thanks for the drink, Liam," my mom says.

He nods as he grips the edge of the table. "Anytime."

Liam glances at me, nods, and then turns his back to us. Carrie waves as they walk away.

"We should probably get going too," my mom says. "I plan to be at the nursing home first thing in the morning."

"I'm ready whenever you are."

We drive the short distance from the pool hall to our house in silence. When we arrive home, my mom turns to me before getting out of the car.

"Liam sure pays you a lot of attention," she says.

I shrug. "I don't see why. He's not very friendly."

"I don't know," she says. "He seems to have taken to you. And he's not bad on the eyes."

"No, Mom," I say. "You are still not allowed to be my matchmaker."

She laughs. "I know, but I'm so good at it."

We head up the winding stairs together. My mom goes right to her room, and I go left to mine.

"Thanks for indulging me tonight, Birdie. I love you, honey."

"See you in the morning," I say.

Chapter Six

Night shifts at the nursing home are quiet and almost eerie. We're on a rotation, and about every three weeks, I'm the RN in the evenings. I do my rounds, waking residents who need meds during the night, checking those on oxygen, and making sure everyone is settled in and sleeping.

I step into Abigail's room because I see her stirring when I walk by. She lies on her side, facing the wall, but when I walk to the other side of her bed, her eyes are wide open.

"Hey, Abigail." I put my hand on her hip. "Is everything okay?"

"I can't sleep," she says.

I pull up a chair and turn on her table lamp. "Are you feeling okay?"

"Physically, yes," Abigail says. "Mentally, I'm not doing great."

"Well," I say, "I've finished my rounds. Let's talk. Maybe it will make your mind tired."

"I'd like that," she says. I help her sit up, and she leans against the wall behind her, pulling her covers up.

"I don't know a lot about your family. I know you have two daughters, but I'd love to hear more."

Abigail smiles. "My oldest daughter is Samantha. My youngest is Cara. Gosh, Birdie. I can't remember the last time I saw them."

"That must be really hard."

"It is." Abigail nods. "But it's my fault. I don't blame them."

"Abigail," I say, reaching for her hand, "that can't be true."

"It is," she says. "Their father and I had them young. We'd only been married nine months when Samantha was born. And a year later, Cara came. I had all of these hopes and dreams of what I wanted our life to look like, and it couldn't have been more different."

Abigail closes her eyes and squeezes my hand. "I got attached to the taste of liquor. It became a sickness. I wanted to stop and be the mom who showed up for my kids, but instead, I was the mom who drank all day, missed concerts, plays, and ballgames. When the girls were teenagers, their dad finally left me and took Samantha and Cara with him."

A tear falls down her face. "By the time I got my life together, the girls were grown, and they both have two kids each of their own, whom I've never met. I did a program, wrote them letters, and tried to make amends. Cara did write me back and told me not to contact her again. I never heard back from Samantha. I've been sober for thirty years, but all of it was too late. Those girls don't have a positive memory of me, and I certainly don't blame them for that."

"That's really hard, Abigail."

She shakes her head. "I deserve to be alone. My choices brought me to this nursing home. I'm going to die on my own. That's my fate. I have no one to blame but myself."

I squeeze her hand. "All you can do is own your mistakes. But they don't define you, Abigail. You deserve love."

"I'm not so sure about that," Abigail says. She moves down and turns on her side. "Can I ask you something?"

"Anything," I say.

"I'm not scared of dying, but I don't want to do it alone," Abigail says. "When it's my time, will you be by my side?"

"Oh, Abigail," I say. "Of course. I'll be right next to you, holding your hand. You're not alone, okay?"

Abigail nods. I want to tell her that she's got a lot of time left and not to think about this, but I don't know if that's true. Her health continues to decline, and I also can't tell her that her daughters will forgive her in her last stage of life. Ever since being here, I've invited them to the monthly meetings, but I never hear back.

"Do you want to know about one of my best days?" Abigail says, her mouth turning up in a smile, and I nod.

"Samantha and Cara were young, and it was a hot summer night and their dad was traveling for work. In the middle of the night, I was woken up by the light outside. I peeked out the window, and it was the most vivid display of aurora borealis I'd ever seen. I woke the girls up and brought them to the yard, and we watched it together. It was the most perfect day."

"It sounds great, Abigail."

She grabs my hand and yawns. "Tell me about one of your most perfect days."

"Hmm," I say, but don't have to think for long. "I was young. Maybe five or six. My grandma took me to the apple orchard on the ranch, and we picked apples. We didn't think to bring a basket, so she put them in her apron skirt. We went inside, and she taught me how to bake a pie. When my grandpa and mom got home from work, we served it to them with ice cream on the side. We sat on the wrap-around porch, and I remember breathing the country air and feeling so happy."

"That is a good day, Birdie."

The next time I look up, Abigail is sleeping and breathing heavily through her mouth. I pull the covers up to her shoulders, turn off her lamp, and leave her.

By eight in the morning, I can't quit yawning. I'm ready to pass the baton to the day nurse and go cuddle up in bed for a few hours before I do the same thing tonight. I work my way to the staff bathroom, splash water on my eyes, and redo my messy bun. My eyes are a little red, and my long hair is standing up in every direction. I put some water on that too and smooth it down.

I grab my personal things out of my locker. On my way out, I pass the cafeteria and smile when I see Sunny sitting with his group of friends, having their morning coffee.

"Sunny," I say, walking over to him and putting my hand on his back.

"Birdie." He smiles. "Are you just getting to work?"

"I'm actually leaving for the day. I worked an overnight."

"I didn't even see you creeping into my room," he says.

I laugh. "You were sound asleep. I woke Sis up around two to give her meds, and she went right back to sleep."

"Hey there, Walt, Juan, Lawson. It's great to see you guys here."

"We thought we'd come here for coffee and maybe a card game," Walt says. "It's supposed to rain all day."

"The farmers are happy," Juan says. "But not the fishermen."

No resident in the nursing home has as many visitors as Sunny. And these men are some of my favorites. They try to make things as normal as possible for Sunny, which is needed because living in a nursing home is a tough adjustment for anyone, but especially for someone like Sunny, who doesn't need to be here.

Liam rounds the corner, holding a box of donuts. He looks at Sunny and doesn't see me initially. He holds them up.

"Hey, guys. I brought donuts for the card game."

Liam's smile is so big that I can hardly believe it's him. I've never seen any emotion from him except brooding.

"Wow," I say, and Liam's face spins in my direction. "The man smiles. I had no idea you had it in you."

Walt puts his hand on his knee and shakes as he laughs.

"Birdie's not wrong," Sunny says. "You've been a little serious since getting to town. I know circumstances are tough, but you're starting to bring us down."

"I've been here for less than two weeks, Grandpa." Liam puts the box down on the table and pulls up a chair.

"For two weeks, you've been acting like your dog died," Juan says.

"Agreed," I say, arms folded over my chest. "Did your dog die?"

Sunny and Walt laugh.

Liam glances at me. "Why are you part of this conversation? The boys and I are going to have coffee, donuts, and play cards."

Sunny puts his hand on mine. "Birdie is the best thing that's happened to this nursing home. You could try to be a little warmer toward her."

Liam rolls his eyes at me.

"You're new to town, Liam. So is Birdie. You two could relate to each other," Walt says. He bites into his donut, and jelly runs down his chin.

"I'm not planning on staying long," Liam says. "So no point in getting to know people."

"You could at least be nice," Sunny says.

"Yes." I grab a napkin and put a donut on it. "You keep reminding us that you're leaving. You don't have to worry. None of us will forget."

I turn my attention toward Sunny and his friends. "Well, boys, I'm coming off a twelve-hour shift, so I'm going to go home and get some sleep."

I'm almost to the door when Liam's voice calls out.

"Are you still walking everywhere?"

I nod. "The exercise has been great. See you tonight, Sunny."

"I like her," one of the men says as I punch in the code to leave. I can't tell who said it, but I smile.

Chapter Seven

The town is buzzing with activity because it's Wheaton Days. Most of the residents are getting so many visitors, and moods are lighter because of it. Abigail hasn't had any, so I've tried to spend some extra time with her. We are short-staffed but can't afford to hire more people. I've quit keeping track of how many hours I'm working each week because I don't want to stress my mom out, but my schedule isn't sustainable.

"Can I get a ride home when you're done working?" Joe approaches me with his walker.

"Joe," I say, "you live here. You know I can't give you a ride."

"I hate it here." He tries to open the door, and I pull him back. "The food is horrible, and half the residents sleep in their wheelchairs all day."

I sit next to him. "How can I help make this a better place for you?"

"You could take me home," he says. "I miss the farm. Call Betty and tell her I'm ready to leave."

"You know I can't do that. This is your home. Do you have any other ideas?"

"We could do more activities around here," he says. "Not all of us are at the shitting-in-our-diapers stage, you know?"

"Joe." I hold a hand over my mouth to cover my smile. "More activities are a good idea. Let me talk to some of the staff, and we'll come up with a plan."

"Fine," he says, diverting his attention toward the TV. "And if you could turn on something new for once, that would be great."

I grab the remote from behind the desk and turn on a baseball game.

"There." I pat his leg. "I'll catch up with you later."

Joe has dementia, although he's still fairly high functioning. But he also had a stroke a couple of years ago and is a fall risk. There was no way he could live independently anymore. His wife Betty was going to die taking care of him. She comes every morning and then again for dinner. Multiple times a day, he asks me to leave.

My phone rings in my pocket, and it's Will, one of the other RNs, calling.

"Hey, Will," I say.

"Where are you?"

"Leaving the lobby," I say. "Why? What's up?"

"There's a Larry Bergland here, and he'd like to speak to you if you have time. We're at the South Desk."

One of Sunny and Sis's sons. I've never met him in person, but he intimidates me plenty over the phone.

"I'll be there in two minutes."

I turn the corner, and Larry stands at the desk with Liam. Liam has his hands stuffed in his pockets and is looking down at the floor. Larry is taller than I was expecting. He's about the same height as Liam, only broader.

"Hi, Mr. Bergland," I say, sticking my hand out. "I'm Birdie. It's nice to finally meet you in person. You must be here for Wheaton—"

"I'm hoping we can discuss the care of my parents," he says, cutting me off.

I glance at my watch. "I have about thirty minutes if you think that's enough time."

"That will do," he says.

"Do you want your parents present?"

"No," he says. "Liam wants to be there though."

"Of course," I say, and point down the hall. "Let's pop into one of the offices."

We get situated at a round table. Larry rests his hands on the table, but Liam continues to look down.

Larry points to me. "Are you their main nurse?"

I nod. "I'm Sunny and Sis's appointed RN, yes. They also have a caseworker, a physician who oversees their care, and June Van Osten, who is the nursing home administrator."

And also my mom, but I leave that part out.

"My mom," Larry begins, "Sis, she needs a lot more care than she's getting. Her Alzheimer's is progressing more quickly than before, and Sunny only gets a two-hour break from her a day, which is going to kill him before Alzheimer's kills my mom."

"I understand your concerns," I say, focusing on Larry but very aware of Liam's presence. "We'd love to have the resources to do more memory care, but we don't. Sis received intervention late, and there will be faster progression of the disease because of—"

"That's not good enough," Larry says. "I won't hesitate to pull my parents out of here."

"Dad," Liam says under his breath, but his dad holds his hand up and silences him.

"Mr. Bergland," I continue, "if you think it's better for your mom to receive more memory care therapies, I'd be happy to share a list of recommendations. The best one is in Minneapolis, but they don't accept anyone into their program without severe issues, so Sunny couldn't live with her, which is an important consideration."

Larry stands and runs his fingers through his graying hair. "This place is a joke. I pay a premium to have my parents here. Do you know how much you'd lose monthly if I pulled them out?"

"We'd hate to see them go," I say, "but we can't offer what you're looking for. We know we're small compared to other options. We do our best with the limited resources we have, but I recognize it's not always enough."

"They love it here," Liam says. "And think about their friends and how much they'd miss them."

"Enough, Liam," Larry says. "You're the last person I need to weigh in on this."

"Sir," I say, standing, "I don't know how many days you're in town, but I'm sure my..."

I let my voice trail off.

"June Van Osten would be happy to sit down with you and discuss options. We are committed to giving them the best care they need, but we are unfortunately limited."

Larry Bergland glances at his watch. "I will take that meeting with the administrator. Thank you. I'm here all week."

"I do have to get back to work," I say, staring at the large circular clock on the wall. "But I'll be in touch with what day will be best."

"Thanks for your time, Birdie," Liam says. He almost looks as defeated as I feel.

The residents are the easiest part of this job. The families, who I need to remind myself mean well, can be challenging. I don't know how the sweetest couple in the world, Sunny and Sis, could have an offspring who is so unpleasant. But then again, Liam also comes from them, and now it makes sense after meeting his dad. I follow them out of the office, and they walk in one direction, and I head in the other.

"Hey, Marilyn," I say as she makes her way toward the birds. "Do you have a lot of family in town?"

Marilyn smiles. "My grandbabies are coming in today to play bingo."

"That's great," I say. "I'll be sure to stop by."

"They're here until Sunday, so you'll see a lot of them."

"Perfect," I say, squeezing her shoulder. "I know how much you've missed them."

"Also," Marilyn says, grabbing my arm, "Abigail and I are going to knit later."

"You're a good friend," I say.

After my shift, I head outside and pull my sunglasses on. I'm getting used to the walk home, but I'm going to have to figure out the car situation soon. My mom and me sharing isn't working so well because her hours are so unpredictable. I had my car towed from Camilla and Jake's, and the estimate to get it fixed was more than the value of the car. I've been trying to save up money to get something respectable. I feel stranded without one.

The walk home is only about a mile, and it's shorter because I cut through the cemetery.

"Birdie." Liam pulls up beside me and steps out of his car. "It's a hundred degrees out. Why are you walking?"

"Would you believe I'm trying to get steps in on this beautiful day?" I raise my shoulders and smile.

"Let me guess," he says. "Your piece-of-shit car will not be making a comeback."

"And here I am."

He comes up on the sidewalk. I squint because the sun is directly behind him, and it's bright, even with my shades.

"I'm sorry about my dad," he finally says.

"He's a concerned parent," I say. "You have nothing to apologize for."

"Come on." Liam presses his lips into a thin line. "He's an ass. And maybe some medical code of ethics won't allow you to say it out loud. But if you ever catch me resembling him in any way, I give you permission to hit me."

"Noted." I pull my bottom lip into my mouth and bite it.

He glances at his car. "Can I give you a ride? I'm sweating through my shirt. You can't be comfortable."

I go to refuse, but I'm hot as well and wouldn't mind a break from the heat.

"Thanks," I say.

We drive to my house in silence. He remembers exactly where I live. After all, the Hurst haunted house is a staple in this town. We pull into the driveway, and Liam puts his car in park.

"Thanks for the—"

"It's not even about you," Liam interrupts. "Or Sunny and Sis. My dad came to town to punish me. I'm a huge disappointment to him, and he needed to remind me of that fact."

I take my seatbelt off and blow out a breath.

"Okay. I'll admit, he's not the most pleasant person I've had to deal with." I press my lips together, but my smile bleeds through.

"That's putting it mildly." Liam shakes his head. "Who's looking better? Your sperm donor or Larry Bergland?"

"Liam." I slug him in the arm, and he laughs.

I'm immediately transfixed by the power it has on me. I feel like I've yet to see the real man hiding beneath his stoic exterior. The sound of it makes me wish I had something funny and clever to offer so I could hear so much more of that beautiful sound.

"Seriously, Birdie," Liam says, "you are amazing at your job. And I'm sure you know that. Don't let people like my father ever make you feel small."

My mouth opens, but nothing comes out. The car is warming, and a bead of sweat runs down the back of my neck. But I'm transfixed by this kind person staring back at me. I'm seeing him for the first time, and it's so different from what he's shown me previously.

"What?" Liam says, narrowing his eyes.

"I'm trying to figure out if this is the real you, or if you're the sarcastic curmudgeon who likes to point out that my car is crap and that I live in a haunted house."

Liam puckers his lips and then bites the corner of his lip.

"I suppose I'm both."

"Hmm," I say. "I guess you are."

We stare at each other as if there's something we're trying to figure out about the other person.

"Well," I finally say, reaching for the door, "I appreciate the ride home. And the apology. Which was wholly unnecessary."

I step out of the car, and Liam pulls away.

Chapter Eight

Tonight is the big street dance to celebrate Wheaton Days, but I took Joe's advice and have been working all week to create a fun experience for the nursing home residents. I've had a lot of help, too. We're going to have a little dance of our own. It won't be the same, especially since many of the people here aren't mobile. But we'll be playing oldies music, have decorations, and serve Root Beer Floats.

"Will," I say, holding a streamer above my head. "Can you help me hang this? I can't quite reach the nail."

"No problem, Birdie," Will says. "I'm on it."

He takes the streamer from my hand and effortlessly loops it along the archway to the cafeteria. I'm starting to get to know the staff here, and they are a great group of co-workers. Will is about my age, also from South Dakota, and he's worked at the care center as an RN for over a year. I've gravitated toward another RN who is probably ten years or so older than me, Lucy. My favorite shifts are the ones we're all together.

"This looks great," Will says, hands on his hips, taking it all in.

"It really does." I straighten the banner announcing the first annual Wheaton Days nursing home dance. "I'll get the speaker ready. The residents should be here soon."

Bedtime at the nursing home is early, so our dance goes from six until eight, ending when the real street dance is set to begin. I get the music prepared, and Lucy is behind the table with coolers ready to serve the floats. The staff go to the rooms to see who wants to come and bring everyone to the lobby where the party is. We also asked the residents to invite their families.

"This is great," Joe says. "Good music."

"Thanks for the idea," I say. "Tonight is because of you."

"It's about time some fun happened around here." A smile extends across his face. "There's my Betty."

"Birdie." Sunny comes up to me, Sis at his side. "Everything is perfect. This is the place to be. Forget the street dance."

I laugh. "I agree."

The line forms for floats, and some of the residents dance along to the music. Sunny swings Sis around, and the moves come to her without thought. I'm always amazed at what Sis remembers.

A slower song comes on, and people flood to the makeshift dance floor.

"Care to dance?" Will puts his hand out to me.

"Oh, I don't—"

"Dance with the guy," Joe says, pushing me toward Will.

"Yes, dance." Abigail smiles from a chair on the other side of the room.

"The people have spoken," Will says. He smiles as I give in and place my hand in his.

"We pulled it off," I say. I grip his shoulder, and he squeezes my waist.

"You pulled it off." Will stares at me. "I don't know how you manage to have all the energy for stuff like this in addition to your nursing job."

"It's all worth it to see the smiles on everyone's faces." I look around and immediately lock eyes with Liam, who is in a chair next to Sis, leaning back, one leg crossed over the other. He raises an eyebrow as if he's asking me a question. I shake my head and turn my attention back to Will.

"Thanks for the dance," I say as the song ends. "I should probably go see if everyone has gotten a float."

Will smiles. "Thank you, Birdie."

"How are we doing on ice cream?" I ask, walking over to Lucy.

"We're short, but I think everyone who wants some has been served. And there's only thirty minutes left anyway."

I glance at my watch. "Wow. Time has flown."

"You and Will, doing a little dancing." Lucy shakes her hips, and I swat her.

She throws her head back and laughs.

There are plastic cups everywhere, so I work to get everything cleaned up. People still dance, and I smile at Liam dancing with his Grandma Sis. He towers over her petite frame, and she rests her head against his chest as they sway to the music.

At eight on the dot, the staff and I work to get the residents back to their rooms, in their pajamas, and their meds administered. Everyone is tired from the festivities. I go to check on Abigail, and she's sound asleep.

I'm working another overnight because one of our RNs quit without notice. I'm going to need to say something to my mom, but she's been so stressed about the state of the nursing home that I haven't wanted to burden her with the fact that I'm working nearly eighty hours a week.

I go to the lobby after my night checks so I can start disassembling the decorations, and Liam is out there, taking down streamers.

"What are you doing?" I ask, tugging on the banner. "I can hear the music down the street. Aren't you going to the dance? I hear there are a lot more people born in your decade there."

He looks at me over his shoulder. "I may pop in later, but I thought you could use some help."

"I appreciate that." I jump and grab one of the dangling streamers.

The teardown goes quickly with Liam's help. When everything is in a box, I collapse in a chair. My body is tired and broken down. Liam sits next to me and swivels so he's facing me.

"Tonight was great, Birdie." Liam kicks his foot out and taps it against mine.

"These residents deserve it," I say. "To see the smiles on their faces. It made it all worth it."

Liam glances at the door. "Any interest in getting changed and going to the street dance?"

"What?" I look down at my scrubs. "You don't like my outfit?"

He smiles. "Come on. I can drive you home, you can put on actual clothes, and we could be there in thirty minutes."

"Unfortunately, I'm working an overnight." I blow out a breath.

"Is it just me or are you always working?"

"I'm always working," I say. I look around, then lean closer to Liam and rest my head on my hand. "Can I trust you?"

Liam rolls his eyes but nods.

"The nursing home isn't doing well. My mom has spent her career coming in and improving things. But this one may be too far gone. We're worried it won't survive."

Liam nods and bites at his thumbnail. "What does that mean?"

"Without staff, we can't take on more residents. And without more residents, we can't pay our staff. There's a major cash flow issue. And I don't know. I actually like it here, but the only thing keeping me here is a nursing home at risk of closing."

"What would happen to the residents?" Liam leans forward.

"We'd have to reassign them to other homes," I say. "I shouldn't even be telling you this. If you tell your—"

"Birdie." Liam holds his hand up. "I said you can trust me."

"Okay."

"You like it here?" Liam narrows his eyes.

"I do." I smile. "Actually, I love it here."

"Love is a strong word."

"Wheaton is cute, and the people are great," I say, as Liam and I keep inching forward. "It seems like you can't wait to leave. Why'd you come in the first place?"

Liam leans back and puts his hands behind his head. "I was laid off from my job in New York. I couldn't afford my rent without a steady income, so I decided to come here while I'm looking for jobs. But as soon as I have one, I'll go back to the city."

"I'm sorry about the job," I say. "That really sucks."

Liam nods. "My options were moving in with my parents, who live in the Chicago area. But you've met my dad." Liam chuckles. "My other option was to stay in the Bergland cottage for the summer. It was an easy choice."

"Hmm."

"I've always been close to Camilla and now Jake. Dax is one of my best friends, and, well, my grandparents are here. Plus, I can live cheaply while I get back on my feet."

"But you couldn't see yourself here?"

He scrunches his face up. "Hell no. I loved the city, walking down the block to the market, and eating at good restaurants. I didn't go to many shows, but I loved that I could if I wanted to. What do you like about Wheaton?"

I shrug. "I don't know. I have no ties to my hometown now that my grandparents have passed away and we've sold the ranch. I didn't love my college town. Yeah, I can't get Indian food at the drop of a hat, but the people here have been really nice to me. That's all I care about."

"Yeah, I guess," Liam says.

"For me, it's the people. I'll live anywhere for the right people."

"I hear you." Liam nods as if he's thinking. "My cousin Robby and his wife Jenna were in the city. And the girls there. You have no idea. You'd do great there too, Birdie. You have this girl-next-door thing going on that men would go crazy for."

I grab a throw pillow and toss it at him. He catches it mid-air and laughs.

"It sounds like you have it all figured out," I say, biting my bottom lip. "But the thought of me living in New York City is laughable."

"As soon as I get a job, I'm on the first flight out of here."

We sit for a moment, both of us resting our heads on our hands, comfortable in the silence.

"Hi, Birdie girl." We both turn as my mom walks into the lobby. I was so lost in our conversation, but now, as I glance at the clock, I realize we've been out here talking for two hours. "Hi, Liam."

"Hi, June," he says. "Great party tonight."

"I can take zero credit," my mom says, smiling. "It was all Birdie."

"You headed out for the night?" I ask.

"Yes, and I'm sorry you're doing another all-nighter. We have to get you fewer hours."

She looks at me, then at Liam.

"I'll see you in the morning," my mom says. "Goodnight, Birdie. Liam."

I glance over my shoulder, and she winks at me as she opens the door.

"You should get to the street dance and stop boring yourself hanging out here."

Liam grabs his phone and sighs. "I've missed about twenty calls from Dax. I suppose I should get out of here."

"And I should go do the job they're paying me for."

Liam nods, pats his lap, and gets up. He holds his hand out to me and pulls me up.

"May the rest of your evening be uneventful," Liam says.

"And may yours be the opposite."

Liam chuckles and walks toward the door. He puts in the code, then turns to me.

"Hey," he says. "Is that male nurse working an overnight tonight?"

"No." I shake my head. "Why?"

"No reason." Liam smiles. "Goodnight, Birdie."

Chapter Nine

After sleeping for a few hours, I get up, shower, and pick up paint at the hardware store. It's the first day I've had off in about nine days, and I've been wanting to start some projects on the house, beginning with my bedroom.

The space is massive, probably the largest I've ever had. My room is at the front of the house and has a beautiful turret, where I envision a chair and table. But the first thing I have to do is get rid of the reddish-brown walls and lighten it up.

I pull on my short overalls and then start taping the room. I open the can of pale yellow paint, which I mostly chose because I liked the name of it: Provincial Garden. I start with the trim near the white baseboard. It goes on smoothly and will brighten up this space so nicely.

The first coat looks beautiful, and I smile at my work. One more coat, and this room will be transformed. Then I'll be able to accessorize with a rug for the hardwood floors, window coverings, and new bedding.

"What do you think, spirits? Pretty, isn't it?"

I laugh. I figure if this house is haunted, I want to be friends with these spirits instead of enemies. I look at my arms and legs, and I'm covered in paint. I haven't painted in so long, and I'm not very neat when doing it. I begin the second coat, determined that when I lay my head on the pillow tonight, this part of the makeover will be done.

There's a knock at the door, and I jump, startled. I look outside, but the overhang of the front porch prevents me from seeing if someone is parked here. I wipe my hands on my overalls and head downstairs to see who's here.

"Liam," I say, as I swing the door open.

He never looks like he fully fits in here. He pulls down his designer sunglasses to look at me.

"Am I interrupting something?" He raises an eyebrow.

"I'm painting my bedroom. I'm almost done, actually," I say.

He reaches out and grabs my arm. "From the looks of it, yellow."

"Provincial Garden," I say, and he laughs. "Do you want to come in?"

Liam looks past me, inside the house. "I can't believe I'm about to go into the Hurst haunted house. I never thought I'd see the day."

"Enter at your own risk," I say, holding the door open farther.

Liam smiles and follows me inside.

"What brings you here?" I walk into the kitchen, and Liam follows. I lean against the counter.

"I've been thinking a lot about our conversation from last night," Liam says, leaning against the counter opposite me.

"I'm sorry I even put that in your mind," I say. "You don't need to worry about it. My mom and I will figure it out."

"Can we sit?" Liam looks around.

"Yeah, sure," I say. "Can I grab you a drink?"

"Water, if you have it," he says.

I pour us both a glass of ice water and bring Liam to the living room, where we sit. He takes a long, slow drink and then sets the glass down on the coffee table.

"My background is in finance." Liam clears his throat. "That's what I did in New York. And I'd like to think I was pretty good at it."

"That's right. You are." I bite my bottom lip. "Forty-three minus eighteen is twenty-five."

Liam rolls his eyes.

"I don't want to overstep or anything, but would your mom benefit from me taking a look at the books?" Liam says, leaning forward. "I'm not here to insinuate that your mom isn't knowledgeable in—"

"She's not," I interrupt. "At larger nursing homes, they can afford to bring in an accountant. That isn't possible here. My mom does the best she can, but she's not an expert."

Liam smiles. "What do you think?"

"Why would you do that?" I shake my head. "I mean, I'm sure my mom would appreciate the help, but you know she couldn't pay you."

Liam folds his hands and rests his head on them. "I care about the health of the nursing home. I'd be lying if I said I always have. But now that my grandparents are there, I can't imagine if they were forced to go to another city. Their friends and family are all here."

"You're sure?" I ask.

Liam nods and then leans back. "There's something you should know first though, Birdie."

"Okay."

"I didn't get laid off from my job in New York." He closes his eyes for a moment. "I worked for Feldmans."

"Wait," I say, leaning forward. "The Feldmans on Wall Street? The one that's been in the news for the Ponzi scheme and defrauding their clients? That Feldmans?"

He scrapes his nail against his bottom lip. "Yes."

This is why Liam is in Wheaton. He didn't just lose his job; he was fired. The entire company went under.

Liam shoots up from the couch and sits in the chair next to me.

"I know what you're thinking," he says. "And I swear, I wasn't in on it. I had nothing to do with what happened."

"You don't know what I was thinking." I run a hand down my face.

"Wait." Liam narrows his eyes. He studies my face. "I mean it. I really wasn't involved."

"Liam," I say. "I believe you."

"It's okay if you don't," he says. "We are pretty much strangers. My own dad doesn't believe me."

I tilt my head to the side. The sun from outside shines on his blond hair and tanned face. That's why his dad is so disappointed in him.

"I trust people until they give me a reason not to," I say. "You came over here to say you'd take a look at the nursing home's finances. For free. If you were looking to steal from someone, I have no doubt it would be from a person or organization that actually had money."

Liam rolls his eyes but smiles. "Talk to your mom. Get her thoughts. And let me know how I can help."

He stands, and I follow. The paint on my limbs has dried and is now hard and crusty.

"I'll talk to her," I say, walking him to the door. "But maybe I won't mention that you used to work at Feldmans."

He chuckles. "That's only fair. It's a stain that won't go away anytime soon."

We stand at the door, and I wonder how we've gotten to be friendly after the start we had. Maybe I judged him too soon.

I stick my hand out to shake his. He narrows his eyes but takes my hand in his.

"My name's Beatrice. But my friends call me Birdie."

"Beatrice. I like it." Liam smiles, his hand enveloping mine. "You said your grandma nicknamed you Birdie, and it stuck. Where'd she get that?"

"I'll save that story for another day," I say. "Thanks for stopping over, Liam. I'll talk to my mom and let you know."

"Good luck painting," he says. "And Birdie, don't feel like you need to tell anyone that I worked at Feldmans."

"Of course not." I smile as I lean against the doorway. "You can trust me, too."

I close the door and watch Liam pull out of the driveway through the kitchen window.

Chapter Ten

"How's your morning going, Marilyn?" I ask as I enter her room. She sits in a chair, looking out at the nursing home courtyard through the large window.

"Did you hear I had a doctor's appointment yesterday?"

"I did," I say, kneeling beside her. "It sounds like it wasn't the best news."

Her shoulders rise and fall. "Now we know why I've lost vision in one eye. The tumor keeps getting larger. I've known for a while that there's nothing that can be done, but I'm not ready. Not yet."

"I know." I fold her hands in mine. "How are your kids taking this?"

"Oh, Tina jumped into action and feels like she can make this all go away with the appropriate organization. And Tommy hasn't said much at all, which makes me worried for him. The grandbabies are having a hard time, too. They all come daily, almost keeping vigil. They're on a death watch."

"They love you, Marilyn."

I think of Abigail and how much she wishes her family were here, too.

"You are surrounded by us all, Marilyn," I say. "We're here for you."

"You're a dear, Birdie." She lets her head fall back. "I'm going to take a short nap I think."

I grab a blanket and put it over her, and then leave her room.

I've been lingering around my mom's office all day, hoping to get a moment with her. I was already asleep when she got home last night, and I want to talk to her about Liam's offer. I finally see her standing at the South Desk, talking to one of the receptionists.

"Hey," I say, grabbing her arm. "Do you have a minute for a chat?"

"With you?" she smiles. "Always."

My mom takes my hand, and we go to her office.

"What's going on, Birdie?" My mom leans back in her desk chair and puts her feet up on the desk.

"I'd like to get your thoughts on something." I grab a chair and drag it across the floor. "I may have been talking to Liam and mentioned that the nursing home isn't doing well."

"Go on," she says.

"Well, it turns out he's a finance guy. He studied it and has worked in the field his entire career. He mentioned that he'd be happy to look at the balance sheets if that's something you'd be interested in."

"Hmm." My mom smiles and picks up a pen on her desk. "And he's doing this out of the goodness of his heart?"

"Well, yeah," I say. "He wants to make sure his grandparents are getting the best care."

She curls her lips up and nods. "Right. I'm sure it has nothing to do with the stunning woman who works at the nursing home."

"Mom," I say, picking up a paperclip and throwing it at her. "It has nothing to do with me."

"If you say so," she says. "Birdie, you know I'll never turn down help. My goal is to create a nursing home that will survive and thrive long after I'm gone. I love that Liam is willing to help. I can get him the files by the end of the day."

"Thanks, Mom," I say, getting up and wrapping my arms around her.

"For what it's worth," she says as I go to walk out of her office, and I turn back to her. "I don't think this has anything to do with him just wanting the best place for his grandparents."

"Seriously," I say, shaking my head.

My mom has the biggest heart of anyone I've ever known. When I was only thirteen years old, I was on the ranch horseback riding with my grandma. We were in a prairie we'd ridden through a hundred times, but on this day, her horse got spooked and took off running, and my grandma was bucked off.

It was the scariest moment of my life. My grandma lay there, bleeding from her head. Her horse took off, and I rode mine back to the house, where my grandpa was inside making lunch for all of us. He called 911, and my grandma was airlifted to the nearest trauma center.

She survived but had a traumatic brain injury, and it wasn't long before she could no longer stay at home. The only nursing home within a three-hour radius that was equipped to take her was this one in Wheaton.

For the rest of her life, we'd go to Wheaton every weekend and visit her until she died when I was fifteen years old. It was at that moment my mom became passionate about nursing homes. She was already working as a nurse but went back to school to get a master's degree in healthcare administration.

She's good at it, too. She's turned things around everywhere she's gone, but I know Wheaton is her passion project. Being here in this town is a full-circle moment for both of us.

"I hope Liam can find somewhere we could save money," she says. "Because I'm stumped."

"Back to work," I say. "Love you, Mom."

"Love you, Birdie girl."

Even though Liam may not have the answers, having someone who specializes in finance looking through things gives me hope. My mom asked me to review the finances recently, but I chose a degree in nursing so I'd never have to deal with numbers. It's odd because I'm actually very good at math. But I can barely balance my own checkbook, let alone that of a nursing home.

"There you are," Lucy says as she rounds the corner. "The ex has the kid tonight. We need to grab a drink. And before you say no, I'd like to remind you that you've turned me down the past seven times I've asked. And you may not know this about me, but I make an excellent friend."

I laugh. "A drink tonight sounds perfect."

"Did I hear you guys are getting drinks?" Will approaches us.

"Join us if you're free," Lucy says. "We need to blow off some steam and complain about some of the residents' families."

Will laughs. "Perfect. I'll be there."

*****

I liked Lucy the first time I met her. She cares deeply about the residents. They are her first priority in every decision she makes. I also appreciate that she's naughty. She makes me laugh.

The distance from my house to the pool hall is a little over a mile, but it's a beautiful night out and I'm happy for the fresh air. I walk through the door, and everyone's eyes turn to me. I'm not sure how long someone has to live in a town to no longer be considered the new person, but I know I'm not at that stage yet. I'm still very much an outsider. I spot Lucy at the bar, and I beeline toward her.

"I didn't know you had clothes outside of scrubs," she says, pulling me into a hug. "Those shorts are hot. Your legs are gorgeous, girl."

Lucy slowly checks me out and then gives me two thumbs up.

"Is this what a Friday night at the pool hall looks like?" I look around. Every table is full, and the bar has rows of people waiting to order drinks.

Lucy hands me a drink and starts laughing. "Who knows? I go out about as much as you apparently do."

She points toward the door. "Oh, there's Will."

I turn as he walks in our direction. I haven't taken many nights to myself to be a twenty-five-year-old, get out of the house, or leave the nursing home. I've now been here almost three months, and I've never seen Lucy or Will in actual clothes. All we wear are scrubs. He smiles when he sees us.

"It's loud in here," he says. He quickly blinks as he takes me in. I didn't wear anything special. I paired my favorite shorts with a tube top.

"Here." Lucy hands him a drink. "I can't promise it's any good, but I ordered it for you."

Will smiles. "I'll drink anything after the week at work I've had."

Lucy grabs my hand and pulls me to a quieter area in the corner, and Will follows.

"So this is what the young people do while I work or sleep," Lucy says, looking around. "Oh, to be in my twenties again. Don't get me wrong, I love Gavin more than I ever thought possible, but oh, to be carefree for one night."

Music plays loudly from the jukebox, and the entire place smells of burnt popcorn and cheap beer. My feet stick to the floor.

"We're happy you're here," Will says, turning to me. There are so many people, and I'm pressed against the wall and him. "I feel like most of the town grew up here and knows each other. It's great to meet people also from somewhere else."

Lucy smiles into her drink. Will holds up his empty glass.

"I'm going to brave my way to the bar," he says. "Can I get you guys anything?"

"Yes," Lucy says before I have a chance. "Surprise us both."

Will walks away, and Lucy grabs my arm. "He is so into you."

I narrow my eyes. "Sorry. Who's into me?"

"Will," Lucy says. "He mentioned something at work a couple of weeks ago about you being exactly his type, but now I see how he's acting. The boy likes you."

I glance at Will as he makes his way to the bar. I hadn't even considered it. I'm very out of practice when it comes to dating. I've never had anything serious with someone and have been more involved in situationships. Will may be considered handsome by some, but I've never thought of him as anything other than a co-worker and potential friend. His attractiveness isn't the in-your-face kind like some other people's.

"He's just being friendly, Lucy," I say.

Will comes back with our drinks, and as I look up, my gaze meets Liam's. He stands next to his friend, Dax. Now, Liam is the obvious kind of attractive that a person would have to be dead not to notice. His dark jeans, shirt, and sneakers look so good together, and my breath hitches in my chest as he says something to Dax, and then they both walk in my direction.

Lucy and Will have a conversation around me, but all I can focus on is Liam as he closes the gap between us.

"Birdie." Liam holds his glass up and clinks it against mine. "Cheers."

"Liam," I say. "Have you met my co-workers? This is Lucy and Will."

"Of course I have." Liam turns to them. "It's nice to see you outside of the nursing home."

They stay with us in our small corner, like the five of us are old friends. As the crowd grows, we keep getting farther pressed against the wall. Somehow, Liam ends up wedged behind me, and his fingers spread against the bare skin on my waist.

"Sorry, Birdie." He breathes into my ear. "Someone came up behind me."

I look over my shoulder at him, my breath becoming labored at the proximity of Liam to me. His fingers linger around me until he drops his hand. Our eyes meet, and I nod.

Everyone takes their turns buying rounds, and at some point, I feel a little tipsy on both alcohol and attraction.

"I work tomorrow," I abruptly announce to the group. "I think I'm going to take off."

"Hey," Will says, grabbing my arm. "I can drive you home."

"Thanks," I say, leaning toward Will so he can hear me. "But I'll walk. I'll catch up with you at work in a couple of days. I know you have tomorrow off."

He presses his lips together and smiles. I give Lucy a hug and turn to say goodbye to Liam and Dax.

"Let me walk you out," Liam says.

I go to protest, but he grips my arm as I maneuver myself through the crowd. We reach outside, and the air is sticky. We stare at each other as the moon beams down and reflects off of the buildings on Main Street.

"Can I drive you home?" Liam asks.

I look down the street. "Like I told Will, I'll walk."

"Then I'm walking with you," he says. "I'll come back and get my car."

"Suit yourself," I say. "But it's not necessary."

I start down the street, and Liam follows.

We're silent, and after a few blocks, we veer to the left and off Main Street.

"Your mom emailed me," Liam says. I turn to him, and he's smiling. "She sent me a few confidential documents and said she looks forward to me diving in and providing recommendations."

"That's great." I nudge my shoulder against his.

"Did she seem pretty open to it? Her email made it seem so, but I wanted to check."

"She was very open to it," I say. "My mom wants the best for the nursing home. She doesn't care who's part of the solution. She's very unselfish like that."

The road gets darker. During the day, I'd cut through the cemetery to get home, but I'm not going to do that in the dark.

"My grandma was in this nursing home for a couple of years when I was a teenager. Most places wouldn't accept her and her condition, but Wheaton welcomed her with open arms." I glance at Liam, and all of his attention is on me. "She's always felt a soft spot for this place. When they showed up in the local news about the risk of shutting down, she jumped in, no questions asked."

The porch light is on outside our home, and my mom's car is parked out front.

"Your mom said I can work out of one of the empty offices tomorrow so I can go through all the documents she sent me. I'll have coffee with Grandpa Sunny in the morning, and then get to work."

"I'll be there," I say.

Liam walks me to the door, and we stand on the top step. I stare up at him, confident that I've misjudged him from the start. I mistook his quietness for judgment when, really, he was struggling with something in silence. He's the kind of guy who grows on you the more time you spend with him.

Even his appearance gets better the closer you look, which is rare. When Liam walks into a room, people turn their necks and stare at the six-foot-three man with broad shoulders and a chiseled jaw. But upon closer look, it's his deep blue eyes that I can't glance away from.

"Thanks for giving me purpose," he finally says. He rubs his lips together. "Ever since coming back, I've been feeling very—"

"No thanks necessary," I say, spreading my hand across his upper arm. "Thanks for walking me home."

Liam pulls open the screen door. "See you tomorrow, Birdie."

Chapter Eleven

Sunny leaves to have coffee with Liam and the boys in the cafeteria, and I close the door for privacy so I can help get Sis ready for the day. Usually, our CNAs handle this type of work, but we're short-staffed on them too.

"Can I help with your bra?"

Sis nods.

I help lift her shirt off, her mastectomy scars a reminder of all she's been through. I clasp it shut.

"What do you want to wear today?"

Sis sits on the edge of her bed, staring into her open closet where several beautiful outfits hang.

"Yellow," Sis says.

I grab a pale yellow jumpsuit and help her get into it.

"Yellow is your best color," I say, zipping up the soft cotton sweatshirt over her white undershirt. "It suits your tone so well."

"Birdie?" Sis looks up at me once she's fully dressed. "Am I crazy? Is that why I'm here?"

"You're not crazy." I sit on the bed beside her and hold her hand. "Did someone tell you that?"

"No." Sis shakes her head and looks down. "But why else would I live here? I must be, right?"

"You're here because your family thinks it's the safest place for you," I say. "You have memory issues, Sis. Was it hard to take care of yourself when you lived in the big house on Main Street?"

"It was," Sis says, and I start styling her hair. "Sometimes I'd forget to turn off the burner when I made tea."

"Exactly." I run a comb through her soft curls. "But here, we can help you with your memory and make sure both you and Sunny are safe. And so many of your friends are here, too."

"So, I'm not crazy?" Her eyes meet mine, and I'm sure I've never seen bluer ones.

"You are not crazy," I say. "No one here is crazy. But as we age, we can't always be independent like we were when we were young. Heck, I'll probably end up here someday."

Sis stands, and I follow. She takes my hand and squeezes it.

"I feel crazy. I have a thought in my head, and the next moment, I forget it. I can't always come up with the words I want to say. My brain is messy."

I walk Sis down the hall and past the doors with extra security to our memory unit for her classes. On my way there, I see her son and Liam's dad, Larry, sitting with the men, drinking coffee, and I purposely take the long way because I don't have the energy for him today. I didn't even realize he was still in town.

Sis has moments, almost daily, where her thoughts seem clear, and we can have a concise conversation. However, those moments are becoming less frequent, and she rarely retains what I say, so I have to repeat myself often.

"Birdie," Will says, rounding the corner and pushing Joe in a wheelchair. "How was the rest of your night?"

"It was good," I say. "My mom and I watched a show when I got home, and then I went to bed. How was yours?"

"I left shortly after you," he says. "Did Liam take you home?"

"I walked," I say. "He came with me though. He had something to share with me."

"Oh." Will nods.

"Can someone take me to get my damn coffee?" Joe says impatiently, and I laugh.

"Will is going to take you right now, Joe," I say.

I pop in to check on Marilyn, and her daughter Tina is here, so I make it quick so they can enjoy their visit.

Marilyn continues to lose weight, and I'm not sure how much more time we have with her.

"Birdie." I turn to see Liam coming in my direction. "What time do you break for lunch?"

I glance at my watch, and it's already two in the afternoon. Days at the nursing home fly by.

"Now," I say. "What's up?"

"Meet me in the office? I'm down this hall." Liam points.

I grab my lunch in the break room and venture down the hallway where some of the staff offices are until I see Liam sitting at a table in one of them, studying a laptop. He has black-rimmed glasses on and squints at what he's looking at.

"I think you need a new prescription," I say, closing the door and pointing at him. "You don't seem to be able to see very well."

"Readers." He glances at me. "My eyes get tired from studying spreadsheets all the time."

Liam looks back down at the computer. I open my brown-bagged lunch and pull out a peanut-butter-and-jelly sandwich.

He eyes it and raises an eyebrow. "That can't be enough to sustain you."

"You'd be surprised." I bite into it and moan. "It's my go-to. Grape jelly. Creamy peanut butter. Perfection."

Liam removes his glasses and leans back in his chair. He folds his arms behind his head.

"Do you want to tell me why you're barely taking a salary?"

"I..."

Nothing else comes out as my mouth hangs open. I hadn't considered that Liam having access to all the financials meant he'd also have access to mine.

"I've spent the entire morning looking at the books. You're making less than the poverty line. You're taking only about twenty percent of what you should be making."

I tuck my half-eaten sandwich back into its bag. I close my Tupperware of fruit because I'm no longer hungry.

"It's fine, Liam."

He studies the paper in his hands once again. "It's not. You working for almost free is not fine."

"Li—"

"Why is your little male nurse friend making a full salary while you're putting in more hours than anyone and making this?" He slaps a spreadsheet on the table to make his point.

"Look." I shoot up from my chair and pace back and forth, pausing at the window. Outside is a stone fountain with water running down the sides.

"I needed out of a job that had me moving every few months. My mom was down an RN at the nursing home. I wanted to live in the same place as her. I knew things were bad here, but I didn't realize how dire the situation was. But I chose this."

Liam stands and closes the distance between us. We stand shoulder to shoulder. He leans against the window and stares at me.

"You're not setting yourself up for the future, Birdie."

"It's a pause," I say. "We're going to turn this place around, and my salary will go to what it should be and I can start paying off my school loans."

"Your mom's been here over a year already, and she hasn't turned anything around."

I snap my head in his direction. Concern is splashed across his face. He presses a finger to his lips.

"Your mom invited me to dinner tonight to discuss my initial thoughts," Liam says. "I'll be over at six. I think it would be good if we all sit down together so everything is out in the open."

"Then I better get back to work so I can be home on time."

"Birdie." Liam grabs my wrist as I turn away from him. He opens his mouth and runs his tongue along his upper teeth. Just when I think he's going to say something, he snaps his mouth shut.

"See you at six," I say.

He releases my wrist and nods.

Chapter Twelve

When you work in a nursing home, a shower is always required after the shift. I let the warm water run over my body, replaying my conversation with Liam from earlier. My mom tried to talk me out of coming here. She told me she couldn't afford me, and it was my idea to take a measly salary. I was able to defer my nursing school loans for a year, and then I'll figure it out.

My mom and I are a team. She's an anchor in this world of unknowns, and I trust that we have each other's best interests at heart. She begged me not to come but being around her is like coming home, and I insisted. I pull on my favorite cutoff shorts and a tank top. I stand in front of the full-length mirror in my room and brush my hair, which has gotten so long. I can't remember the last time I had a haircut. I put on a little blush, mascara, and tinted lip moisturizer. I smack my lips together and head downstairs.

"What can I help with?" I ask as my mom stands at the kitchen counter, making her famous summer salad. It's got uncooked ramen noodles, cabbage, scallions, and almonds, and it's always been my favorite.

There's a knock at the door, and she looks over her shoulder and smiles. "Saved by the bell."

Liam stands there, a bottle of wine in his hand. A breeze comes up behind him, and I inhale the fresh scent of whatever he's wearing.

"Are you going to invite me in?" Liam raises an eyebrow.

"Sorry. Yes, of course. Please." I open the door wider.

"Welcome back to the Hurst haunted house," I say, and he smiles. "You should see it at night. It's a lot scarier."

"Liam," my mom says, rounding the corner, holding her large bowl of salad. "Thanks so much for coming. It's so beautiful out, I thought we could eat on the back deck."

"What can I help with?" he asks.

"There's a stack of plates over there. Birdie, grab us glasses and utensils, please."

We get situated at our round table on the deck in our backyard. I love it out here. On one side is the cemetery, and on the other side and behind us is farmland as far as the eye can see.

"Everything looks great," Liam says, as my mom hands him the plate of chicken.

"It's been so hot out, I didn't want to make anything too heavy."

Liam holds out the bottle of wine. I nod, and he pours me a glass.

"I appreciate you offering to look at the finances," my mom says. "I've been studying them to death. What I can't figure out is what to change. Our biggest expense is salaries, and we can't get people to work at the nursing home if we don't offer competitive pay. I'm not sure what else to do. I've never been at such a loss."

Liam glances up from his bowl. "I'd like to have a frank conversation. Lay everything out on the table."

My mom nods. "Should I be nervous?"

I cut my chicken and lean toward Liam, giving him my full attention.

"The way things are going now with the nursing home in its current state is only sustainable for another six months, best-case scenario. It's been operating in the red for a very long time. Bills are overdue. And the capital equipment agreements are out of compliance, which puts you at risk of losing those vital resources."

My mom puts her fork down. She leans back in her chair and runs her fingers through her hair.

"You're barely paying yourself, June. Or paying Birdie."

"Liam," I say, and his eyes cut to mine. "I told you—"

"It's okay, Birdie," my mom says. "He's right."

"When Midwest Care, the owner of the nursing home, brought you on, I don't think they had any confidence that you'd turn things around."

"The nursing home is for sale," Liam says. "Midwest Care has been trying to sell this one off for years because it's not making any money. They're trying to get as much for it as possible, but at the same time, they're taking a huge cut of the money that's coming in, which means no matter what you do, you won't have enough revenue."

"I noticed that," my mom says. "But I'm not sure what I can do about it. They aren't going to agree to take less money."

Liam looks at me and then turns toward my mom. "If you're serious about turning things around, you should buy the nursing home. Midwest Care needs to be out. Immediately."

My mom nearly chokes on her water.

"Me? Buy the nursing home?" She laughs. "I'm not business savvy. I wouldn't even know where to start."

"That's what I'm here for," Liam says. "Midwest Care is going to be willing to negotiate. I can help you with the paperwork to start your own business. It's not worth any money right now. Anyone who buys it is taking on a huge liability. They'll be motivated to sell."

My mom folds her hands over her face and lets out a deep breath. "I have my inheritance from the ranch, but that's all. And I wanted to give that to Birdie someday. What if I lost it all?"

Liam leans back and folds his hands behind his head. "Based on the salary you're paying yourself, you're dipping into your inheritance on a monthly basis already. Once everything is transferred to your name as the owner, we can work on the revenue stream. I have an extensive background in corporate fundraising."

"You've been quiet, Birdie," my mom says, looking at me. "If I do this, I'm in Wheaton. Is this even where you want to be?"

"Yeah, Mom," I say. "I think I do."

My mom passes around a bowl of raspberries, and I pop one in my mouth.

"This is a lot to digest, Liam," my mom says. "I need to think long and hard about everything."

"Of course." Liam takes a sip of wine. "I've dabbled in actuarial work, along with finance. I'm going to write up an analysis of financial risk for several options moving forward to give you a clearer picture."

My mom puts her hand on Liam's and squeezes. "I can't thank you enough. You're good at what you do. I can tell. The world of finance needs more honest people like you."

Liam takes a long blink and sucks in his breath. My mom's phone starts vibrating on the table, and she glances at it.

"Lucy's calling," she says. "I better take this."

My mom walks inside and closes the French doors leading to the deck with a thud.

"How'd I do?"

"It sounds bad." I scrape my teeth along my bottom lip. "Buying the nursing home, though? I hope you're right."

Liam refills my glass of wine and rubs his palms against his temples. "It's not about right or wrong. It's weighing risk and whether your mom—and potentially you—want to do it. I'll tell you this: if you don't, this nursing home will be shut down within the year after Midwest Care files for bankruptcy. Guaranteed."

Liam looks up at the sky and closes his eyes. His lips turn up ever so slightly.

"You enjoy talking about this, don't you?" I throw a napkin at him, and he laughs. "You're one of those people who geek out discussing finance and risk analysis, aren't you?"

He throws the napkin back at me. "I can't help it. I love this stuff."

I grab his arm and stand. "Okay. Let me show you something I love."

I grab the half-full bottle of wine and our glasses. Liam follows me through the thick grass toward the cemetery. I kick off my flip-flops, skip, and twirl, feeling the softness beneath my feet.

"Why am I not surprised that you like to hang out with dead people?" Liam smiles.

"You know they aren't actually here, right?" I say quietly.

"It doesn't scare you living by the cemetery? In a haunted house?"

"You know who has never hurt me?" I put my hands up in the air and spin. "Dead people. It's the living that scares the shit out of me."

"Huh," Liam says, taking my hand and spinning me toward him. "I've never thought about it like that before."

I lick the sweet wine off my lips, and we reach my favorite spot in the cemetery, a stone bench that faces a few gravestones, with large, rolling hills in the background. I take a seat, and Liam sits next to me. I refill our glasses and let out a deep breath.

Liam turns to me. His white shirt brings out the bronzed tone of his arms.

"Given everything you know about my professional past, thank you for trusting me with something so important."

"Well," I say, glancing at him over my wine glass, "if you mess with my family, I will kill you."

Liam barks a laugh, but then his expression falls.

"I had a great job in Manhattan," Liam says. "I started getting recruited by Feldmans, and it felt good to be so desired. When they offered me a job, my dad warned me about financial startups like them. I told him he had nothing to worry about and took it anyway."

I put my hand on his arm and feel the muscles underneath. Liam glances at me over his shoulder.

"Things were too good to be true," he continues. "And part of me knew it then. I may not have had anything to do with their schemes, but I didn't say anything either. I collected my paycheck and kept my mouth shut."

Liam presses the glass against his lips.

"When they went down, I lost everything. My retirement, my salary. My pride. When I called my dad to tell him, the first thing he said was, 'Well, I told you so.'"

He puts his hand on my forearm. It's heavy. Large. Electric. The subtle touch ignites something in me in a way that I don't allow often. Part of me wants to go back to a few weeks ago when he was the ornery grandson of Sunny and Sis. Now he's Liam Bergland, the handsome, sometimes mysterious friend who makes my body heat.

"Thank you," he says.

Our gazes stay locked on each other, his hand unwavering. My brain jumbles up with thoughts. I look beyond Liam to where the sun is almost touching the hills.

"This," I say, pointing, and Liam turns. "Is what I wanted to show you."

The sun hits the top of the rolling hills, and everything turns to hues of orange and pink as it begins to disappear, getting smaller. Neither of us says anything. The gravestones light up with the shadows of the sun. They glow as if they're coming alive.

"You're really selling the beauty of a cemetery, Birdie." Liam stands, holds out his hand, and helps me to my feet. "But I refuse to be here at night."

"Understood." I laugh as I reach to the ground and grab the empty bottle of wine.

We walk through the grass in comfortable silence. I'm deep in my thoughts about what my mom buying the nursing home could mean, and also thinking about how rare it is for me to find someone attractive, yet a new electricity passes between Liam and me.

The dishes are all cleared from the outside table, and we step inside. I peek out front, and my mom's car is gone. Whatever Lucy was calling about must have been some nursing home emergency she had to attend to.

"It's late," Liam says, walking toward the door. "Please tell your mom thanks for dinner. And that I'll be in touch."

Liam pauses at the door. His mouth opens as if he's going to say something, but then he snaps it shut.

"See you tomorrow," I say.

"Yes." Liam steps outside and looks at his phone. "I should get back to the cottage just in time for my dad's third drink, which is when he starts lecturing me about all of my bad life decisions."

"Ouch." I scrunch up my face. "Good luck with that."

Liam extends his arm and playfully pushes my arm. "Night, Birdie."

Chapter Thirteen

"Do you want to know the worst part about turning ninety-three?" Joe crosses his arms as he watches me put the rest of his birthday decorations on the door.

"What's that?" I ask, finishing taping the final streamer.

"Everyone else is dead," he says. "At your age, it's about going to all the weddings. At my age, I average two funerals a week."

I glance at him as he lies in bed. His blue robe is pulled tightly across his body.

"You may not believe this," Joe says, "but I was a popular guy back in the day. All the ladies liked me, but Betty was the lucky one."

"You're pretty lucky too." I help Joe stand up and grab his walker from the corner of his room. "Betty's a good one."

"Yeah, she is," he says.

"Head down to the cafeteria," I say. "Your cake awaits you."

"Will you take me home afterward?"

"Oh, Joe," I say, and then jerk my neck when I hear commotion down the hall.

Joe throws his robe off, and I'm relieved when I see he's wearing a jumpsuit underneath it. He starts moving in the direction of the cafeteria, and I jog toward the sound of complete chaos.

It's Sis. She's in the room with one of the CNAs and is agitated. One of her porcelain figurines flies across the room as I enter, barely missing me.

"Sis, it's okay," I say in my calmest voice. "It's me, Birdie."

"What the hell is going on in here?" Larry's voice calls out at the worst possible time because it only upsets Sis more.

"This man"—she points at the new CNA, Jose—"tried to take my shirt off."

A big scream escapes Sis, and she grabs a book from her side table and throws that across the room.

"Grandma?" Liam walks into the room.

"He touched me," Sis says, looking at Jose, who appears horrified.

"I didn't," Jose stammers out. "Lucy told me to get Sis dressed for Joe's birthday party."

She flails her arms around, pacing and crying. I rush to her just as she turns and flails an arm, her elbow catching me directly in the eye. I wince, then reach her and wrap my arms around her, completely immobilizing her.

"Sis," I say, "it's okay. It's me, Birdie. It's okay. Shh."

Her screaming lessens, and her breath begins to regulate.

"Jose, why don't you go check on Abigail and get her down to the cafeteria for cake?"

He nods and leaves the room, but then Sis begins flailing again. Her strength is astounding, and when I look behind me, Larry and Liam stand back in horror. Will comes running in and helps restrain her. He holds her arms to her side, and I get in her line of vision.

"Sis," I say, "Jose's job is to help you get dressed. But if that makes you uncomfortable, I'll make sure that only females come into your room. Would that be okay?"

"Yes," she chokes out. "No men."

Will and I get Sis calm and then put her in bed. Liam comes to her bedside and rubs her arm.

My face is on fire. I put my cool palm against it. Will stays with Sis, and as I try to leave the room, Larry grabs my arm.

"You won't report this, will you?"

I look at him, confused.

"You won't file a report, right?"

I put my hand to my face, already feeling a bump forming, and storm past him. I duck into an empty room and slam the door shut. First, Larry threatens to remove his parents from the nursing home, and therefore take his finances with them. And now he doesn't want me to report Sis because she may be deemed too high needs? Unbelievable.

"Shit," I say, still holding my face.

Everything happened so fast, but I didn't follow protocol. I went in there alone, and although Sis didn't try to hurt me, I should have called for backup before running into the room. I lean back against the wall and try to catch my breath.

The door flies open, and Liam stands there with a bag of ice. He holds it up, presses his lips together, and I nod.

"Birdie." He closes the distance between us and holds the ice pack to my face, and I wince.

The door opens again, and this time it's Will.

"Hey, Birdie," he says, looking at me before his gaze cuts to Liam. "You okay?"

"I'm fine," I say.

He raises an eyebrow as he glances at Liam. "Let me know if you need anything."

"Thanks, Will," I say. "I appreciate you stepping in."

He nods.

Once he's gone, Liam takes my hand and leads me to the desk, and I sit on the edge of it. He places the ice bag on my face, and I close my eyes. The cold against the heat of my face hurts. Fire and ice.

Liam steps to the side and puts his hand on my shoulder. His leg rubs against mine. "If this is something you're supposed to report, don't let my dad bully you out of it. You need to do what's right."

I put my hand over his to apply more pressure to my face.

"I shouldn't have gone in there alone," I say. "I know better."

Liam moves his hand from my shoulder to my arm. He pulls the ice bag away, tilts his head, and studies my face. He brushes his thumb over where Sis's elbow made contact with my bone. It's a feather-light touch, and my arms explode in goosebumps.

"Am I still intact?" Gravity pulls me into his orbit until my face is inches from his chest, and I inhale and breathe him in.

Liam smiles and pulls his hand away. "You're going to survive this time but watch out for my family's elbows. They're pointy."

"Good to know." I'm not sure if I'm concussed or if my fuzziness is due to proximity to Liam.

He hands me the ice bag. "Keep icing, okay?"

"Thanks." I press my lips together.

Liam's chest rises, then falls as he studies me. He nods toward the door, then walks out.

After gaining composure, I leave the room and get back to work. I check in on Joe's birthday party, which many of the residents are attending. Then I stop at the south desk, where Lucy sits, doing paperwork.

"Birdie." I turn as Will walks my way. "Are you up for getting a pizza tonight?"

"Yeah," I say, looking at Lucy. "What time are you thinking?"

"Seven," he says. "I'll pick you up."

"You don't have—"

"Birdie," Will says. "I'll pick you up."

He walks away when one of the residents needs his assistance with something, and I turn to Lucy.

"Yay," I say. "I get to hang out with you again. Which is needed after today."

"Oh no," she says, laughing. "I'm pretty sure Will just asked you on a date. There was no mention of me in this pizza get-together."

My head shoots in Will's direction, and I snap my hand over my open mouth.

"No," I say. "I didn't realize. I thought you two had already made plans, and the three of us were going to hang out."

Lucy jumps up from her chair and sits on the desk beside me. "Do you like him? He's a cutie, right? I mean, I'm in my mid-thirties. I don't know what you young kids are into these days."

I glance across the room where Will is assisting a resident. I narrow my eyes. "I don't see him that way. And I don't envision that changing."

"Well." Lucy shrugs. "You'll have to tell him that because he sees you that way. I've been trying to tell you. The man hasn't stopped talking about you since the day you got to town."

"Today just keeps getting better." I hold my hand up to my face.

"Birdie." Lucy stands and cups my cheeks. "You are this beautiful girl with freckles, the brightest blue eyes I've ever seen, and a body that looks good in everything. Men are going to shoot their shot. Get used to it."

She smiles as she walks away laughing.

Chapter Fourteen

"What does someone wear on a date to give off 'friend only' vibes?" I say the words out loud into my full-length mirror.

I pull on a pair of jeans and check myself out.

"Damn it, my butt looks too good. I can't wear these." As soon as the words are out of my mouth, the light in my room flickers off and then on again.

Old wiring. It has to be.

I rip the jeans off and put on a sundress. It's pretty, which is why I bought it, but also shapeless. I stand in front of the mirror. This is the best option. It's short, but it also covers my curves. Then I put on some makeup, mostly to hide the fact that my cheek is red and slightly swollen.

There's a knock at the door, and I look at the time. No way would Will be here this early. I run down the stairs and throw the door open, and Liam stands on the other side, his hands stuffed into his pockets.

"Hey," he says. He tilts his head, his gaze on me. "You look nice."

I glance down at my dress. "I do? That's not what I was going for."

Liam narrows his eyes. "Sorry for the compliment, I guess."

"What's up?" I stay in the doorway and hold my arm against the frame.

"Can we talk?"

His face is serious, so I open the door wider and he walks through.

"What's going on? Is everything okay?"

Liam heads toward the living room and sits in the middle of the couch. I lower myself onto the chair.

"How is this going to end?" He looks at his hands folded over his lap.

"Sorry, how does what end?"

Liam puckers his lips and blows out a breath. "With Grandma. Sis. It keeps getting worse. How does it end? With Alzheimer's?"

"Oh." I stand and take a seat next to Liam on the couch. "Did something else happen today?"

Liam shakes his head. "But that person in the room freaking the fuck out? That wasn't my grandma. It's like her eyes were empty."

I tuck a leg underneath myself and lean my elbow on the back of the couch.

"No one knows how anything ends," I say.

"Birdie." He shifts so our knees press together. "You've seen this play out. What should I expect? Because what I saw today? It broke my fucking heart. Yeah, she forgets things, but today was different."

His dark blue eyes stare into mine. I put my hand on his knee.

"Do you want my response as your friend or as your grandma's nurse?"

He closes his eyes and takes a couple of deep breaths. "Nurse."

I remove my hand from his leg and tuck it into my lap.

"At some point, Sis will most likely become non-verbal, and when she does speak, it won't make much sense." Liam's body tightens.

"Most Alzheimer's patients become bed bound," I say. "Unable to get up and walk around. She'll lose bladder and bowel function at some point as well."

Liam grabs my hand. I pause, but I think about all the people I've had to deliver bad news to in my short career, and it's a common reaction.

"Don't hold back. Please. I need to know what we're in for as a family."

"The end will most likely be when your grandma can no longer swallow. She won't be able to take food in, and that happens in the later stages. As you know, she's DNR, and your dad and uncle want minimal interventions."

"So she'll starve or die from dehydration," he says.

It's not a question, but a realization.

Liam nods. "How long before that happens?"

"It's impossible to tell," I say. "But since meeting Sis, it's clear to me that her disease is progressing."

"Yeah." Liam runs a hand across his face. "When I was away, I could ignore it, you know? I'd call and check in almost daily, but everyone told me what they thought I needed to hear. But now that I'm here, there's no hiding from it."

"It's a terrible disease," I say, grabbing both of his hands and holding them. "There are no absolutes. So we hope. That's all we have."

We've somehow inched closer, our legs intertwined, our faces inches apart. He moves his hand to my face, tracing the bruise left by today's events. I inhale sharply when he traces his thumb along my bottom lip in a way that no longer feels like his grandma's nurse catching him up on her case. Or even two friends. This feels like more.

"Li—" I begin to say, but he presses my lips together with his finger.

"Can I block all the bad stuff out and just enjoy the view in front of me?"

I take a deep breath but nod.

Since when am I the view?

His hand slides to the nape of my neck, fingers weaving through the strands of my hair, pulling me closer. When I look at him, he's staring at all the places he touches me. His finger traces the edge of my hairline, moves to my jaw, and down to my chest before he stops.

His eyes flick to mine. Our lips meet in a hungry collision, a symphony of desire and urgency. He tastes so good. Too good. Like the Sour Patch Kids I say I'm only going to have one of, but then finish the entire bag. Or like the glass of Prosecco that turns into two because of how much I love the sweetness on my lips.

The pressure of our kiss pushes me over until I'm lying on my back, Liam between my legs. His mouth opens mine, and I experience sensory overload. His heavy body atop mine. Our tongues dance as if this isn't the first time they've met.

His large hand grips my thigh, then moves higher until it's under my dress and tracing the outline of my panties.

The front door pushes open, and Liam jumps off of me and I shoot up to a sitting position.

"Pillow," he murmurs under his breath, and I turn to him. He points. "Pillow, Birdie. Pillow."

I throw it to him, and then I see what he's trying to hide right before he presses it into his lap.

"Birdie." My mom walks into the living room and sees us. I most likely look as disheveled as I feel. "Hi, Liam."

He gives a wave in her direction, and she covers the amused expression on her face.

"I'm going to go upstairs," she says, while pointing in case it wasn't clear. "Take a shower. A long one. You know the drill."

She presses her lips together, trying to suppress a smile, and walks upstairs.

The stairs creak with her weight, and then we hear her on the floor above us. Liam moves the pillow, grips my waist, and drags me toward him.

"Wait." I push my hand against his chest.

"What?" He runs his hand along my cheek.

"Did you kiss me to forget about how sad you are?" I take slow breaths.

"Yes and no." He runs his hand along my outer thigh. "But now that I've tasted you, I'm addicted."

I know what he means.

"We can't do that again." I push him back again, and he puts space between us.

"Wait," Liam says. "What?"

I lean forward and wipe my lip gloss off of his swollen lips.

"Has something changed that I'm not aware of?" I say, straightening my legs and pressing my head into the back of the couch. "Because last I checked, you're trying to find the first ticket out of here."

Liam rubs a finger along the curve of his lip. "You know I'm still leaving, Birdie."

He turns toward me and puts his hand on my leg. His long fingers rub circles into the inside of my thigh. It would be so easy to lean forward and push away all logic, but I'm smarter than that.

"I'm attracted to you," he says, and my body heats up. "I feel like you may be attracted to me, too. We can be casual."

"Casual?" I choke out a laugh. "What does that mean to you?"

Liam pushes his lips out as he nods. "I haven't given it a lot of thought. We'll spend time together. Do a lot more of that." He smiles.

"And what happens when you leave?"

"I'll leave." He pulls me toward him. "But I will spend so many nights lying awake and thinking about that particular kiss."

"At least you're honest." I move to the corner of the couch and tuck my legs in. "I was half-expecting you to tell me you'd try to sustain some sort of long-distance relationship."

I stand and straighten my dress. "Thanks for not feeding me that level of bullshit."

"What?" Liam shakes his head. "You only talk to people you could have a future with?"

"Actually," I say. "Yes."

"Huh." Liam stands and drags a hand down his face. He moves a window curtain to the side and stares out at the front yard. He slowly turns around. "What if you could have a future, but you just don't know it at the time? Imagine all the people you shut out before getting to know them."

"There is something you should know about me." I fold my arms over my chest and take a deep breath. "I let very few people get close to me. I have my reasons. If we hadn't already become friends, who knows? Maybe something more could happen."

"We're not that good of friends," Liam says.

I glance up at him, and he's smiling. I grab a pillow from the couch and throw it at his face, but he catches it with ease. He laughs and holds his arm out to me. I willingly melt into his embrace, and he kisses the top of my head. It's not lost on me what I'm saying no to.

I deserve sainthood.

Liam reaches for my hand. "Friends."

I hear the door to my mom's bedroom open and then loud footsteps coming down the stairs.

"Liam," she says as she appears in the room. "Do you want to stay for dinner?"

He opens his mouth to answer, just as there's a knock at the door.

"Will," I say, completely forgetting that he was going to pick me up.

"Will from work?" my mom says, screwing up her face.

"You're going on a date with Will?" Liam says, raising an eyebrow. "The male nurse guy?"

"It's not really a date," I say, moving toward the door. "It's just pizza."

"That sounds like a date," my mom says.

"I agree." Liam folds his hands over his chest.

"Hey, Will," I say as I open the door. He smiles, and then looks behind me at my mom and Liam.

"See you later, Mom," I say. "Liam, thanks for stopping by." I hold the door open for him so he can leave.

Liam steps out, watching me the entire time. He turns back when he reaches his car and raises an eyebrow when Will puts his hand on the small of my back as he opens the door to his truck.

It may make zero sense to Liam, but going on a date with someone who I find nice enough is a much safer option than getting lost in the world of Liam Bergland.

Chapter Fifteen

The last date I went on was so long ago that I can't even recall who it was with. Growing up, I wasn't overly social. I preferred to be on the ranch, tending to the animals and spending time with my grandparents and mom.

My grandma's accident nearly destroyed me. My mom put me in therapy afterward, but I don't know if it helped.

In college, I had a couple of situationships, but I've never had a boyfriend. I've never come close to being in love. And it wasn't because of the guys—it was because of me. I've always had complicated emotions when it comes to men. At the heart of the issue, I don't trust them.

"How are you liking Wheaton so far?" Will asks from across the table, bringing me back to the present.

"It's been good," I say. "I can't believe I've been here three months already."

I stare at Will as he studies the menu. He's not bad-looking, and although it's completely unfair, I can't help but compare him to Liam, who is a man. Will still looks like a boy. He's shorter than Liam and less built. His face is so smooth it looks like he doesn't even need to shave. If we kissed, would I get completely consumed by it? If my mom hadn't come home, I wouldn't have stopped anything from happening. Being touched by Liam was like being in a trance.

"What are your thoughts on the meat lovers?" He looks up from the menu.

"That sounds perfect."

Our drinks come, and we sip beer.

"Where'd you go to school?" Will asks, blowing on his piece of pizza.

"I stayed in South Dakota," I say. "My mom and I were selling the ranch we lived on, and she was figuring out where to go next."

"After nursing school, you became a travel nurse?"

"I did," I say. "I saw a job posting for a three-month assignment in Flagstaff and thought, why not? After my time there, I loved that I didn't have to stay because the hospital wasn't for me. So I headed to Vermont. Then I saw an opening in West Virginia and kept moving."

We go back and forth, and the conversation flows. Will is also from South Dakota and has lived here for a few years. He's a couple of years older than me. We stick to surface-level things, which is fine—maybe even preferred. There's no spark, though, and I wonder if Will realizes that too.

"Liam," Will says, and my ears perk up. "What's his story? He always looks pissed at the world, but somehow, he's always smiling around you."

"He's harmless," I say casually and shrug. I leave out the part about him looking into the finances of the nursing home.

My mind goes to our kiss from earlier. I'd imagined what kissing him would be like, even though I had no intention of finding out. Usually, the more I get to know someone, the less attractive they become. Why couldn't that be true with Liam?

Liam is also the kind of guy who's used to getting what he wants, which is why he's struggled so much with being here, as well as the circumstances behind it. Women say yes to him, and I can guarantee that I'm unlike anyone he's ever pursued.

People describe me as the girl next door. I look much younger than my twenty-five years, with freckles sprinkling my face, shoulders, and chest. I'm cute. The women he's dated are probably bombshells.

"Do you want another drink?" Will asks.

I shake my head. How long have I been sitting here daydreaming about Liam?

"No," I say. "Sorry. I must be the worst company. I have low energy for some reason."

"I'm enjoying myself." Will smiles from across the table. "How's the cheek? It looks better than it did earlier."

Did that just happen today? It already feels like a lifetime ago.

"Much better," I say. "Thanks again for stepping in. I should have called for backup. Sis usually calms down faster than that."

The bill comes, and Will takes it before I have a chance, sliding his card across the wobbly wood table.

"Shall we?" he says after paying.

Will drives me the short distance home and gets out of the car to walk me to the door.

"Thanks for tonight," I say. "And sorry if I seem distracted. I think I'm just sleep deprived."

"I had fun," he says, going up the three steps to the landing. "I like getting to know you. You've made everything better at the nursing home."

"Yeah?" I wrinkle my nose. "That's nice of you to say."

Will leans in at the same time I stick my hand out to shake his. I pretty much punch him in the gut, and he ends up kissing the tip of my nose. It's every awkward end-of-the-night goodbye wrapped into one perfectly terrible package.

"Have a good night," I quickly say, opening the door, wanting to get as far away as possible. "Thanks again."

I shut the door, lock it, and then let myself slide down until I'm sitting on the cold tile floor. I let my head roll back, and I close my eyes. It was a full day. From getting a shiner to comforting Liam to making out with him and then going on a non-date with Will. I rub my palms into my eyes, and then open them. My mom stands with her arms crossed and a smile on her face.

"Birdie girl." She reaches her arms out and pulls me up. "I'm opening a bottle of wine, and you're going to tell me everything."

Chapter Sixteen

"I'm going to do it."

My mom's voice rings out as I put coins into the vending machine, needing an afternoon sugar fix. I turn to face her and wrinkle my forehead.

"You're going to do what?"

My mom leans against the counter and grabs my free hand. "I'm going to buy the nursing home."

"Mom," I say, but she holds up her hand and presses it against my lips.

"Birdie," she says. "I've thought a lot about this. It's what I want. The answer has been in front of me this entire time. I love living here. I love the community. I need this nursing home to succeed, and if I'm not the right person to make that happen, then I don't know who is."

"That's huge, though, Mom."

"It is." She smiles. "I met with a lawyer already. I met with my financial planner. It's all within reach."

I open my mouth to say something, but then snap it shut. Her face glows, and I know her mind is made up. It was so hard for my mom to sell the ranch. But after my grandma had her accident, my grandpa's health went downhill quickly, and he passed. It all happened so fast, and all of a sudden, my mom owned a two-hundred-acre property in rural South Dakota.

She knew she'd have to sell it, and my mom and I have had several conversations on the importance of the inheritance going to something meaningful. But each month, she's had to tap into the funds because we're barely getting paid to work.

The ranch was so special, too. It was home. Where I felt safe. Until it wasn't. But this nursing home feels like home, too.

"Liam is coming here soon," my mom says. "Pop into my office when you get a chance. I'd love for you to be part of the conversation."

"Let me do a couple of rounds, and I'll be there."

My mom claps her hands together and leaves the break room. I step into the hall and look around. This place is falling apart. It needs so many things, I wouldn't even know where to start. And why should we trust Liam with my mom's inheritance? He worked for a company that defrauded its clients out of their life's work. He may not have been actively involved, but even he said that he should have recognized that something was amiss.

The money my mom got from the ranch? Well, it's more than that. It's my grandparents' legacy. It's our future. I can't imagine putting it all into the sale of something that may or may not work out.

I speed up my pace and rip the door open to my mom's office just as Liam is about to sit.

He stands when he sees me. We haven't seen each other since the night of our kiss, and we both pause and stare. My mom glances at me, and then Liam.

"Good, you're here," she says, pointing to a chair.

"Hi, Birdie." Liam lowers himself into the chair. "We were just about to get started."

"About that." I clench my hands together. "I haven't had a chance to look at your report."

"Birdie," my mom says. "I've looked at it in detail. I showed it to my attorney and my financial planner. It's excellent work." She turns to Liam. "What's next? I'm all in."

"Well," Liam chuckles. "Are you sure?"

"Yeah, Mom," I say. "Are you sure? You're talking about investing every cent of your money into something that has been operating in the red since I was missing my two front teeth."

"Birdie," she says. "This isn't some impulse on a whim. I've been wanting to lay down roots and do something meaningful for a long time. This is it. I can feel it."

Liam nods as he turns his chair toward my mom's.

"June," he says slowly. "There is something that I need you to know."

"Okay." My mom rests her head on her hand and leans toward him. "Go on."

"You see." Liam's eyes flick to mine. "Before coming to Wheaton, I lived in New York. I worked in finance."

Liam looks down at his lap, the struggle written across his face. He's going to tell her everything.

"I worked at Feldmans. And unless you've been living under a rock, you know the rest of the story. I promise you, I wasn't part of it. I didn't know what was going on. But I should have. And I thought you should know before you go any further with everything."

My mom leans back in her chair. She crosses her hands over her chest and narrows her eyes.

"Are you trying to steal from me, Liam? Trick me into giving you my inheritance and running off into the sunset?"

Liam nearly chokes. "No. Of course not."

She reaches her hand across the table and squeezes Liam's. "That was a joke. You worked for Feldmans. If you were trying to defraud someone, you're smart enough to go after someone with a lot more money than my cut of the ranch once I paid it off."

"Even so," he says, eyes again cutting in my direction. "It felt like something you should know."

"And I appreciate that." My mom pushes back from the table and stands. "I have to run but let me know what the next steps are."

Liam jumps up. "I know a broker. Let me give him a call today and see how fast we can get the ball rolling."

My mom glances at Liam and then at me. She smiles and turns to walk toward the door. She crosses her fingers. "I have a really good feeling about this."

She walks out and leaves the door open. I press my fingers into the table and watch the blood move away, turning a pale shade.

"What is it?" Liam closes the distance between us and sits on the edge of the table.

"This could fail," I say, standing. "I'm not sure if she should move forward with it. She could lose everything. We could lose everything."

Liam tilts his head and studies me. He taps his long finger along the ridge of the table.

"What?" I say when he continues to stare.

"I'm learning who you are." Liam pinches his bottom lip between his fingers. "You seem to have an extremely low tolerance for trying things without a guarantee."

"It's worked out for me so far."

"Has it though?" Liam raises his eyebrows.

"What is that supposed to mean?"

"Everything could fail," he says. "But it could also work out and be the most amazing risk ever taken."

I'm no longer sure if he's talking about the nursing home or us.

I shake my head. "I know that. But you don't understand how much this money means to my mom. When my grandparents. . ."

I don't finish my sentence. I cross my arms over my chest and stare into his dark blue eyes.

"You have nothing at stake here. You're going to move back to New York, and my mom and I will have to pick up the pieces if this goes terribly wrong. I'd rather make little money than go bankrupt if the nursing home doesn't rebound."

Liam presses his lips together and shrugs. "You're right, Birdie. I'm going to be back in New York. Hopefully sooner rather than later. Your mom knows that, and she still wants to try."

"What is she thinking? Why would she want to do this?"

"I didn't give her advice, one way or another. I laid out the risks and the rewards. This decision is hers to make."

Liam walks toward me and places his hand on my arm. "I'm not sure how much longer I'll be here, but I'm going to do everything I can to make sure this goes well."

June is almost over, and all Liam has been telling me since the moment I met him is how eager he is to start his life over in New York. He feels like a safety net to me. One that is very temporary.

"It seems like the decision is made," I say. "But I want to go on record and say I'm very much against this."

Liam puts a hand on my other arm and squeezes. "Your mom is smart and capable, Birdie. You both seem to love it here. Let her make an informed decision about this."

Liam lets go of me. "This could be a really good thing for you. You need to think about your future, too."

I stare up at him, aware of how easy it would be to get lost in his eyes. They're dark, mysterious, and I let myself imagine this town without him here, which is going to be the reality sooner than I know it.

"I have to get back to work." I glance toward the door.

He grabs my hand as I brush against him. "Have some faith, Birdie. I think this is going to be a really good thing for both of you."

Chapter Seventeen

The mood today at the nursing home is lively with anticipation. I barely have time to think between running from one resident to another. These hours aren't sustainable. The accumulation of long days and little sleep is catching up with me. Sunny sits alone in his room reading a newspaper, and I dip into his room and take a seat.

"Sis is still in memory care?" I glance at my watch.

Sunny puts his paper down, then grabs his coffee mug and takes a sip. "For another hour. The boys went fishing this morning, but I decided to stay back."

I grab a pile of Sis's clothes that were left on her bed, fully laundered, and start putting them away.

"How's Sis doing? Is she having a good day?"

Sunny reclines his chair and rests his head back on his folded hands. "Did I ever tell you the story of the day I fell in love with Sis?"

"No," I say, smiling. "But I'd love to hear it."

I glance at my watch again. No one should be looking for me for at least fifteen minutes.

"Well," Sunny says. "If I recall correctly, it was the first day of school when we were five years old."

Sunny grins up at the ceiling. "She walked into the room, her white blond hair in two pigtails. She looked around, and I could tell she was very nervous. And lucky me—her assigned seat was next to mine. Signe Larsen. Bright blue eyes. A pretty yellow dress. And I was smitten."

"We learned that both of our parents had moved here from Norway. Oh, I loved her from that day, but she didn't know I existed for several more years."

"How'd you finally get her to notice you?" I lean forward and rest my head on my fist.

"Well, that's a funny story, Birdie," Sunny says. "You see, I was a small kid, and she went out with a couple of our classmates throughout high school, but nothing serious. I had to sit back and watch it. By this point, we were good friends. She had dreams of going to a women's college and moving to a city. I had dreams of inheriting my dad's grocery store in town, running it, and expanding to other towns in the area. Sis did not want to stay in Wheaton. She made that very clear."

"What did you do?"

"Well," Sunny says but then looks at the door, and his face lights up. I turn to Camilla walking in with Sis. "That is a story for another day."

"Hi, Grandpa," Camilla says, rushing to his side and wrapping her arms around him.

"Hey, Birdie," she says, waving.

I get up and guide Sis to the bed, as this is the time she takes her afternoon nap.

"Hey, Camilla." I pull the blanket up over Sis. "Do you and Sunny want to go to the game room? Or how about a walk outside?"

Camilla kisses her grandma's forehead, turns to me, and nods. "I'll see you later, Grandma. I'm going to bring the kids by, too."

"Thanks, dear," Sis says and turns to her side.

I follow Sunny and Camilla out and flick the light off on my way. We walk out into the lobby, where Joe is standing by the door, waiting for someone to let him out.

"Grandpa," Camilla says. "Are you up for a walk? It's beautiful out today."

"A short one would be nice," Sunny says. "I'm going to stop in the bathroom. I'll be right back."

Sunny walks off, and Camilla turns to me.

"Birdie," she says. "I've been meaning to ask you. Do you have any plans for the Fourth of July?"

"Umm," I say, biting my bottom lip. "I'll have to look at the schedule, but I'm pretty sure I'm free during the day."

"Good," she says, smiling. "Jake and I have hosted a party at our house for the past few years. It's such a good time. It starts in the morning and goes as late as you want to stay. A lot of people come, and it's a great way to get to know people. There's a lot of food, drinks, and all you need to do is bring yourself."

Joe tries to leave when someone walks through the door, and I hold up my finger to Camilla, then pull him away from the door.

"I'll try to stop by," I say. "I appreciate the invite."

"Joe." I gently take his arm. "Where do you think you're going?"

"As far away from here as possible." He glances at Camilla, who smiles and shakes her head as we walk past her. "Meatloaf for lunch again? Who do I need to talk to that makes the decisions around here?"

"Okay." I place him in the chair and immediately turn off *Gunsmoke* before he fixates on how much he hates that. "If you could choose a perfect meal that we could serve on a regular basis, what would that be?"

"Are you pulling my leg right now?"

I shake my head. "Seriously. What would you want?"

"It's about time someone asked me that." Joe grabs a throw pillow and puts it behind his back. "Easy. Spaghetti, meatballs, and garlic bread. That's it. Simple. Can you make that happen?"

I nod. "I know some people in charge. I'm going to make this happen, Joe."

He winks, and I pat his shoulder and continue on my rounds.

Marilyn is in her wheelchair, trying to make her way down the hallway.

"Can I help you get somewhere faster?"

"Miss Birdie," she says. "I'm trying to work my way back to my room. But at this rate, I may not get there for a while."

"I can help you with that."

We take a left at the nurse's station and head toward her room. I lift her out of the chair and into bed. She keeps getting thinner. Her collarbone protrudes, and I gently pull the covers over her.

"Tommy stopped by this morning, Miss Birdie." She rolls to her side. "He cried. I haven't seen that boy cry since his best friend told everyone who his crush was in middle school."

I drag a chair to the edge of her bed.

"Do you want to know the hardest thing about knowing you're dying?"

"What?" I practically whisper the question.

"Having to make everyone else feel better about it." Marilyn reaches for a tissue. "I'm sad myself. And plenty scared. But Tommy is about to lose his mama. So I have to smile and pinch back the tears and tell him everything is going to be alright. But I'm not ready. I have grandbabies I won't see get married. They're so young that they'll forget me."

"I'm so scared." Her voice is small.

I hold her hand and then massage it. Her hands are arthritic from years of knitting. I press into them gently, and she smiles.

"That sounds like an incredible burden, Marilyn," I say. "When you're sad, scared, and overwhelmed, talk to me."

She nods.

"Your kids are losing their mama, and they are going to need you to give them permission to heal. When you have big feelings, I want to hear about them. Lay your worries on me."

Marilyn lifts her head and covers her mouth. "That's all I need. Someone I can say how I really feel to. Someone who lets me feel self-pity because I'm not ready. And nothing anyone says to me is going to make me ready to be dead."

She puts her head back on her pillow, her breathing slows, and she falls into a deep slumber.

Chapter Eighteen

The morning of July Fourth is hot and sticky. I think about making an excuse not to go. My mom already left to spend the day at the nursing home, and it would be more comfortable to go there and see if she needs help than to attend this party and put myself out there. But I can't cancel. I invited Lucy to go with me, and it's all she's been talking about for the past couple of days.

Lucy pulls into the driveway promptly at two, and I run outside to greet her.

"I feel like I'm going to a party at the popular kids' house." Lucy claps her hands together.

"Wait." I buckle my seatbelt. "Haven't we outgrown the whole popular group thing at our age? Because let me tell you, those were never my people."

Lucy laughs. "Mine neither. I was squarely in the theater kid, slightly emo group. I can't wait to see how the other half lives."

"Yeah?" I shake my head and smile. "I was the horse girl throughout middle school, and in high school, I think I was actually invisible."

"Ouch."

We drive out of town until the lake comes into view. I don't need to give Lucy directions. Everyone in town knows where Jake and Camilla Abrams live. We pull up to their large home, and there must be twenty cars parked in the driveway and nearby field. Lucy puts her car into park, and her mouth hangs open.

"I really wish I didn't have to leave early," she says. "This is going to be a party."

"I don't plan to stay late either." I pull down the mirror and glance at myself. "I need to be at the nursing home no later than eight."

"Well." Lucy grabs lipstick from her purse and paints her lips a deep red. "I need to get Gavin from his dad's at five, so if you stay later, you may need a ride home."

The music is loud when we step outside of the car and into the sun. People on the lawn play volleyball in their suits. A woman hits the ball over the net, and a man lifts her off the ground and twirls her in celebration. Then I realize it's Liam. I stop walking, and Lucy practically runs into me. He wears only swim trunks, and his muscular chest is golden brown. He puts the woman down, grabs the ball, and moves to the serving position. She smiles at him the entire time, unable to take her eyes off him.

"Damn," Lucy says, leaning toward me. "Is that your Liam?"

"There is no 'my Liam.'"

"Let me rephrase that." Lucy links her arm in mine. "Is that Liam Bergland? Sunny and Sis's grandson, who spends more time talking to you when he visits the nursing home than talking to his grandparents?"

I slide my sunglasses down. "That is Liam Bergland. The man who reminds me daily how much he hates being here and that he can't wait to move back to New York to live the rest of his life."

"Well." Lucy pushes me through the screen door of the house. "There's always Will. All the guy does is talk about you."

Will. The nice guy from work who makes it known how he feels about me. The man who wants to settle down in this nice community, meet a woman, and raise a family. Someone I know could be mine if I wanted him. Yet I feel no spark and can't fake that I do.

There are as many people inside the house as are scattered out on the lawn. Camilla turns, and when she sees us, she smiles and heads in our direction.

"Birdie. Lucy. I'm so happy you came." Camilla pulls me into a hug and then hugs Lucy.

"Hopefully, you know quite a few people here." She points as Dax, Carrie, and Malik work their way toward us.

"Birdie, hi." Carrie hugs me. "Jake is working the grill right now, so please, eat some food."

"Hey, ladies." Malik hugs me and Lucy. "Jake and Camilla got new jet skis. I just went for a ride. It was amazing."

"Yes." Camilla nods. "You should take one out. It's the perfect day for it."

"Umm." I glance at Lucy. "I've never been on one. I think I'll stick to land today."

"You've never been on a jet ski, Birdie?" We all turn as Liam walks through the door and enters our conversation. "That's just wrong. I can take you."

"No." I glance at Liam, who is now next to me, and for some reason, it's hard to breathe. "I didn't even bring a suit. But thank you."

"I've got you." Camilla grabs my hand. "I have about a hundred suits, in all shapes and sizes, in our guest room. They're all clean. Help yourself."

"Umm," I say, but Camilla is already pulling me in another direction.

"Let me know when you're ready." I turn over my shoulder to Liam and nod.

She opens up the top drawer of a dresser, and she wasn't lying. Camilla pulls out so many suits—bikinis and one-pieces of all different shapes and colors.

"Hmm." Camilla holds up a pale pink two-piece. "I think this will be perfect. Try it on, and if it doesn't work, there are many more to choose from."

I can't remember the last time I wore a swimsuit. I pull it on and stare at myself in the full-length mirror in the corner of the room. I feel very exposed. I turn to look at my backside, and it barely covers my butt. I push my breasts up and run my hand down my smooth stomach. I blow out a breath.

I feel a bit like an imposter and maybe even a little beautiful. I pull on my light blue summer dress and walk out of the room.

No one is in the same spot they were in when I left the group, so I pop outside. Liam talks to the woman who was playing volleyball with him, but he glances over his shoulder and spots me waiting in the distance.

"Ready?" He raises his eyebrow, and I nod.

He turns and says something to the woman, walks toward the water, and I follow.

"You don't need to take me." I catch up to him as we reach a shed. He pulls me inside. "I don't even know if I want to go on a jet ski. What if I hate it?"

"What if you don't?" Liam grabs a life jacket. "I'm going to get you out of your shell, Birdie. By the time this summer is over, you're going to have all sorts of new experiences under your belt."

"That sounds like a threat," I say under my breath.

We stand by the water's edge, where four jet skis are parked in their ramps. He puts his hands on his hips and stares at me. He's back to the Liam I met at the beginning of the summer. The man who said very little but did a lot of judging with his deep blue eyes.

"Didn't Camilla give you a suit to wear?" He gestures toward my clothes.

"She did."

I drop the life jacket to the ground, pull my dress over my head, and toss it onto a nearby bench. When our eyes meet again, Liam is staring at me, mouth slightly open. His eyes rake down my body. He bends down to grab my life jacket and mumbles something under his breath as he throws it to me. I secure it in place, and Liam grips it and pulls me toward him. He tightens a couple of the straps.

"Ready?" Liam gestures toward the lake.

"Ready."

Liam gets on the jet ski first and then nods at the small space left on the seat.

"I'm supposed to sit there?"

"Yes," he says. "Unless you want to try to take one out on your own."

I step down onto the jet ski. "How do I hold on?"

"Here." He takes my hand and wraps it around his torso, and then my other hand, until I'm hugging him.

He glances at me over his shoulder. "Hold on tight, okay?"

The engine starts up with a roar. I bury my face in his warm, tanned back. He smells like sunblock, coconuts, and sunshine. He starts slow, but when we get into deeper water, he speeds up, and I grab him tighter.

Liam turns to me. "Are you okay?"

"Watch where you're going," I yell over the engine.

He laughs and then stares straight ahead. We whip by Lucy, who has Malik as a passenger, and Liam heads farther down the lake. I move one hand off Liam's torso and onto his thigh for greater support. His body tightens underneath my touch.

Liam steers us closer to shore, where the resort is. He stops at the end of a dock and turns off the engine.

"Do you want to drive?"

"No." I shake my head vigorously. "Definitely not."

Liam laughs. "Come on, Birdie. I'll show you how. You live in a lake town now. You should know how to drive a jet ski."

He hops off and sits at the edge of the dock.

"Do you want me to be scared?" I say, and Liam's face goes flat.

"Never." Liam squeezes the base of his neck. "If you don't want to drive, you don't have to. I don't want you to be scared. Ever. I want you to be the opposite of scared."

I release a breath. "Fine. But you need to be with me, and I'm going to go slow."

Liam nods. "I know you are."

I move myself to the front of the jet ski, and Liam gets on behind me. He leans across my body and connects the lanyard kill switch around my wrist.

"In case we fall off."

He points to the right handle. "This is the throttle. It's sensitive. You don't need to turn it much."

He reaches over me and takes my hand. "If you want to reverse or go into neutral. And this is the start and stop button."

"Seems straightforward." I turn the jet ski on, grip the handles, and pull away from the dock.

Liam is so much taller than me that his head rests on my shoulder. His breath is warm against me. He reaches his hand across my body and puts his hand over mine.

"Don't forget the throttle."

I head down the lake, and when we pass the very last boat in sight, I grip harder, and the jet ski goes faster. Liam's arms tighten around my waist. I haven't felt this much power between my legs since the last time I was on a horse. The jet ski feels predictable, though, in ways a horse never could.

"You're a natural," Liam yells into my ear.

His hand tightens against my waist, and he pushes me back into him. We're so close, I'm practically on his lap. His thighs press against mine, and his other hand grips my hip.

The wind in my face brings me back to that open meadow all those years ago. I felt invincible then. My entire world was in front of me. Nothing could touch me. But then everything changed. For years afterward, I had a recurring nightmare of me and my grandma flying through the air, knowing that the ground was going to come with a thud. I shouldn't have let myself forget that. When Jake and Camilla's cabin comes into view, I slow down and steer directly toward it. Anxiety overtakes my chest cavity, and it's hard to take a deep breath.

It's been years since I've had a panic attack.

"You were doing great," Liam says. "Why'd you stop?"

"I'm done."

We reach the ramp, and I disconnect myself from the jet ski, hand Liam the keys, and jump off. I hear Liam's voice behind me, but I rush toward the shed, needing to be alone. I unhook my life jacket and go to leave but run into Liam's hard body, blocking the only way out.

"Birdie."

He shuts the door behind him so we're completely alone in the dark shed. The sunlight peeks through the gaps in the wood.

"Did I do something wrong?"

"No." I shake my head. "I was just done."

"Did I make you uncomfortable?" He steps toward me but then stops himself. "I wanted to redistribute your weight. I was pushing you back. I'm so sorry if you felt unsafe. . ."

His voice trails off.

"Shit." I look around. "What time is it?"

"I don't know, about seven maybe. Why?"

I promised the residents they'd get their fireworks show. I can't let them down. How could Liam and I have been out on the water for so long? Time moves too quickly when I'm with him. I lose sight of what's important when he's in my orbit.

"I need to get to the nursing home. I may have missed my ride."

"Let's get changed," Liam says. "I can bring you."

"You don't have to," I say. "I don't want you to miss the fireworks over the lake."

"They won't start for hours." He opens the door of the shed. "I can be ready in ten minutes."

I change out of the bikini and get into Liam's car. Neither of us says anything on the way there. I expect him to pull away as soon as we arrive at the nursing home, but instead, he gets out with me.

Chapter Nineteen

"What are we doing here?" Liam rushes to keep up with me.

"Fireworks for the residents." I press the code to get in the door. "You should go back to the lake and hang out with your friends."

He doesn't turn around, though. Instead, he follows me inside, where several of the residents are waiting. I never would have forgiven myself if I'd gotten lost in the moment and let them down. It's all they've been talking about for days.

"There you are." Abigail uses her legs to move closer to me in her wheelchair. "I was nervous you wouldn't come."

"I wouldn't do that to you." I get her situated by the door and turn to Joe. "Are you ready?"

"Been ready." He crosses his arms over his chest.

"We have to wait for Marilyn," Abigail says. "We're going to sit together."

"I wouldn't let Marilyn miss out on this," I say.

Sunny and Sis round the corner, and both smile when they see Liam. "Oh, good. You came for the show too."

He raises his eyebrows at me, and I laugh. Liam grabs my arm.

"What is going on?" He grips my shoulder. "Is this what you do when you have a night shift? Throw parties for the residents? No wonder you have no social life."

"Funny." I elbow his side. "I promised the residents that I'd put on a fireworks show for them. They're craving something normal. You don't have to stay, Liam. I have this under control. Seriously, go back to your party. I know there are people waiting for you. That cute volleyball player from earlier."

"Birdie, I—"

"Liam," I say, as more residents are wheeled out to the lobby. "I'm busy. Either help or leave."

He glances at the door, then back at me. "What can I do?"

I grab a key from my purse. "Go into the storage room. It's all the way down the hall. That's where the fireworks are. Grab a cart. There's one in the corner. Load that up."

"Got it."

"Birdie." Will takes my arm and spins me around. "Is it time to get the residents outside?"

Will stands there in his scrubs, waiting for my answer. I glance at my watch.

"Wait." I take in his attire. "You're working tonight? I thought you were going to set off the fireworks from the park across the street."

"That was the plan," Will says. "But one of the new CNAs walked off the job today, so here I am."

Panic sets in. The one thing I hate most in life is disappointing people, especially the residents who at times have so little to look forward to. I raised money for these fireworks, bought them a couple of weeks ago, and had everything ready to go.

I'd set them off myself, except I'm deathly afraid of fire and explosions that close to my face.

"Here they are." Liam's voice brings me back to reality. The cart is full. I look between him and Will, both staring at me.

"What's up, Birdie?" Liam scrunches up his face. "Everything okay?"

"Liam." I close my eyes and inhale deeply. "Is there any way you could help me out for the next thirty minutes? I know you want to get back to the party, but I'm in a—"

"What do you need?" Liam steps forward, and then Will does the same. "I'm not in a hurry."

"How are you at lighting fireworks?"

Liam's smile stretches from ear to ear. "It's my specialty."

"Perfect." I point across the road to where the public park is. "We can't light them up on the nursing home's land, so that's where you'll need to be. If you could go set up, Will and I will get everyone outside."

Liam pushes the cart through the door, and Will and I start getting all the residents into the parking lot. The majority use wheelchairs at this point, so we need to take them out one at a time. In total, there are about fifteen people, and some of their families came out with lawn chairs to watch as well. I shake my head, watching Liam stand in the park in his swim trunks and white shirt, getting everything lined up. This is not how I envisioned my night going.

Liam's gaze meets mine, and I give him a thumbs-up. He lights the first firework, and all the residents gasp, then clap. The sky lights up with red, white, and blue fireworks, but I don't watch them. Instead, I stare at the faces of the residents. No matter what we do to make things better, they're all in the same position—facing the end of life. If there's one thing I want to do in my life, it's to make their last days better.

Being a nurse is so much more than knowing what medicine to give and making decisions under pressure. It's about providing hope in the worst situations. It's the joy I can offer them by just showing up.

"Birdie." Will stands next to me, our shoulders touching. "I'm sorry I couldn't come through tonight."

My eyes meet Liam's from across the street. I don't think he could ever realize how much this means to me—how much just showing up and making what's important to me important to him is everything.

"It's fine," I say to Will, never taking my eyes off Liam. "It all worked out."

The fireworks show only lasts about fifteen minutes, but it was perfect.

"Do I get to go home now?" Joe asks, wheeling over to me. "Betty is here. She said she'd take me."

I glance at his wife, and she shakes her head.

"You're coming inside with us, Joe." Sunny takes his arm. "This is home now. They're serving ice cream, too."

Joe doesn't protest. I wheel Abigail in and tuck her in for the night. As I walk away from her bed, she grabs my hand.

"That was really special, Birdie. I'll never forget it."

I pull the blanket up over her arms. "I'll never forget it either."

"Will you tell me about one of your most perfect days?"

"Okay." I sit in the chair next to her bed. A memory quickly pops into my head. "When I was much younger, I used to show my horse Shadow at the South Dakota State Fair. We'd leave a couple of nights before it started—my grandpa, grandma, mom, and I—and we'd camp. The fair was so magical. My mom would buy me all the junk food, and I'd go on rides. I felt like I was living the most glamorous life. And then the day came for me to ride Shadow. The arena was packed full of people, and everything went perfectly. We ended up winning the blue ribbon that year. I was so proud of us."

I rub Abigail's shoulder. "How about your most perfect day?"

She smiles. "When my girls were in elementary school, one day every year, I'd do a skip day with them. I'd call the school and say they were sick, which they thought was a hoot. Then we'd spend the day doing something special. One year, we went to an amusement park, went on all the rides, ate all the food, and drove back home late, blaring our favorite music in the car. They declared me the coolest mom in the world. I'll never forget it."

"Perfect." I let out a heavy sigh.

"Perfect," Abigail says as she closes her eyes.

Next, I check in on Sunny and Sis. They are in their single beds, with a table anchored between them.

"Goodnight, lovebirds," I say. "I'll see you in the morning."

Will is the only RN on duty tonight, so I do a few more checks as well.

"You're still here." Will rounds the corner. "Your mom is on her way. Going to do some work tonight. She just called."

"She works too much," I say.

Will yawns. "We're all working too much."

"I know," I say.

"Hey, Birdie." My mom approaches and pulls me into a hug. "I could see the fireworks from our house; they were beautiful."

"Everything turned out perfectly." I smile.

"Well," she says, nodding toward the hall, "I'm going to get a few things done, but there's someone waiting for you in the lobby."

"Wait, Birdie."

I turn toward Will.

My mom squeezes my hand and walks off.

"I was wondering if you, well…"

As if on cue, Liam rounds the corner. When he sees me, he leans against the wall, arms crossed over his chest.

"Sorry, Will, I have to go. I'll see you soon."

It hadn't occurred to me that Liam would still be waiting, but I'm happy he is. It's late, and he's still here, instead of being at that party with the girl who couldn't keep her eyes off him.

"You're here." I reach him, and he grabs my hand, dropping keys into them.

"I disposed of the garbage and locked the storage room."

"I'm sorry I roped you into this." I glance at the clock. "It's so late. If you hurry, you can still get to the party. I'm sure it's still going strong."

Liam smiles. "Tonight was really fun. I can't imagine Jake and Camilla's party being any better than this."

Liam looks toward the door. "If you're done for the night, can I drive you home?"

I go to refuse, but my feet are killing me and I could use a ride.

"That'd be great."

"Let's get out of here." Liam puts his hand on my lower back, and we leave the nursing home for the night.

Chapter Twenty

The town is asleep. Liam drives me the short distance to my home, and his car is the only one on the road. We pass the cemetery in complete silence, and he pulls into my driveway. The house is dark except for the light on the front porch.

"I'll walk you in." Liam hops out of the car before I have a chance to tell him it's unnecessary.

I love the porch on this old home that extends from one end of the house to the other.

He steps into the light, his hair golden. He points at the swing hanging in the corner.

"Sit for a minute?"

"Yeah."

I take a seat in the corner, tuck my feet in, and put a pillow in my lap. The weight from Liam makes the swing rock forward. The night is clear, and the crescent moon reflects off the wood panels of the porch floor.

"Thanks again," I say, and Liam turns to me. "I feel like I derailed your Fourth."

"You didn't." Liam bends his leg and leans his head on his hand. "I get the importance of the nursing home in ways I didn't before."

I smile. "The residents loved it, didn't they?"

He nods. "Their faces. It was maybe the best thing I've seen. My grandparents looked so happy."

I stretch my feet out. They're sore after being on them most of the day. Liam grabs hold of them, slips off my sandals, and places them on his lap.

"Hey, Birdie." Liam's gaze flicks up to mine. "If I did something to offend you in any way on the jet ski, I'm sorry."

He thinks he hurt me in some way, but it has nothing to do with him. I'm broken and have been for so long that I'd almost forgotten until today.

"You didn't hurt me," I say.

"But we were having fun, and something shifted. I've gone over it in my mind a thousand times, and the only thing I keep coming back to is that I must have crossed a line in some way."

I close my eyes and move down until my head is resting on the pillow of the wooden rocking bench.

"Today took me back to something I try not to think about."

He turns his head toward me, and his voice is mostly a whisper. "What happened?"

"When I was thirteen, something traumatic happened, and for whatever reason, being on the jet ski brought me back to that day. It came out of nowhere. I had to get off."

Liam squeezes my feet. I glance at him, and he studies me. Crickets cry out all around us, and a steady breeze blows the leaves of the big trees in the front yard.

"Have you ever gone through something that you're convinced is going to define you for the rest of your life?"

"What happened to you, Birdie?"

Liam pinches my toe, and I sit back up.

"You know how I told you my mom had me as a teenager? My dad could never decide if he wanted to be in our lives." I lean back on the bench and curl my legs up.

"My mom's parents, my grandparents, took us in. My mom was eighteen, had a newborn baby, and no money, so we lived on their ranch with them in South Dakota. Honestly, it was the best childhood. I had three people around me who loved me to death."

Liam nods, and I find myself getting lost in his eyes.

"My grandparents had horses, and I grew up riding them." I chuckle, thinking of a memory.

"I didn't have a lot of friends, but I had my very own horse, Shadow, and he was the only best friend I needed."

"When I was thirteen, I got home from school, and my grandma asked if I wanted to go trail riding. We'd done this a million times before, and this day was no different. She was riding her horse, Brewster, and I was on Shadow, like always. For whatever reason, though, Shadow was acting strange and not responding to commands, so somewhere along the path, we decided to switch horses, and my grandma started riding Shadow."

"We came to an open meadow, and both horses took off galloping. But then Shadow took off at full speed ahead. Something spooked him. I still don't know to this day why he acted like that. He bucked her off, and on his way down, his hoof went into her head."

"Birdie." Liam brushes hair out of my face.

"It was the scariest thing I'd ever seen. She was lying there, in the meadow of flowers and long grass, with her eyes shut and blood at her temple. I rode Brewster back to the ranch as fast as I could. My grandpa was in the barn, and I had him call 911. He rode to the meadow until a helicopter came and got her."

My face is wet, but it takes me a moment to recognize it's from my tears. I hadn't realized that I'd started crying.

"Grandma survived, but she had a traumatic brain injury and was never the same. No one would take her in, and we couldn't provide the care she needed. The Wheaton Nursing Home stepped in, and they cared for her so well, until she died from her injuries two years later."

Liam flicks a tear from my face.

"When I turned ten, my grandma gifted me the most beautiful locket, pendant thing. It was white gold, and according to my mom, very expensive. It had this intricate design, and I opened it up, and it had this saying from Dr. Seuss about no one being more youer than you, or something like that. Somehow, in the chaos and aftermath, and me jumping off my horse and riding back to the ranch, it got lost. Every day for an entire year, I went to that meadow to look for it. I thought if I found it, she'd come back to me. But I never did. It's the stupidest thing."

Liam rubs his fingers down my arm and then wipes away another tear. "It's not."

"The worst part of all of it is it's my fault." I swallow away my pain. "It should have been me on Shadow. He was my horse. It should have been me."

Liam closes the distance between us and scoops me into his arms. He holds me against his chest, and I bury my face in his neck. I've never shared anything more than the very high-level details of that day with anyone. I didn't even tell my mom and grandpa the horror I saw. Yet, I exposed all of this to someone I just met.

His cotton shirt now smells like sunblock, and I breathe him in. He feels safe in ways that someone I've only met shouldn't.

"It wasn't your fault." He presses his hand against the back of my head and kisses my temple. "You were a child, Birdie. It wasn't your fault."

Liam grips me firmly, and his body is so large next to mine that I feel all of him wrapped around me from every angle.

Car lights shine in my eyes, and I squint. The sound of an engine turns off, and I back away from Liam after realizing I'm practically on his lap at this point. Footsteps echo against the steps, and Mom turns and jumps when she sees us.

"Birdie. Liam." She puts her hand on her heart and smiles. "Come inside. It's so buggy out. You must be getting eaten alive."

"We're fine," I say. "Liam gave me a ride home after the fireworks."

She looks at Liam. "That was nice of you. Well, I'm headed to bed, but you kids have a good night."

"Love you." I blow her a kiss as she walks inside.

I wipe my eyes with my palms. "I'm sorry."

"Don't be." Liam takes my hair into his fist. "Never apologize for sharing these parts of yourself, Birdie."

I nod. A silent, understanding look passes between us.

"You've totally ruined my plan, you know?" he says.

"What plan is that?"

"I was supposed to come to Wheaton and hate everything about it. I was going to go back to New York and tell them that this place I was stuck in all summer was the absolute worst. But then I met you."

"Hmm." I stand and hold my hand out to pull Liam up. "Maybe you'll decide to stay."

Liam grabs my hand and laughs. "I wouldn't go that far."

Liam walks me the few steps to the door, and then pulls me into a hug. His arms are so solid, warm, and strong, and they keep me pressed against his firm chest.

"Thanks for reminding me what's at stake here," Liam says. "I knew the nursing home was important to you and your mom, but now I realize it on an entirely different level. I'm not going to let you down."

"Okay." I pull back from him.

Liam grips my shoulders and then lays a kiss in the middle of my forehead.

"Goodnight, Birdie."

I lock up the house and tiptoe up the stairs. My mom's bedroom door is open, so I peek inside, and she's sitting up in bed, scrolling through her phone.

"Goodnight, Mom," I say.

She looks up at me and smiles. "Birdie."

"I'll see you in the morning."

"Hey," she says as I'm about to step out. "I love getting to see this side of you."

I raise an eyebrow. "What side?"

She presses her lips together. "The side where my favorite person in the entire world is falling in love for the first time."

"I'm not falling in love."

"Oh, Birdie," she says. "You'll see."

I roll my eyes. "Goodnight, Mom."

Chapter Twenty-One

It's official. My mom is the proud new owner of the Wheaton Nursing Home. The seller was so eager to offload this property that they put little investment into it. The staff at this morning's meeting seemed happy about the change, and my mom assured everyone that it's business as usual for now.

But now, as I stare at the article on the front page of *Wheaton Happenings*, it all feels real. My mom owns this entire building. I look around at the drab walls and furniture. Whether it succeeds or fails is solely in her hands.

According to Liam, it was a steal. It didn't feel like that to me. Almost all of my mom's inheritance is wrapped up in these very large, and very dated, four walls.

"How's it going, boys?" I turn the corner into the cafeteria, where Sunny sits with his buddies, Walt, Juan, and Lawson.

"The water's turned green," Walt says. "The walleye haven't bitten for a week."

"You're fishing in the wrong place," Juan says. "I was at the dam yesterday and was pulling in fish left and right."

Lawson shakes his head. "That feels like a fish tale if I've ever heard one."

"Can I top off anyone's coffee?" I hold up the pot.

"I'll take a little." Sunny holds up his cup.

"Don't get too rowdy," I say as I walk away. "It's almost some of the residents' nap time."

Juan laughs. "We wouldn't dream of it."

I head down to the south wing to do rounds. Abigail sits in the bird room, watching them. I grab a chair next to her.

"How are you feeling today, Abigail?"

She turns to me. "I've been a bit down, I'm afraid. Next week is my birthday. This is not where I thought I would be when I turned seventy."

"You know, Abigail," I say, grabbing her hand. "Sometimes I wonder if any of us are where we think we'll be."

"You're probably right." She purses her lips. "Where did you think you'd be?"

"Hmm." I tap a finger against my cheek. "I guess when I was younger, twenty-five seemed so old. I figured

I'd be married, with two kids, and living in a beautiful home. Instead, I'm very much single and live with my mom."

"You're still so young." Abigail smiles. "You have your entire life in front of you. You'll have all of those things someday."

"Maybe," I say, shrugging. "I don't mind where I'm at. I don't think I'd be ready for the responsibility of a family yet anyway."

"You know, Birdie," Abigail says, as if conjuring up a memory, "I once imagined my seventieth birthday party. I'd be surrounded by my kids and grandkids, and a few friends. And, of course, my handsome man. I'd look around and feel so proud of what I'd built. My life couldn't be more different from that."

Lucy walks out of a room down the hall and motions for me to come her way. I stand.

"Start thinking about what you want to do for your birthday next week, Abigail. Let's make it special."

"Thanks for the visit," she says.

I wander down the hall in search of Lucy. None of the staff stays in one place for too long. We're always running from one spot to another. I turn the corner, and when I see Will, I head in the opposite direction.

"There you are." Lucy grabs my arm and pulls me into an empty room, where she's updating resident charts.

"Hey," I say. "Sorry, it's been a busy day."

"Are we still on for drinks and pizza after work?"

"Yes." I look at the clock on the wall. "I should be able to get out of here by five today."

"Perfect." Lucy claps her hands together. "Will is coming too."

"Ugh." I grab Lucy's arm. "Are you forcing me into a situation where I need to have a blunt conversation with him that I'm not interested in dating?"

She laughs. "It may be the only way he gets the hint. But after seeing you and Liam on a jet ski together, I'm going to go out on a limb and say there is zero chance of you being interested in Will."

"Lucy," I say, covering my mouth to stifle a laugh. "Liam was just being nice."

"You could use more of that kind of nice in your life." Lucy smacks my butt as I walk out of the room.

I spend the rest of the day doing rounds and getting everything ready for the night crew. When I walk by Sunny and Sis's room, I pause when I see Liam and Camilla talking and laughing.

"Hey, guys." I step inside. "What are you up to?"

"Birdie." Camilla smiles and holds up a frame. "We are redecorating. I roped Liam into helping."

Camilla sits at the end of Sunny's bed, and Liam at the end of Sis's, and it makes me envious that I'll never have cousins who I can share inside jokes with and laugh with. Being an only child of an only child has its disadvantages.

"I was hoping to see you." Liam gets off the bed. "Your mom and I are grabbing dinner when she's off work to discuss phase one of fundraising. Can you join us?"

"Wish I could," I say. "I already have plans."

"Popular, aren't we, Birdie?" Liam reaches into his bag and hands me a thick packet. "Look through this when you have a chance and give me some feedback. That's what your mom and I will be going over tonight."

"You got it." I run my hand over the smooth, laminated surface. "Good to see you both."

*****

The pizza is steaming hot, so I blow on it before taking another bite. Will sets down three drinks and pulls up a chair.

"I've been dying to hear how your date went last night, Lucy," I say.

Lucy dramatically rolls her eyes and takes a long sip of beer.

"There are no good men left, I've decided. Present company excluded." She glances at Will. "But you're too young."

"Oh, no." I stifle a laugh. "What happened?"

Lucy and her husband have been divorced for over a year, and ever since I arrived in Wheaton, she's told me about one dating disaster after another. It's probably one of the most entertaining experiences I've had since coming here.

"Everything was going great," Lucy says. "He took me to the steak joint outside of town, and we had a few drinks and conversation was flowing. He asked if I wanted to come over to his place afterward, and I figured, why not? I'm single. I'm ready to mingle. Gavin was at his dad's for the night. A girl has needs, right?"

"Inverted penis? Specific and disturbing kinks? What was it?" Will leans forward, a grin on his face.

"No, and I wish it had been the latter." Lucy takes another sip. "We walk into his house, which, from the outside, was quite lovely. For a moment, I thought I had hit the jackpot. So there we are, and his mom greets us. She was very nice. I figured she was visiting her son from out of town."

I laugh. "So far, it doesn't sound like the worst."

"Wait for it." Lucy puckers her lips. "After niceties with his mom, he brings me to the unfinished basement, and it smelled like wet basements often do. Mold. Cat piss. Water damage. You know the smell. There was a sheet hanging in the corner, and he moves it out of the way and brings me inside. Yes. If you guessed he still lived with his mom and brought me to his makeshift basement bedroom with a twin bed, you would be correct."

"What did you do?" Will puts his head in his hands. "You didn't—"

"Lucy," I interrupt. "Who is this man? Where is this house?"

"I ran," she says. "What did you think I did?"

Will and I laugh, and after another sip of beer, Lucy joins us. Her stories take away all of my hope of finding someone decent in this world. For a town this small, there is a lot of action on the dating apps. And I love that Lucy puts herself out there, time and time again, especially because I benefit from hearing her stories.

"Birdie." I look up to see Liam, his hands gripping the edge of our table. He glances at Lucy and Will. "Hello."

He came out of nowhere, but somehow, Will and Lucy, and everyone else fades into the background, and Liam takes all the light.

"Wait," I say, looking around. "Are you here with my mom?"

He points to the corner table, and then I spot her. "We're talking business. Are you free later to go over the documents I gave you? I had a couple of thoughts I wanted to run by you."

Liam focuses entirely on me. He intensely stares, and my breath hitches in my chest.

"Not tonight," I say, proud of myself for having these boundaries. "But I'll look over everything and let you know if I have any questions."

He slowly nods and presses his lips together. "Let me know when it works, okay?"

Liam turns and walks away, and Lucy leans forward.

"Now, if a guy like that would ask me out, my date stories would be so much dirtier."

I grab a napkin, throw it at Lucy, and laugh.

"I'm going to grab another round," she says, and pops up from the table.

Will stares at me from across the table. I'd almost forgotten he was there.

"What's up?"

"Guys like that," he says, looking over his shoulder where my mom and Liam sit. "All they want to do is take things from people."

"Who? Guys like Liam?"

He nods.

"What does he want to take?"

"It's obvious, isn't it?" Will leans forward. "He's everywhere you are. You're his current object of affection, but guys like that, they wear you down, and then when they get you, they move on."

"Sorry." I bite into my bottom lip. "What does 'get you' mean?"

"Come on, Birdie." Will puts his hand on my arm.

As if on cue, Lucy comes back to the table with our drinks.

When I get home, I lie in bed with the table lamp on and read through Liam's fundraising ideas. He's thought of everything. The first thing on the agenda is to create a website with fundraising capabilities. In addition to that, he's already researched top contributors to nursing homes in the country and created a list of organizations that provide grant funding. He's made a separate list of enhancements to the building, solely based on donations, such as furniture, paint, and labor. In another bucket is fundraising, and he's laid out plans for a gala at the end of the summer to bring the community together to support the nursing home. He also plans to seek out a public relations professional to donate their services.

The entire plan is meticulous. I lie back on my pillow and read through everything again. Liam is smart and capable. I imagine he was great at his job. He gives me hope that together we can turn things around, and that my mom buying the nursing home was a good idea. I want to call him, but when I glance at the clock, I'm reminded how late it is.

This could actually work.

Chapter Twenty-Two

He's here. The sperm donor.

I walk through the door of the nursing home and need to lean against the wall to support myself. I haven't seen him in years, but he hasn't changed at all. He's tall, with slightly wild brown hair, and his bright blue eyes look around expectantly. His beard has hints of gray, and there are creases under his eyes, like he's spent too much time in the sun. I scrunch up my face, trying to remember the last time I saw him. I can't recall. But what floods my mind are all the times he didn't show up.

My first day of kindergarten.

When I broke my arm in fourth grade.

The daddy-daughter dance he said he'd pick me up for when I sat in the living room of my grandparents' house in my fluffy red dress, my hair perfectly curled.

The day of the accident when I lost what I'd ever known of my grandma. The day my grandpa died. My high school graduation. My college graduation.

None of those things would have mattered. I knew he wasn't in my life much. But at all of those events, he said he'd be there. He allowed me to believe in him, to hope. And each time, I was left feeling like a fool.

It's not the times he showed up that I remember; it's the million times he didn't.

But here he is, sitting in the chair of the nursing home, looking around to his left and then to his right, searching. And all of those feelings of abandonment come right back to me, as if it all happened yesterday. My dad.

"What are you doing here?" My voice is quiet and clipped.

"Beatrice, baby." His mouth turns up in a smile, and it's hard to take a deep breath.

"No one calls me that," I say.

"Still going by Birdie, huh?"

I nod.

My dad stands and continues to look around.

"So, this is where you work?"

I clasp my hands together, and with my thumb, rub the inside of my hand. It's what I've done my entire life to calm myself down in his presence. I dig my nail deeper until it hurts.

"Why are you here?"

He looks so much older than his forty-three years and much more weathered than my mom. His face is tan, and I hate that his eyes are my eyes.

He chuckles. "Can't your old man pay you a visit? A buddy showed me the paper, and I saw your mom bought this dump. I figured you must be here, too. You know, I only live thirty miles from here."

"How would I have known that?" I shake my head. "I haven't seen you in..." I start holding up my fingers. "In a really long time."

My dad reaches out to grab my arm, but I retreat. "Birdie, you know that isn't my fault. I was young. I was a mess. You know I've always loved you. That's never stopped."

"This isn't the place to have this conversation." I look around. My shift starts in a few minutes.

"I realize that," he says. "But I didn't know where else to find you. When will work for you? Don't you want to catch up with your old man?"

"What do you want from me?"

"A conversation. Nothing more."

All my life, I've had the inability to shut him out completely. He's my weakness, and he's disappointed me every single time. It's embarrassing how many times I've had to learn the same lesson.

The bell above the door jingles, and when I glance over, Liam walks in with Dax, Carrie, and Camilla. We lock eyes, but I quickly look away.

"I can't imagine what you'd have to say to me."

His face drops. His eyes wrinkle, and he runs a hand through his beard.

"But if you want to see me, I only work a half day on Friday. There's a corner café on Main Street. Meet me there at noon."

He smiles, then presses his hands together. "I'll be there, Beatrice. I wouldn't be anywhere else."

"If you're not there, then don't ever come back. This is it. I mean it," I say.

"I said I'd be there." He steps back and then turns toward the door.

My eyes once again meet Liam's, who watches me with curiosity. I take my first deep breath since a few minutes before when I saw him. I unclutch my hands and rush off toward my mom's office, as she came in early this morning. I knock once, and she opens the door.

She takes one look at my face, pulls me into her office, and wraps her arms around me. The tears start to fall, and I hyperventilate into her shoulder.

"Birdie." She rubs her hand up and down my back. "I'm here. You're safe."

I take short breaths until I'm able to catch mine. My mom grips my face in her hands.

"What happened, Birdie girl?"

"He's back," I say.

My mom's face changes immediately. Her softness turns into the angry protector she's been forced to be all my life. Her chest starts rising and falling with purpose. She looks around.

"Adam is back?" she says. "He's here?"

"Yes, Mom." I walk to her desk and grab a tissue. "I came into work today, and there he was."

"What in the hell is he thinking?" My mom starts pacing around her office.

"Who knows?" I pull out my phone and look at myself. "He saw the article in the paper."

"Of course he did. And now he wants something from you. From us."

"Probably," I say.

"You owe him nothing, Birdie. Never forget that."

But what if he's changed? What if he's ready to atone for his mistakes and be the dad that I've always wanted in my life? These are the reasons I've allowed him back in more times than he's ever deserved.

"Maybe it'll be different this time?" I raise my shoulders, and my voice is small.

"Highly unlikely," she says. "I can almost guarantee you that. He's the same selfish asshole he's always been. He doesn't deserve your energy and definitely not your tears."

I'm usually not a crier, but for the past two days, it feels like all I've done. Even worse, I did it in front of Liam, of all people. This is why I don't open up to anyone.

Because once words are out there, I can't take them back. And now I'm crying over someone who doesn't deserve any of the pain and anxiety I feel over seeing him.

"I should get to work."

My mom grabs me and wraps her arms tightly around me.

"I'm fine, Mom."

"He gave me the most important thing in this entire world," she says. "You. But besides that, he doesn't deserve to breathe the same air as you."

"I love you." I pat my face, hoping to remove some of the redness. "We'll talk later."

I get back to work, avoiding the lobby where my dad was earlier, even though I know he left. I can feel his presence everywhere. This nursing home was my happy place, but now it's tainted by him.

A hand grazes against mine as I rush down the hallway, and I turn. Liam is standing there. He pulls me into one of the empty, unassigned rooms. We get inside just as my pager starts to go off. I want to avoid him almost as much as my dad. He knows too much about me.

"What's up?" I say, holding out my vibrating pager.

Liam narrows his eyebrows. "Birdie."

He takes both of my shoulders in his hands.

"I really have to go."

He lets go. "Okay, but who was that man?"

I press my lips together, close my eyes, and then reach for the door.

"The sperm donor."

Liam's face falls, but I don't stick around for his full reaction. Instead, I answer the page and stay busy, which is what I always do to avoid thinking about all the ways my dad has let me down.

Chapter Twenty-Three

The next day, I'm off, and I've never needed a mental break more. I wake up after my mom has already gone to work, but she texts me a link to a story in *The New York Times*. It's not one of their feature articles, but it's still a write-up on this small town in Minnesota and the efforts being made to revitalize the town's nursing home.

"Holy shit." I scroll through the article.

It talks about the website that will be going live at seven in the evening and how to donate online. Equity and keeping the costs for nursing home residents down are the main focus. My mom is highlighted, and it mentions how important this place is to her because her own mom was once here. Why didn't my mom tell me she was interviewed for this article?

The New York Times. How did this happen?

My phone rings, and I jump to answer it.

"Mom, what is going on?"

She laughs into the phone. "Liam is apparently a miracle worker. Who knew?"

"How did he get this story in *The New York Times*? I'm so confused."

"His cousin's wife Jenna Abrams is a writer. She agreed to do a piece on us, and the *Times* picked it up."

Jenna Abrams. I know that name. And then it occurs to me—she wrote a piece on domestic abuse that went viral a couple of years back. Wait. I think I saw her at Asher's second birthday party, even though I never got the opportunity to meet her. That's who's married to Liam's cousin Robby.

"Do you think this will help?"

"It won't hurt," she says. "I've got to run, but I invited Liam over for when the website goes live. We'll order food, but maybe pick up the house a bit."

She hangs up before I can respond. I laugh. Wheaton just got put on the map by a paper with one of the largest circulations. I have so many questions. I read the article for the fifth time. It states that donations will be accepted via the website beginning at seven, and one hundred percent of the proceeds will go to hiring and retaining staff, fixing up the building, and providing affordable care for the many residents.

It's like a GoFundMe for a corporation. I didn't realize these things existed.

It's hard for me to trust people and I wasn't sure if Liam would be able to help, but if this works, it's a great first step in raising funds. I spend my day running errands, picking up food and wine, and then going back to the house and tidying up.

This big, old house has so much potential. If only my mom and I were home long enough to give it the love it deserves.

"Birdie, are you home?" my mom yells from downstairs as I step out of the shower.

"I'll be down in a minute."

I throw on a tank top and cutoff shorts and brush out my long hair. This will have to do. I take two stairs at a time, and my mom is unloading takeout on the kitchen island.

"There you are." She grabs a bottle of champagne from the fridge and opens it. "Liam should be here any minute. I told him the food would be arriving by six."

"You have so much to fill me in on." I hold out my glass, and my mom fills it to the brim. "The new website launches at seven, and then what happens?"

There's a knock at the door, and I go to open it. Liam stands there with his own bottle of wine in hand, and I wave him in.

"I have so many questions," I say, and he looks at me over his shoulder and winks.

"Do you really think people are going to donate money through the website?" My mom hands Liam a glass of champagne.

"And your cousin's wife has that much clout to be able to get an article in *The New York Times*?"

Liam takes a long sip of his drink and laughs.

"One thing at a time," Liam says. "Tonight could be anticlimactic, or it could blow our minds. But my gi—"

He stops talking and takes a deep breath. "I have a friend in New York who does corporate fundraising for a living. She has been calling large businesses and personal donors who focus on the nursing home space. She said the conversations went extremely well."

"But is there a possibility that no one will donate?" I pull my bottom lip into my mouth.

Liam shrugs. "Of course. But I also sent the news story to the largest Minnesota publication, as well as to the Dakotas. The hope is that it will get published, and that people will share our goals widely."

My mom refills our almost-empty glasses.

"But if tonight is slow, that's okay too," Liam says. "This is only the first step in our plan to turn the nursing home around."

My mom looks at her watch. "It's almost seven. Should we hook your laptop into the TV and watch?"

Liam grabs his computer, and I take another bottle of wine out of the fridge, and the three of us move to the living room. He sets up the computer, and we watch the countdown for the website to go live.

"Who built the site?" I narrow my eyes and study Liam.

He looks like I imagine he did when he was younger. His hair is tousled, and he smiles at the screen as he presses buttons, carefree and happy.

"Computer Science was my minor," he says, glancing at me.

At seven, Liam begins pushing buttons on his laptop, and then the display shows up on the TV: Traverse County Tranquil Waters Nursing Home.

"What?" I look at my mom, and then at Liam. "You renamed it?"

"We did." My mom nods. "We'll rebrand all of the brochures and change the signage on the building."

"It's Sunny and the men having coffee." I hold my hand over my heart as the photo displays on the site.

Liam smiles. "Don't worry, they signed off on all the privacy elements."

My mouth hangs open as I study the page. It looks beautiful in its white and blue hues. Liam presses more buttons, and on the front page, fundraising information appears.

"Anything donated will be directly deposited into the nursing home's account," he says.

"Will this stay open?" I move to the couch and sit between my mom and Liam. "So anyone could come out here at any time and throw money our way?"

"Yes," Liam says. "But we need momentum tonight, so I'm really hoping people donate."

We stare at the screen, and I slowly hold a glass up to my lips and swallow the sweet champagne. The dollar amount received remains at zero, and you could hear a pin drop in the house as we all sit still.

Five hundred dollars appear, and my mom gasps and Liam grabs my arm. Two minutes later, the total is up to two thousand.

"Oh my God." I cover my mouth with my hand. "People are donating."

"We're going to need more wine," my mom says, jumping up and going to the kitchen. I've never seen her have more than one glass in an evening. She must be overwhelmed by all of this.

"Holy shit." Liam moves closer to me and rests his arm over the couch. "It's up to twenty thousand, and it's only 7:15."

The three of us sit quietly, sipping our champagne as the amount continues to climb. Liam's thigh presses against mine, heavy with warmth.

"This is unbelievable." My mom's voice cuts through the silence, and she looks toward Liam. "I'm not sure whether to laugh, cry, or wrap my arms around you."

"I had no idea that random people who have no ties to this town would be so generous," I say.

"You'd be surprised." Liam slings his arm around me. "People are passionate about their causes, and the article pulled at their heartstrings. They trust that their money will be put to good use. This isn't a novel idea. Care centers all over the country do this. Corporations like Midwest Care don't focus on the patients."

We've been like this for three hours and have gone through several bottles of wine, too stunned to speak. It's ten in the evening, and the amount continues to climb. My mind is fuzzy, but all I can think about is what we could do with this money. The updates we'd be able to make, the staff my mom would be able to hire, and the programming the residents would have.

"I could watch this all night." My mom grabs my knee and pushes off the couch. "But my hangover has already set in, and I work in the morning."

She turns to me, smiles, and points. My mom trips and grabs the edge of the couch. For the first time in my entire life, I witness her being tipsy. "You kids stay up and have fun. You don't work tomorrow, Birdie."

She exaggerates a yawn. "I'm going to sleep so heavily. Have a good night."

She glances over her shoulder before leaving the room. "No driving home tonight for you, Liam."

"Goodnight, June," Liam says, and gets up.

When he comes back, he shuts off the main living room light.

"God." He covers his smile with his hand. "I'm pretty sure your mom just tried to ship us together."

"That was actually mortifying."

Liam laughs and collapses onto the couch. We lean back and stare at the screen. It almost puts me in a trance. The number continues to climb, and none of it makes sense to me. People are giving us money.

Liam tilts his head toward me, and I do the same. The room is dark except for the blue glow of the TV screen, and his face is illuminated. He opens his mouth slightly and narrows his eyes. He slowly inches closer to me until I can feel his breath on me.

"Liam." I press my hand against his chest. "You can't look at me like that."

He sighs and presses his head into the couch. "I haven't forgotten. You don't want to date me."

"You don't want to date me either." I press my head back against the couch.

Liam runs his tongue along the inside of his bottom lip. "I don't?"

"You definitely don't." I close my eyes, and the room spins.

Liam leans back on the couch, his gaze locking onto me with a mix of adoration and quiet resignation. His lips press together, a subtle tension held in place, while the corners turn up just enough to hint at a smile.

"Oh, Birdie."

"Trust me. I know you don't usually have to work hard for things."

I press my teeth into my bottom lip and try to suppress all the thoughts spinning in my head. My eyes linger on him for a moment too long, and I shake the thoughts away.

"Well," Liam says. "You heard your mom. I can't drive."

"This couch will be perfect for you." I slap my hand down.

"You want me to stay down here, alone, in a haunted house?" Liam stuffs his fist into his hand as he looks around.

"Are you seriously scared?"

Liam looks at me. "A little, yeah."

"Fine." I stand, grab his hands, and pull him up. "You can come upstairs with me. But there will be no looking at me with those eyes. You know the look. Actually, I'll bring blankets up and get you comfortable on the floor. That would be the best place for you."

Liam laughs. I grab a handful of blankets from a basket in the corner, and we tiptoe upstairs. I quietly close the door behind me and flick on the light.

"Provincial garden," he says, looking around.

He remembers the color of paint I chose.

"The ensuite bathroom is there," I say, pointing. "I'll grab you a new toothbrush."

I throw a couple of pillows on the floor before deciding that my bed is massive and I only take up a sliver of it, and I don't want his back to hurt tomorrow. I pull down the blankets and start making a barrier down the middle with a few of my throw pillows.

"Birdie," he says, glancing at me, and then at the bed. "I'm fine on the floor."

"My bed is huge. You stay in your corner, and I'll stay in mine."

The barrier is for me. I don't trust myself around him.

I grab my pajamas and slip inside the bathroom to change. Liam is out of my league, and he knows it. He must be suffering from proximity bias. It's the only explanation. I pinch my cheeks and watch them come to life with color.

I come out of the bathroom, and Liam is already in bed, with the cover up to his mid-torso. He watches me walk toward the bed, his elbow propping him up. He stares at me. Goosebumps travel up my arms.

"Quit looking at me," I say.

"You're impossible." Liam covers his eyes with his hands. "I'm not sure where you want me to look."

I shut off the lamp and lie down. "This corporate fundraiser you know. Is that the woman you were dating before you left?"

The bed shifts underneath me. "Yes. Olivia."

"Olivia." I say her name slowly and imagine what she must be like. A picture of a tall, beautiful woman comes to mind. "You guys still talk, huh?"

"We just started talking again recently." Liam reaches his hand over the pillow and messes up my hair, and I swat him.

"No touching."

"Sorry," Liam says. "She's good at what she does. Really good, clearly."

"Do you think you guys will get back together when you're back in New York?" I move onto my back and tuck my hands underneath my head.

"Birdie." Liam's voice is quiet.

"What?"

"Do you want to cuddle?"

"No." I grab one of the pillows acting as a barrier and hit him gently on the head. "You're impossible. Goodnight."

Liam laughs. "Okay. Goodnight. Don't snore."

"You don't snore." I turn on my side and fall asleep within seconds.

Chapter Twenty-Four

Liam is a quiet sleeper, and when I wake up, I almost forget that he's in bed beside me, next to the mound of pillows I put between us.

Almost.

I tiptoe out of the room, but as I reach the door, I glance back. The blanket has slipped low, revealing the elastic of his black underwear. One arm is tucked beneath him, and his golden chest rises and falls with each slow breath. Strands of his blond hair have fallen across his face, partially obscuring his closed eyes.

The smell of coffee awakens my senses, and my mom stands at the pot when I reach the kitchen.

"What are you still doing here?" I ask as she pours coffee into her thermos.

"Nursing a hangover." My mom leans against the counter. "And how was your night?"

"You mean, after you mentioned how hard you'd be sleeping and that Liam should spend the night?"

"I did say that, didn't I?" She smacks her palm against her forehead. "In my defense, he was drinking. Safety first."

"That's not how it came off." I blow on my coffee. "And we have a very platonic relationship, if you must know."

"Okay," she says slowly, a smile plastered across her face.

"Seriously, Mom." I shake my head.

She shrugs her shoulders. "Whatever you say."

I moan when I take my first sip. "We're friends."

"Birdie." She puts her hand on my arm. "It's okay to let yourself feel something, even if he isn't going to be your forever."

I try my best not to roll my eyes. "I can't with this. Have a good day at work."

When I return to my bedroom, Liam stands at my bookshelf, wearing only his shorts. He's looking through a photo album, and when he hears me, he smiles and closes it. He leans against my desk.

"Good morning."

His hair is tousled, and his muscles are on display as he folds his arms over his chest.

"Good morning. I brought coffee."

Liam smiles and grabs a mug from me. It should be illegal to look like this after only just waking up.

"You were an adorable child." He nods toward the closed album.

I sit on the edge of my bed. "Yeah, that word has been used to describe me a lot."

"Did you sleep okay?" I ask.

"I did." He puts his cup down, grabs his shirt from the chair, and pulls it on.

"Why'd we drink so much?" I put my mug on the nightstand and fall back into the bed. "Everything hurts."

Liam laughs. "Have you ever had a lake day? It's the best cure for a hangover."

"I've been to the lake." I raise an eyebrow.

"But have you had a lake day? Where you lie in a swimsuit all day, swim, fish, sleep, eat, repeat?"

Liam grabs a bag slung over my full-length mirror. "Pack a bag. We're having a lake day. I'll meet you downstairs."

I don't bother protesting. I throw on a bikini with a summer dress over it and put a few things in a bag. I tie my hair on top of my head. It's hot outside, and we ride with the windows down all the way to the lake, music blaring so there's no need for conversation. We pull in down the road from where Jake and Camilla live to an adorable cottage. Liam grabs my bag for me, and we get out of the car.

"Welcome." He smiles as he points to it. "It's been in the Bergland family forever. And it is my summer home."

He opens the door to the cottage, and I fall in love instantly. It's modern and looks like it's been recently remodeled. It smells like fresh paint but also like Liam.

As if he's reading my mind, Liam says, "Camilla and Jake fixed it up a few years ago. That's actually how the two of them met. Camilla came to spend the summer, and Jake took pity on her and helped her with the renovation."

"It's beautiful." I run a finger along the countertops and glance out the large window with panoramic views of the lake.

Liam hands me my bag and points to a room. "You can get changed in there, and then we're going to paddleboard out to a platform and do some swimming."

"I thought there would be no physical activity." I moan. "My entire body is sore."

Liam laughs. "It's not far. I promise."

I sigh as I stare at myself in the mirror in my black bikini. I run my hand down my pale stomach and turn to the side. When I was growing up, everyone thought I was younger than I was. But I've come to appreciate my body and all it's capable of. I step out of the room, and Liam does a double take.

"You're doing it again," I say, and he knows exactly what I'm talking about.

"Take this." He throws me a beach towel and pulls his gaze away from me.

We grab paddleboards from the shed and put them in the water. The platform is only about twenty yards out from shore, and the lake is like glass, with no wind.

"It's beautiful out here, isn't it?" Liam closes his eyes and tilts his face toward the sky. "I've been out here all summer, but I haven't taken the chance to enjoy it."

We reach the platform, and Liam helps me onto it. We pull up our paddleboards, and I jump into the lake. It's cool, which feels nice on this hot day. I float on my back and squint as I look up at the bright sky.

"So far," I say, "I like this lake day thing."

He laughs, and his muscles flex while he pulls himself up the stairs. I follow him and then plop myself onto my stomach. The surface beneath me is warm. Liam lies next to me.

"How are things with your dad?" I turn to him and shield my eyes. "I haven't seen him around lately."

"He's coming back next week." Liam props himself up on his elbow. "Which means we get to share this space for a few days. Lucky me."

"Is he really that bad?"

"Compared to some dads, no." Liam bites on the inside of his cheek. "But there's something about him I'll never understand. He likes to put me down. Remind me of my mediocrity. And trust me, I usually feel bad about myself without needing help from him."

"I'm sorry." I chew the inside of my cheek and nod. "About your dad. And that you would ever feel bad about yourself."

"Why do I have the feeling you could top every story I ever told you?" Water beads drip down his face, and he brushes his hair back.

"That's not a good thing," I say.

"What's the story of that mysterious man at the nursing home?" Liam squeezes the nape of his neck. "The sperm donor."

"There's not really much to tell."

Liam traces his lips with his index finger. "Why do I feel like there is? Like he's at the center of so many of your fears?"

"Hmm." I lie flat on my back and bend my arm over my face. "You're perceptive."

"So, I'm right?"

"Yes, and no." I focus on my breathing. "My mom's light more than made up for his darkness. I'm able to put things into perspective now. But did I internalize why I wasn't good enough for him to show up for my entire life? Of course."

All my logic and reason tell me that I've shared enough. For now. But my words are met with silence. I turn to look at Liam, and he's staring back at me, curious, focused in a way that makes me feel so seen by him.

"He taught me what it feels like to have a broken heart. He gave me lessons at a young age on what broken promises feel like. He's the reason I understand disappointment at its core. As I've gotten older, I've been able to recognize that it's about him, and not about me at all. But for a really long time, I wondered what was wrong with me. Why I wasn't good enough."

"But you know you are, right?"

Liam shifts onto his stomach, positioning himself above me and shielding my eyes from the sun. He props himself up on one arm, his presence close and warm. Opening up to him feels like the scariest and best thing I've ever done.

"We all have our shit." I stare into his eyes. "But I'm not at a point where I can say that having a messed-up, absent father has had no effect on my life. It has. It does."

Liam brushes my hair back. "I only want you to top my stories with the good stuff. Never the bad."

Energy transfers between us, but neither of us speaks. Moments pass, and the intimacy of it gets to me. I quickly lift my head, almost hitting his.

"Paddle back to shore?"

"Yeah. Sure." Liam helps me get to my feet.

I sit on a stool in the cottage as Liam makes me lunch, the radio quietly playing in the background. I watch as he cuts up fruit and puts vegetables on a turkey sandwich. We sit side by side.

"What's next on the agenda?" I ask.

Liam presses his hands together and smiles. "Everyone knows that a nap comes after lunch on lake days."

"A nap? Really?" I laugh. "That makes sense, I guess."

"Yep." Liam grabs my hand. "But it's not just any nap. It's outside. In the hammock. It's going to change your entire life."

I almost believe him that it will.

Liam leads me outside and jumps into it and gets situated. It rocks back and forth, and then he holds his hand out.

"Your turn."

I squint my eyes. "There is no way I'm going to fit into that. Not with you in it."

"You will. Trust me."

I sit gingerly, and when I feel steady, I lift my legs into the hammock and lie back. The moment I do, gravity pushes both Liam and me to the center. Our bodies pressed together.

"Is this your ploy to get a cuddle out of me?"

Liam flicks his eyes up. "What if it is?"

My bikini and his trunks are now dry, and I anchor my leg between his. Liam lazily wraps an arm around my back and pulls me toward him. I bury my face in his warm chest that smells like the lake, sunscreen, coconuts, grass, and every other favorite memory of summer.

"Is this okay?" His words vibrate against my head.

"It's not the worst." I wrap my arm around his lower back and drag my fingernails down his skin.

We're a tangle of limbs swaying in the breeze. I close my eyes, syncing my breath with the gentle rise and fall of his chest beneath me. His strong arms wrap around me. Liam's body is solid and warm, and it isn't long before sleep claims me. But even as I doze off, I'm aware of him.

I don't know how long I'm out for, but enough time passes that my dull headache is gone. I slowly open my eyes to slits and glance up to Liam's gaze on me.

"Hey," he says, smiling. He slides his hand down my back.

I detach myself from his body and wipe my mouth. "How long was I out for?"

"A while." Liam sits up. "Aren't hammock naps the best?"

It was being wrapped up with Liam that I liked so much. I could stay here with him the rest of the day and be very happy.

"Are you hungry? 'Cause I'm starved," Liam says.

"I could eat."

He takes my hand and pulls me up. "Well, since we're having a lake day, we're going to have to go fishing and hope we catch dinner."

Liam wasn't joking. He goes to the shed and starts bringing things to the boat: first life jackets, then two fishing poles, and a tackle box.

"Are you serious?" I stand and stretch my arms up. "I haven't fished since I was little. And there is no way you know how, Mr. New York City."

"I wouldn't kid about something as serious as catching dinner." Liam tosses the last life jacket in the boat, then grabs my hand. "Let's pick out a fishing hat."

We go into the cabin, and he opens up a wicker basket full of hats of every shape and size.

"What about this one?" Liam pulls out a wide-brimmed straw hat and pushes it on my head.

"You're kidding, right?" I look around for a mirror but don't see one. I go to remove the hat, and he laughs and pushes it back onto my head. He then puts one on, too. But instead of looking ridiculous, the wide-brimmed straw hat fits him perfectly.

"Let's fish." Liam grabs my hand.

We pull out onto the boat, and Liam hands me a fishing pole. I haven't gone since my grandpa taught me how when I was younger. That was a long time ago, and this pole looks nothing like the one I remember.

The shore is laden with rocks, and large trees rise up behind them. Liam grabs my pole back from me and casts it into the water before handing it back to me. The lake is calm, and it looks like the boat is slicing through glass.

"You look like you fit here," I say. "How can you so easily leave it all behind?"

"Some of it will be hard to leave." Liam turns the boat. "But this has never been my home."

I lean back in my chair and put my legs up on the other seat. "Maybe. But I've seen your eyes light up over helping the nursing home, and I wonder if you ever felt that kind of excitement with the work you did in New York."

"Birdie." Liam kills the engine and lurches forward. "You have a fish on your line."

He grabs the net, and I clumsily reel in, muscle memory taking over.

"Keep the tip up," he says, grabbing my line and easing the fish to the boat. "You're doing great."

He guides the fishing line to the net, and I jump up in excitement.

"Is this something we keep?"

"It's a walleye. If we can catch one more, we have dinner."

Liam gets the next fish, and I could have stayed out on the lake for longer. We are almost the only ones out there. It's so peaceful. Liam pours me a glass of wine as he cleans and cooks the fish, and I watch.

"See," I say. "You're pretty good at this small-town stuff."

"Sunny taught me how to clean and cook fish when I was a kid." Liam dishes up my plate. "I could visit every summer, sure. See the people I love. But you'll be singing a different tune about this place come winter. I promise you that."

Someday, I'll run into Liam and his future wife as he comes to town to spend a long weekend at the cottage. He'll be someone I knew back when. He won't tell his wife that at one point, this girl from Wheaton felt comfortable enough to share almost all the things. Even the ugly stuff.

He sits next to me, and I remove his hat and put the one I've been wearing on his head.

"Better," I say.

I spoon the fish into my mouth, and it's good. I haven't had walleye since I was a kid. I should recommend this meal for the residents at the nursing home.

Liam turns his stool. "A day at the lake isn't over. We haven't even done the bonfire yet."

"As much as I'd love to, it's getting late." I glance at the clock on the wall. The entire day went too fast. "You should probably take me home."

I think about all I have to do before I work six days straight. There are piles of laundry, I need to stop at the grocery store before it closes and pick up a few things, and I have to get a good night's sleep.

Liam takes my empty plate from me and brings it to the sink.

He leans against the counter. "You could stay here tonight."

"Oh, really?" I put my hands on my hips. "Could I?"

"That's not what I meant," he says. "I have two extra bedrooms."

Staying would be so easy. Continuing to get lost in his presence and talking late into the night.

"I can't," I finally say.

But also, I hate how much I want to. I get up and close the distance between us. I pull down the ridiculous hat that he's still wearing. He rubs his hands down my arms.

"You're freckly," he says.

Liam traces a few of them along my collarbone. New ones seem to pop up anytime I'm in the sun.

"I found my favorite one," he says, holding his finger against one right where my shoulder and neck meet. I glance up at him.

"Today was amazing." I grip his waist. "I like lake days."

Liam pulls off his hat and wraps his arms around me, drawing me close. His lips brush softly against my temple.

"You can't stay?"

I release a breath and pull away. "I shouldn't stay."

Those are two very different things.

Chapter Twenty-Five

"Hey, Sis." I walk into the room, knowing she'll be alone because I just saw Sunny having coffee with the boys. "Can I join you?"

She looks up from her needlework and points to the chair next to her. "I was needing a break from this anyway. Have a seat."

It only takes me seconds when being with Sis to know what kind of moment she's having, and this is a good one. She smiles at me with recognition.

"What are you making?"

"Oh, dear," she says. "I still haven't made Asher artwork for his bedroom. I do it for all of my great-grandkids."

I study her work. "You're good, Sis. I was never a very creative person."

"I wasn't always." She weaves the long needle in and out of the fabric, then puts it down. "But when my boys started having kids of their own, I wanted them all to have something special that I made for them. I do it with love, so they'll always feel surrounded by mine."

"How many grandkids do you have?" I ask her questions I sometimes know the answer to, but it helps her remember.

"Four." Sis looks up and smiles. "I couldn't ask for better ones."

"Will you tell me about them?"

I love getting to know the residents, but the break from being on my feet isn't a bad thing either.

Her eyes light up. "Well, my Liam is the oldest. And I think being the oldest has put some pressure on him. When he was younger, everything came easy to my little Liam. He got good grades, was the star athlete on his sports teams, got into every college he applied to, and then got his dream job in New York. He's never had to work that hard for anything, which isn't good for a person."

"But you know what, Birdie?" Sis leans forward, looks at the door, and then at me. "He got fired. But that's not even the worst of it."

"What's the worst of it?" I lean forward too, curious to learn bits of him that he hasn't openly shared.

"I don't think he's ever done one thing because he enjoyed it. His dad, my Larry, is a good man, but he wanted a son just like him, and Liam isn't that. I wish he'd start making decisions for himself. He has some things to figure out."

"That's hard, Sis," I say. "I hope he finds what he's looking for."

She nods and leans back in the chair, once again picking up her needlework. "And then there's my sweet boy, Robby. He's had to work for things. And he's so sensitive and loves big. He married an Abram girl, Jenna. And they write to me from New York and seem happy."

Sis smiles as if she's conjuring a memory. "My third grandson is David. He's Liam's younger brother and never faced the same pressures. He lives in Florida. Moved there for a job. He's the most carefree of all of them. He has an artistic spirit about him."

"Then our first granddaughter was born. Oh, Camilla looks just like I used to. And she's a fiery thing. She used to move around from place to place, acted like she liked that life. But in reality, she wanted to settle down. Her husband Jake is also an Abram. I love that one of my grandkids came to live here."

"You must be so proud, Sis." I grip her hand. "They all seem like great people."

"Hi, Grandma."

Liam walks through the door, and our eyes meet. He glances at Sis as he sits at the end of the bed.

"Oh, good," he says. "You're both here. I have news I want to share."

"Happy news, I hope." Sis drops her needlework and turns to Liam.

"It is, I think."

He links his fingers together, then stands again. He paces once and then stops.

"Well, I've been talking to a company for about three weeks and had a couple of informational interviews. Well, they called me this morning, and they're flying me to New York for two days of interviews."

"Liam." I jump up from the chair, unable to hide my excitement for him. I give him a quick hug and then push away. "Congrats. I'm so happy for you."

He laughs, and when I turn to Sis, she's studying us, her lips slightly turned up.

"Is this what you want, Liam?" She narrows her eyes. "To find another job there?"

"Well, yeah, Grandma. It is. I miss New York and my friends. And the job is a great opportunity for me."

Sis nods. "As long as it's for you and not your dad."

"Grandma." Liam sits and takes her hands in his. "Of course, it's for me."

"Then I wish you luck," she says.

"You two have a lot to catch up on." I move to the door a bit too fast. "Sis is having a great day, Liam." I turn and mouth, "So happy for you."

My emotions confuse me as I step out of the room and into the hallway. There's this part of me that's sad. But the biggest thing I feel right now is relief. It's been hard to grow closer to him, not knowing for how long I have him here. Now I know it's all going away. I can step away from getting to know him better. I only want what's best for him. From the moment I met him, all he's talked about is how amazing New York City is. I knew our friendship this summer was temporary, which is why I've kept it platonic, even when there have been moments where it felt like we were slipping into something more.

But now it's real. He's going to leave Wheaton. There is relief in the clarity.

"Hey." Liam grabs my arm and spins me toward him. "Can we talk?"

I blink, as I didn't hear him coming. "I can't now. I'm actually meeting my sperm donor for lunch."

"Birdie." He narrows his eyes. "Do you think that's a good idea?"

"No." I press my lips together. "It's never a good idea. But he said he'd be there at noon, and I'm going to find out if he is."

"Don't go." He grabs my hand. "You have the afternoon off. Let's have another lake day. I leave in the morning."

"Tomorrow already?" I narrow my eyes. "I didn't realize when you said they were flying you to New York, it meant immediately."

He runs his long fingers through his hair. "My interviews are Monday and Tuesday, but I'm going to go stay with my cousin Robby and his wife. I figured I'd go for the weekend and catch up with my friends."

"Oh." I force a smile. "That makes sense."

"Spend today with me."

"I can't, Liam," I say. "I have plans."

Will walks by and gives us a look but keeps moving.

"I was supposed to have the afternoon off, but now I'm needed. It'll be late before I get off."

"Birdie," he says slowly.

"When are you back?" I look at my watch.

"Late Tuesday or early Wednesday. I haven't decided yet."

I grip his arm. "Perfect. Good luck. I can't wait to hear all about it when you get back."

"Birdie." Liam grabs me as I walk away. "Why do I feel like you're saying goodbye to me?"

He releases me.

"Because you're leaving." I smile, turn from him, but glance over my shoulder. "Break a leg, Liam."

I walk into Main Street Cafe expecting and almost knowing in my bones that my dad won't be here. I'll wait ten minutes, maybe fifteen, and then I'll head home and take a nap before I have to be back at work at three.

But there he is, sitting at a table for two in the corner, by the window, reading glasses on as he studies the menu.

"Hey," I say, and he looks up and smiles.

"Beatrice." He stands and pulls a chair out for me.

I let out a breath. "If we're going to spend time together, you're going to have to start calling me Birdie. Beatrice sounds like a sixty-year-old woman."

My dad nods. "Where did that name even come from?"

"My grandma," I say without hesitation. "She said when I was hungry as a newborn, I'd pucker my lips like a bird being fed worms. The nickname stuck, and I prefer it."

"I'll try to keep it straight." He hands me a menu. "Get anything you'd like, Birdie. Lunch is on me."

We order our food and then nervously look at each other. What do I say to someone I barely even know?

"How's your old lady doing?" He takes a sip of his Coke.

"She's great, actually." I drink my water. "As you saw from the paper, she now owns the nursing home. She also bought a house, and I'm living there with her, and so far, everything is going great."

My dad pounds on the bottom of the ketchup bottle. "I saw that you guys raised a lot of money for that nursing home."

My skin fills with goosebumps, and I scratch the inside of my hands, nearly drawing blood. "That money isn't hers. It goes directly to running the business."

"I know that," he says.

"Why are you here?" I put down my fork, unable to pretend that this is normal. "After all this time, what do you want with me? With Mom?"

"Can't I want to live a life I'm proud of? One where we're in each other's lives? I've missed you, Birdie. I know I've been a shit dad, but I've gone through a lot. I want to be better."

I want to believe that this time is different. But why should I? I can forgive someone for hurting me once or twice. But when it becomes a pattern, how can there ever be trust?

"I'm twenty-five. We haven't had a relationship. You can't just show up and expect something from me. You don't even know me."

"You're right," he says. "And I know that. Baby steps."

I bite into a fry and study him, wondering if anything in this relationship is redeemable.

"I didn't see you park. Did you walk here?" He wipes his mouth.

"My car broke down. I'm in the process of buying a new one."

"Cars are my specialty," he says. "I can help."

"You don't have to do that," I say.

"Let me help." He claps his hands together. "I want to make sure my baby girl doesn't get taken for all she has."

I nod, knowing that all of this could go very badly, yet I agree to have him claw his way back into my life.

Chapter Twenty-Six

By now, Liam is probably on a plane to New York. Maybe he's already there, transitioning from his laid-back Wheaton look to a man about town in the city. This is where the fade-out begins. I've seen it before with friends when I was a travel nurse. There's an understanding that exists but is never spoken about.

It's easier to lie.

So instead, we say all the nice things: Keep in touch. Text me. Don't be a stranger. If we ever end up in the same place, reach out, and we can grab a drink.

Maybe they aren't all lies. I've said that to people with the best intentions in mind. But then time passes, and all the things you enjoyed about the person's company are slowly forgotten. The reach-outs become less frequent until they stop altogether.

I've experienced it so many times. I've known from the moment I met Liam that his presence in Wheaton would be temporary. This is good. He's meant to be somewhere else. It was a nice distraction, but he'll leave before I get more attached.

"Are you still up for wine night tonight?"

Lucy stops at the desk where I've been doing charts for the past hour.

"Your house, right? At seven?"

Lucy twirls the ends of her hair. "Yes. And it's a total disaster right now. Let this be your warning."

"I'm sure it's fine," I say.

Lucy looks over her shoulder and then leans closer. "I told Will you were coming over, and he wants to join. What should I tell him?"

"Umm." I rub my lips together. "Does he need to be there?"

"I feel bad. He doesn't have many friends in town. What if I tell him to come around eight? That way, we can catch up on our girl gossip before he gets there."

"Perfect." I go back to chart work. "See you later."

Everything in Wheaton is walkable, so I grab a bottle of wine from the fridge and the charcuterie board I put together and stroll over to her house. She lives on the other side of town, a good seven or eight blocks away.

"Birdie." Lucy runs outside and grabs the wine. "I could have given you a ride."

"It's a nice night," I say. "I don't mind walking."

She opens the door for me. "This no-car business is getting ridiculous."

"Agreed."

I look around her house, and she wasn't joking. Gavin's toys are everywhere, and I have to step over a bin of Legos lying in the middle of the floor. Her kitchen is small, and the counter is full of mismatched appliances and an open loaf of bread.

"This house is very temporary." Lucy grabs a corkscrew and opens the wine. "Derik wanted the house in the divorce, and I didn't have the fight in me so I'm renting this dump."

Lucy hands me a glass, and we clink our glasses together. She looks around.

"Gavin doesn't have enough places for his toys, so they end up all over the house. I can't tell you how many toes I've almost broken stepping on his stuff."

She points to the living room, and we take a seat. She has one chair and a small couch in the room.

"When are you going to tell Will that you're not that into him?" Lucy smiles above her glass at me.

"Do I need to?" I tuck my legs underneath myself. "I've given him no validation. I barely talk to him. I don't initiate contact. Shouldn't he just know?"

"You'd think so." Lucy laughs. "The next time he asks me about you, I may just mention that you have much hotter prospects."

"Well, I don't know about that." I look down at my glass.

Lucy leans forward. "We're becoming friends, right?"

"Yeah, of course."

Lucy is easily my closest female friend in town, which isn't saying much.

"I have to ask." Lucy bites away her smile. "What is up with you and Liam?"

"Nothing." I shrug my shoulders.

"Come on, Birdie." Lucy shakes her head. "He's beautiful. You're beautiful. Please let me live vicariously through you because my life is so boring at the moment."

"You are going to be sorely disappointed." I grab the wine bottle on the ottoman and fill up my glass.

"Nothing has happened. At all? I don't buy it. My favorite thing to do at the nursing home, well, besides my job, is watching the two of you converse. It's like you're unaware of anything else existing."

My face heats, and Lucy hits me across the arm and laughs.

"I knew it."

"Fine." I take a long sip. "There was a kiss. Once. But that's it."

Lucy shrieks. "That was it? No. There has to be more."

"I swear." I shrug. "I don't know, Lucy. I'm attracted to him, obviously. But he's only here for a short time, and that's not how I roll. So I friend-zoned him."

"Hmm." Lucy leans back.

"Look," I say. "I know it may be confusing. But I don't need to develop feelings for a guy who's made it very known that he's moving away the first chance he gets. It's hard for me to put myself out there. Especially when I know he's leaving."

Lucy tilts her head and studies me. "But you already have feelings for him, Birdie. I don't know you that well yet, but it's pretty obvious."

"Not big ones." I wrinkle up my nose. "Imagine if something between us happened. I'd have bigger feelings for him, and it would make everything harder."

"Andy Kennedy." Lucy nods her head.

I snap my head in her direction. "Huh? Who is Andy Kennedy?"

"Well," Lucy says. "When I was your age, that's who I talked myself out of trying things with. He was this gorgeous guy I went to college with, but he was going to medical school on the other side of the country, and I didn't want to start anything with someone who was going to be leaving so soon."

"What happened to him?"

Lucy shakes her head. "According to my online stalking, he's aged incredibly well, is even more gorgeous than before, and is a neurosurgeon. All I'm saying, Birdie, is it's not the things we do that we'll regret; it's the things we're too scared to try."

"I want to see this guy." I bite my lip and smile, and Lucy laughs as she pulls her phone out.

"Look at him." She points. "Gorgeous."

She hands me her phone, and I start flipping through his photos. He only has a few, and it's of him and his dog.

"Reach out to him," I say. "Send him a friend request. Ask him if he's still single."

Lucy rolls her eyes. "I'm in Wheaton co-parenting with my asshole of an ex-husband. That ship has sailed."

"I don't know, Lucy. It could be exactly what you need."

As if on cue, there's a knock at the door, and a moment later, Will walks into the living room.

"Hi, Birdie. Lucy. I brought more wine, and it looks like we could use it."

Will pours us a glass, and Lucy grabs more food from the kitchen. Will sits next to me on the couch.

"What have I missed?" He slides closer to me.

"We were discussing how big of an ass my ex-husband is," Lucy says, and Will nods.

My phone vibrates underneath my leg, and I grab it, trying to suppress the smile that forms when I see it's a text from Liam. I wasn't expecting to hear from him at all while he was in New York. It's a selfie of him eating sushi with chopsticks and a reminder that you can't get that in Wheaton.

"Who texted?" Lucy says. "And has you all giddy over there?"

"No one." I put my phone back down. "My mom sent me a funny meme."

A few minutes later, more pictures come through. One is of bright lights and billboards. And the next is another selfie of Liam, this time eating cheesecake. I save the photos to my camera roll. He looks handsome and carefree.

I try to follow the conversation, but instead, I'm obsessed with my phone. I do my best to hide how distracted I am, but I don't think I do a good job.

By ten, I'm exhausted and want to get home so I can text Liam back.

"I should get going." I stretch my arms up dramatically and yawn.

"Me too." Will jumps to his feet. "I can drive you."

I help bring empty bottles to the kitchen and grab my cutting board that the charcuterie was on.

"Thanks so much for having us, Lucy. Next time, I'd love to have you guys over to the Hurst haunted house."

Will opens the car door for me, and I slide in. My phone starts vibrating, and I glance at the screen, and Liam is calling me. I send it to voicemail.

"There's this waterskiing show next weekend on the south side of the lake. I was thinking about checking it out if you're interested." Will turns to me.

"I'll need to look at my schedule, but—"

My phone rings again. Liam.

"Sorry, Will. I better get this."

"Hi," I say into my phone.

"Are you ignoring me, Birdie?" His voice is deep, and my body heats at the sound of it.

"I'm on my way home." I cover the receiver and mouth an apology to Will. "Can I call you in a few minutes?"

"You're on your way home from where?"

"Lucy's."

"Hmm." I can hear his breath. "Is Lucy giving you a ride home?"

"No," I say, and Will continues to glance in my direction.

"Are you walking?"

"I am not."

"Hmm," Liam says.

Will takes a turn near my house and then pulls into the driveway. He turns off the engine and faces me.

"Here we are," Will says.

"Are you in a car with a man?"

"Can I call you in a few minutes?"

"Is that the male nurse with you?"

"I'll call you later."

I don't wait for him to respond before I hang up.

"Sorry about that."

Will takes his seat belt off and turns to face me. He smiles and puts his hand on my arm. He slowly inches forward. My phone starts vibrating, and we both look down.

"Sorry, Will." I glance at the screen and hold the phone against my chest. "I really need to take this."

"Is everything okay?" Will puts his hand on the middle console.

"Probably, but I better make sure. Thanks so much for the ride home."

I get out of the car before I can hear Will's response. By the time I'm at the door, I already have three more missed calls. The house is dark when I get inside, and I take two steps at a time to get upstairs. When I reach my bedroom, my phone rings again, and this time it's a video call. I run to the mirror to see the state of things and then smooth out my hair with my fingers.

"Hi, Liam."

His face comes onto my screen. He's in bed, leaning against the headboard, his arm tucked behind his head.

"Did he kiss you?"

"Who?" I kick off my shoes and sit on the end of my bed. "Will? No."

Liam blows out a breath and smiles. "Hi, Birdie."

"I was at Lucy's for drinks and apps. Why are you blowing my phone up?"

"I miss you."

That was not what I was expecting him to say. I prop up my pillows and lie back.

"How was your day? How's it being back in the city?"

Liam puckers his lips. "It was fun. I went out for dinner with some friends, and now I'm back at Robby and Jenna's and I was thinking about you."

"What will you do tomorrow?" I move to my side.

"I'm meeting friends for brunch, and then I'm going to do some interview prep because my first one is Monday at eight. Speaking of, can I get your opinion on something?"

Liam gets up from the bed but keeps the phone on him. He props it on something and then pulls his t-shirt off. His jeans hang so low on his chiseled torso, and I wonder if he knows what he does to me.

He pulls on a shirt with a blue and pink pattern.

"This one?" He spins and shows it to me from a few angles.

He takes it off and puts on one that is baby blue and white, and his eyes pop. They look less dark blue and get brighter instantly.

"The second one. For sure."

He takes the shirt off and gets back into bed. He has to be doing this on purpose. Liam's arm is perfectly placed so his muscles pop out.

"It's hot in this apartment," he says.

"Yeah. Okay." I roll my eyes.

We talk about our days, and he tells me about the interviews he has coming up.

I glance at the clock, and it's so late.

"I work in the morning," I say. "I should really get to bed."

"I'll call you tomorrow." Liam stretches an arm up in the air.

"Birdie," he says, as I'm about to say goodnight for the final time. "I'm not sure about that Will guy."

"Why?" I raise my eyebrows.

"He's not right for you," Liam says. "Not what you need."

"Not what I need?" I chuckle. "And what do I need?"

Liam pinches his bottom lip, his eyes studying me intently.

"Birdie. Will you promise me something?"

"That depends," I say.

"Don't let anything happen with Will."

I shake my head. "Goodnight, Liam."

The fade-out never happens. Sunday, Liam documents his entire day for me, and every time I have a chance to glance at my phone during my shift, I smile. It's like I'm at his favorite places with him. Sunday night, he video calls me again, and we discuss his interviews coming up the next couple of days.

I think back to my conversation with Lucy about only regretting things that don't happen. Liam isn't just a friend. Maybe after being around all the beautiful New York women, he'll quit flirting with me, but I'm not sure I want him to.

Chapter Twenty-Seven

Call me if you need anything." My mom stands at the kitchen counter and pours coffee into her travel mug.

"When will you be back?" I ask sleepily.

"Tomorrow evening. The sessions go until late afternoon." She grabs her keys and kisses the top of my head.

I stretch my arms over my head. "Well, I hope you learn a lot at this nursing home convention."

She laughs. "Lucky for me, I have a lot to learn. I still can't believe I'm the owner of a nursing home. Me."

"Me neither." I stand and walk my mom to the door. "Safe travels."

"Love you, Birdie girl."

I wave from the front porch and watch as she drives away. She found this convention a couple of weeks ago, and due to a cancellation, she was able to get enrolled. It's all she's been talking about.

The shower is hot, and I let it run over my head as my mind wanders to Liam. He never called me yesterday, and I'm not sure when he's due home, but I'm almost positive it's sometime today. I'm excited to hear how his last interviews went, but I know Liam well enough to be sure he aced them. They'd be fools not to hire him.

As I'm walking down the stairs, there's a light tap on the door, and I speed up. I swing the door open, and there Liam stands. His dress shirt is unbuttoned at the neck, and his tie hangs loosely. A carry-on suitcase is at his feet. My breath hitches, and my mouth hangs open.

God. He looks good. A few days apart didn't cure me of my attraction to him.

"Hi, Birdie." He leans against the doorway.

I lunge toward him and wrap my arms around his neck. I breathe in the scent of him—subtle hints of cologne and aftershave. His hands grip my waist tightly. I pull back to kiss his cheek, but at the same time, he turns his face and our lips connect. I jerk my head back, surprised.

Liam cradles my face in his hand, his breath warm and heavy. My gaze drifts to his slightly parted, full lips, and when our gazes lock, my mind goes blank as desire surges through me.

I lead Liam inside, and he immediately pins me against the wall. His hand fists in my hair, and I clutch the loops of his pants, pulling him closer until his firm body is pressed tightly against mine.

"Birdie." He leans his forehead into mine, his chest rising and falling slowly.

I lift my leg and wrap it around his, forcing him closer into me.

"I missed you," I say, admitting it to him.

"What are you doing to me?" Liam reaches down and runs his hand along my thigh. "What about your mom?"

"Gone until tomorrow."

He lifts me, and I pull at his tie, get it over his head, and throw it across the room. He walks me to the couch, falls back with me on his lap. I work to free him of his shirt. He grabs my butt and grinds me into him, then lifts my dress over my head. His shirt finally comes off, and he lies me back on the couch, but we miss entirely. We roll off, the soft rug beneath me, and Liam's hard body pressing down on top of me.

Liam is large, our size difference never more obvious than now. He reaches beneath me to unclasp my bra, and when he flicks my nipple with his tongue, I'm already on the verge of coming undone. Everywhere he touches feels like an electrical jolt, bringing my body alive. I reach for his belt, then the button of his pants. I push his pants down, and Liam helps with the rest.

There's an understanding between us. We know where this is leading. We always knew. Liam pulls my panties down, then parts me and drags his knuckles over my sex. I gasp.

"Is this okay?" Liam kisses me, and I nod.

He puts a finger inside me and moans.

"Fuck, Birdie." He kisses my neck. His favorite freckle. My breasts.

I push down his underwear and take him in my hand. Liam's eyes roll back into his head. He reaches into the pocket of his pants and rips the foil wrapper.

"Are we going to do this?" Liam opens my mouth with his, and he tastes so sweet.

"Yes," I say into his mouth. "It seems like we are."

He hovers over me, gently pressing into my entrance but not moving. His strong arms on each side of me, his breaths heavy.

I grip his hips.

"Please, Liam," I say breathily.

"Birdie." His abdomen muscles flex. "Say that again, and I'm going to lose it."

He presses into me, and I tense up, my back arching. He starts slow, allowing my body to adjust to him. But then it's frantic. His sweaty body glides over mine, one hand holding my arms over my head, the other grabbing my butt and pulling me toward him.

He releases my hands, and I slide them down his hard chest as Liam kisses me. I move them to his ass and push him into me.

"Don't hold back," I breathe into his neck. "I want all of you."

"Those words," he says. "Coming out of your sweet little mouth."

Liam pushes into me all the way this time, and my body jolts forward. Our skin slaps together, and the rolling motion over me causes a low ache in my belly. It continues to build with each stroke until my toes curl.

"Look at me, Birdie." Liam grips my face. "I want to see you."

The sensation increases. I bite into my bottom lip, and Liam's dark blue eyes look into mine. And then the pleasure topples over into something else entirely. I grab his arms, and something inaudible comes out of my mouth. Liam rolls over me again, elongating my orgasm, pulling every last ounce out of me.

I pull his face to mine and kiss him, a thank you. For making me feel wanted and beautiful. His mouth tastes so sweet, and I don't think I could ever tire of his lips.

"Birdie." Liam bites my lip.

My hands slide down his glistening back, and I squeeze his muscular butt. Liam groans into my neck. His entire body hardens, pushing into me, and then he collapses, first on me, and then he rolls over and lies next to me on his back.

Did that all happen in minutes? Or was it mere seconds?

We both lie on our backs. The only sound is the exhales of our breath. He reaches for my hand and intertwines his fingers with mine.

"That was very unexpected," Liam says, after what feels like the passage of several minutes.

I glance at him, but his eyes are closed.

"Do unexpecting men always carry condoms in their pockets?"

Liam laughs and turns to me, propping himself up on his elbow. I grab a throw blanket from the couch, cover myself up, and turn to him.

"Hope and expectations are very far apart." Liam brushes my wild hair back. "Since the first time I met you, I've been a hopeful man."

Liam gently kisses me, and I push his hair out of his face.

"Well then, I hope it's what you envisioned."

Liam gently kisses me and starts grabbing his clothes.

"I should probably bring in my luggage from outside," he says. "Unless you want me to leave."

"I don't," I say. "Unless you want to."

There's a new shyness between us and an understanding that everything has changed because of this.

"I'd love to stay."

Liam goes outside to grab his stuff, and I go upstairs to my room. I pull my silk robe tightly around my body and look at myself in the full-length mirror. I run my hand along my chest, and my skin is Liam-kissed—red and blotchy. I run my fingers through my hair, then press them to my dark pink lips.

Through the mirror, I see Liam standing in the doorway, watching me. I turn to him. He rolls his bag against the wall, then takes his clothes and throws them on a chair. He seems so comfortable in his skin as he walks toward me in only underwear. He grips my shoulders and presses a kiss against my forehead.

He lies over the sheets in my unmade bed and pats the space next to him.

"I want to show you all of my pictures from New York."

I lie down next to Liam, leaving room between us, but he pulls me toward him and wraps his arm around me.

"What's next?" I glance up at him. "I mean, regarding the job."

Liam unlocks his phone. "If I make it to the next round of interviews, and that's a big if, they'll fly me back out to interview with the CEO."

"Was New York everything you remembered it to be?"

Liam smiles and hands me his phone. I scroll through photos of him with people I don't know, of him on streets I've never seen.

"It was. The food. The culture. The different types of people. My time there went by so fast."

Days passed slowly for me with Liam gone. At times, it felt like they stood still entirely. I continue to scroll through photos. There's one of Liam lying in bed, shirtless with a sheet hanging low on his torso. I glance up at him, and he laughs.

"I took that thinking of you. I almost sent it too. But I chickened out at the last minute."

I text the photo to myself. "There. Now I have it."

It's a photo I may revisit hundreds of times.

I continue scrolling until I reach a photo of Liam and a woman, seemingly at a restaurant. I can tell by their bodies that Liam is taking the selfie. She's beautiful, with long, blond hair. She rests her head on Liam's shoulder, her hand on his chest. He takes his phone from me.

"That's Olivia," he says, his voice low.

"That's Olivia." I move myself from under his arm and lie on my side. He does the same.

Liam runs a hand down his face, never taking his eyes off me. They looked good together, Liam and Olivia. They fit. Like they belong in the same world.

"Did you guys. . ." I pause. "Rekindle things?"

"Birdie." Liam puts his hand on my hip. "If we had, do you think I'd be here with you?"

"You guys look good together," I say. "She still likes you. I can tell."

"Olivia and I had unfinished business to discuss," he says. "But I spent my entire time in New York only thinking about you."

"You shouldn't have," I say quietly.

Liam studies me. "I don't have the ability to just turn off feelings. Do you?"

Liam grabs the silk belt of my robe and runs the fabric through his fingers. He undoes the knot, and it falls open. He spreads his hand across my lower back and brings me flush against his body.

"Your comment earlier." Liam brushes a finger across my lips, and I raise my brows. "Being with you was more than I'd ever hoped for."

Liam grabs my hip and wraps my leg around him.

"You're beautiful." Liam looks at me with an intensity that makes my body heat. "Everyone knows that. But what just happened? I've never experienced anything like that in my life."

I don't want his sweet words in my head, reliving what this meant. It can't mean anything. It was an experience I'm happy to have. I cup his face and slowly kiss him as I press my body against his. His mouth opens for me, and our tongues connect.

Liam shifts to his back, and the weight of it pulls me on top of him. I get off the bed and go to the chair where his pants are draped over the back of it. I reach into the pocket and find what I'm looking for. I blink away my overthinking nature. Liam Bergland is naked in my bed. This once. When it's all over, I'll put distance between us. I let my robe slip off my shoulders, and Liam reaches a hand out for me as he bites his lip.

He lifts my hips directly over him, and then lowers me, and we both hold our breath.

"Kiss me, Birdie."

Liam pulls closer as I move atop him. We go slowly this time, savoring every touch and taste of each other. His full lips devour mine as his hand explores my breasts and moves down to my hip.

"I don't want this to end," he says into my neck.

Those words have multiple meanings for me. I put my finger on his lip, not wanting to hear him speak.

When it's over, he grabs me and holds me close, moving me to my side. Our chests move heavily against each other, both out of breath. He rolls me onto my back and kisses me. When our gazes meet, I need to block out everything besides this moment. I can't allow myself to think about how much harder our goodbye will be.

Chapter Twenty-Eight

Liam rolls over, and I grab my robe and cover myself. I glance at the clock on my nightstand. I'm supposed to meet my dad to go car shopping in less than an hour. I pick out clothes from the closet, go into the bathroom, and shut the door. I sigh as I stare at myself in the mirror.

What just happened felt like inevitability. And now we can both move on. I pull a dress on, and when I walk out of the bathroom, Liam is already dressed.

"Hey," he says. His hair is tousled, and he smiles at me. "Any interest in going out to the lake? I'd like to change out of these clothes. We could cook dinner, have some wine, and start a fire. Have a different kind of lake day."

"I can't." I tie my hair up in front of the mirror, then walk to the door. "I'm actually meeting the sperm donor shortly to look at a car."

Liam stands. "Do you think that's a good idea?"

"Probably not." I shrug. "But he says he knows a lot about them, which is convenient because I need one."

Liam tucks his shirt into his pants. "Do you think he'll show?"

"There's always a fifty percent chance."

"I know some things about cars, too." He holds my arm. "I don't want to see you get hurt, Birdie."

"I appreciate that." I let out a deep breath.

Liam releases me from his grip. "How about when you're done? I can pick you up. We can stay here if you'd rather. As long as the ghost doesn't protest."

He smiles so innocently, but my wall is already going up. I'm not worried about my dad hurting me. I feel impenetrable.

"I can't," I say, turning away from him and walking out of the room. "I need to get groceries, do about five loads of laundry, and I'm tired and need to get to bed early."

"Yeah, okay." Liam reaches for his suitcase and hauls it down the stairs.

He reaches for the doorknob, pauses, and then spins to face me.

"Did I do something wrong, Birdie?" He presses his back against the door. "Everything felt magical, and now I feel like you can't get rid of me fast enough."

"No." I shake my head. "I just have a lot to do. We'll talk later, okay?"

"Yeah." Liam releases his suitcase, grips my chin, and tilts it up.

He presses his lips against mine, and even though I want to resist this touch, my mouth opens, and he sweetly kisses me.

"Bye, Birdie." He looks at me and hesitates, but then walks out the door.

I don't know how I should feel. I was hoping that it would feel like goodbye for both of us and that he would quietly leave afterward, with no mention of continuing things.

It can't happen again.

Ever.

Because the pain of Liam moving away will become that much more unbearable the closer we get.

My dad is already waiting for me when I arrive at the used car lot on the north side of town. I'm relieved when I see him standing there, speaking to an employee. Not because I care about him, but because having no car is beyond inconvenient, and I need someone who knows what they're talking about to help me through this process.

"You came," I say, and my dad turns to me, a big smile plastered across his face.

"Well, of course," he says. "Why wouldn't I?"

"You don't have a good track record of showing up when you say you will," I say flatly.

"You always want to live in the past." He puts his hands on his hips. "Just like your mom. There are a hundred places I could be besides here. Just say the word."

"It doesn't matter to me if you stay or go," I say. His eyes wrinkle, and I realize nothing has changed. I still don't have it in me to hurt him. "But you're already here, and I could use the help."

"Well, okay then."

The lot is lined with cars, at all price points. I gravitate toward the ones that are understated, either white or black.

"This one here is nice." My dad pats the top of a four-door sedan. "It has low mileage, and the price is right. What do you think?"

"How about that one?"

I point to a white Jeep and walk toward it. It looks sporty, and the sunroof extends nearly the entire roof. I imagine driving in warm weather with it completely open.

He reads the information. "The tires are in good condition, but it's got a lot of miles on it." He pulls the door open for me, and I sit in the driver's seat.

I like it. It sits tall and would be good in the Minnesota winters. The interior is dark leather, and everything appears to be in mint condition.

"These seats are going to feel hot in the summer," my dad says, getting into the passenger seat. "The sun will heat these right up."

"This is the one I want." I smile, gripping the steering wheel.

"A Jeep, Birdie? Really?" He studies the card inside with all of the information. "It's not very practical."

"Let's take it out for a test drive."

We get the keys from inside, and I drive the Jeep around town and out to the lake. I open the windows and the roof. My hair blows in the wind. I love how free I feel in it.

"This is the one," I say.

"Why did you have me come with you if you weren't going to listen to me anyway?"

"I did listen." I smile at my dad. "But I chose this one."

He effectively barters with the owner of the dealership to get me a better deal, which is good because money isn't something I have in excess. I study him as he sits next to me at the desk, working out the final details. My entire life, I've dissociated myself from him. It was always easier that way. But there is no mistaking that I got his vibrant blue eyes. Even the shape of them is the same. I also got his freckles. The rest of my features, though, I got from my mom.

An overwhelming sense of pride fills me when I'm handed the keys. My last car was a junker my mom gave me, but this is the first one I've ever bought for myself.

"I'll never forget my first car," my dad says as we walk outside and toward my new Jeep. "I was sixteen and had just met your mom. I wanted to impress her. Everyone in our little town liked her."

"You look just like she did, you know?" He chuckles. "I wasn't sure you were even mine at first until you opened your eyes. The color was indistinguishable."

"I don't know what that says about how you feel about Mom if you weren't sure I was yours."

"Lighten up, Birdie. It was a joke." I reach my new Jeep and run my hand over the smooth paint. "All I meant is you were the spitting image of her. Which is a good thing. I wouldn't have wanted it any other way."

I slowly turn to him and lean back. "Why'd you never try to make it work with her?"

He runs his fingers through his unkempt beard. "I tried. For a while. Even lived in the old ranch house of your grandparents with you and your mom. But all we did was fight. She liked to point out that I wasn't good enough for her or for you. She wasn't wrong. It was easier to leave."

"You didn't have to leave me." I dig my fingers into my palms. "You took away my choice in the matter."

"You cried constantly. There was nothing I could do right. I thought I was doing you a favor."

"I was a baby."

Our conversations through the years always lead to this one place. He left for me. There hasn't once been accountability or an apology. I never press it further than this or ask why he said he'd show up so many times, only to leave me stranded.

"Why are you here?"

"You're my daughter," he says, kicking a rock with his boot.

"Yes, your sperm created me, but why are you here?"

He tucks his hands into the deep pockets of his jeans. "Because I know where you live now. And I have the time. I work for a construction company, and we're between jobs. I figured I'd come here and check on you."

"Well." I unlock the door and get into my brand-new vehicle. "I appreciate your help, but I think I'll take my Jeep out on the open road."

"Care to have lunch again?" He backs away from the Jeep.

I hesitate. "Maybe. I'll let you know."

He nods. "Okay. Let me know."

I get into the driver's seat and glance at him, standing by his car. He watches me pull away.

Chapter Twenty-Nine

Liam is the first person I see when I walk through the nursing home the next day, so instead of cutting through the lobby like I usually do, I take a hard right and cut through the chapel to get to the back of the nursing home.

I have a gift for dissociation that helped me cope with an absentee father, but it's served me in other aspects of life too, including with men. I've always had the ability to keep things light, to enjoy the physical aspects of being with them without developing feelings if I didn't want to. Men have loved me for it. We both get what we want, with no pressure that feelings won't align.

With Liam, it was so different, and I knew it would be. I wasn't thinking. I don't think he was either. He was there, on my doorstep, looking handsome in his interview attire, and every logical thought I've ever had disappeared the moment our lips touched. I couldn't have stopped the forward progression of it. I wouldn't have wanted to.

I take the back hallway and work my way to the main nurse's station. If I were to allow Liam to touch me again, I fear that would be it for me. This aching crush would tip the scale into something else entirely. My feelings would be tied to the choices and actions of what he does next, and I can't allow that. I know what is next for Liam, and it doesn't involve being here.

"Hi, Abigail." I walk into her room, and she's lying on her side. "How are you feeling today?"

"Not good," she says, and I help her sit up. Everything hurts, and my legs are weak. I could barely get into my wheelchair by myself for breakfast."

"When did this start?" I put several pills in her hand and give her a cup of water.

"I wasn't great yesterday, but today is worse."

Her skin color has continued to deteriorate since she's been here. The permanent tan from the liver damage has now turned into jaundice. Even the whites of her eyes have discolored.

I move Abigail to her chair and sit beside her. "You haven't told me a story in a while. Are you up for one?"

Her eyes soften, and she nods. "It's about one of my most perfect days."

"Good." I smile. "Because I'd love to hear it."

"This may be my favorite of all the days."

Abigail leans back in the chair and weaves her fingers together.

"When my girls were four and six, George, my ex-husband, was traveling for work, and it was just me and the girls. We lived out in the country, and there was a terrible snowstorm. We woke up that morning, and it was already snowing, and then it continued throughout the day."

"By noon, I could tell that we weren't going anywhere for a few days. The road to our house had snow drifts taller than me. I wanted to take my mind off how scared I was to be stranded, so I decided to create a day of games."

Abigail laughs, which turns into a deep, dry cough. I hand her more water.

"All day long, we played one game after another. The girls must have known I was nervous because they were extra sweet. I made spaghetti with meatballs. And then I made hot chocolate and put colorful marshmallows on top. We bundled up, went outside, and caught snowflakes on our lips."

"I'll never forget their happy, carefree giggles as they bounced around in their snowsuits, or the snowflakes that stuck to their long lashes. After we came inside, I made a fire, and we cuddled up and watched a movie. The funny thing is, I don't even remember what movie we watched. They couldn't get close enough to me. Acted like I was a superstar that they idolized. And I just stared at the dimples in their small hands, knowing that they'd never be as young as they were at that moment, and feeling so sad about it."

Abigail reaches for my hand, and I hold it tightly. Her face falls, and her eyes well up with tears.

"Sometimes I wonder if they remember that." Abigail shakes her head. "Of course they don't."

"They might," I say.

"There's only so much capacity to hold onto things," Abigail says. "We had so many happy times, but all of them have been erased by the bad ones. When I die, I want to think about that perfect day as I fade away from this world."

Abigail covers her mouth with the back of her hand and takes a slow, deep breath.

"When they find out I'm gone, all they'll remember is the night I got arrested for driving drunk, and the police officer putting me in the back of one car, and them in the other, as they screamed and sobbed for me."

"Abigail—"

"Birdie." She waves me away. "I know it's none of my business what anyone thinks of me."

"Actually"—I grab both of her hands in mine—"I think they do remember that most perfect day. They mourn that mom they knew and loved. Their sadness and anger are because they knew what it could be. They lived it once."

"Maybe." Abigail rests her head on the chair. "I'm going to rest my eyes for a few minutes, Birdie."

I grab a blanket and wrap her in it. "Sleep well, Abigail."

When I walk out of her room, Liam stands near the bird sanctuary with my mom. They both see me. My mom smiles, but then she sees my face and looks between me and Liam. She studies us knowingly. Liam tilts his head. His gaze pierces into mine. I rush off in the opposite direction, not wanting to see Liam.

"Hey, Marilyn." I pop into her room.

She sits in a chair, looking out the window, as two boys ride by on a bike, laughing.

"How are you?" She turns at the sound of my voice.

"Birdie." Her lips turn up ever so slightly. "Have you had a chance to look things over from my latest doctor's appointment?"

I lean against the wall. "I have. How are you feeling about everything?"

"Tina thinks we should call in hospice." Marilyn folds her hands together. "But I don't want to die."

"Marilyn." I kneel beside her. "Having hospice doesn't mean you're giving up. But they are the best ones to support you through this, to make sure you don't feel pain."

"It feels like admitting that I can't fight this cancer anymore." She lies her head back on the chair. "Tommy doesn't think I should go with hospice. He wants me to fight."

I grab her hand. "What do you want?"

"I'm so tired, Miss Birdie," she says. "But I don't feel done."

"I'm going to put together a family meeting for tomorrow. There are so many updates; we should all discuss them together."

"Miss Birdie." She reaches for my hand as I stand. "In case I forget to tell you later, thanks for seeing me. When old people reach a certain age, we seem to become invisible to the rest of society. But you've seen me through all of this, and I can't say thank you enough."

Her eyes fall back, and her eyelids become slits before they close entirely. I grab a blanket and pull it over her.

When I finally have a chance to glance at my phone later in the day, I have missed calls and texts from Liam. Why does it feel like he's not going to go away easily?

"Birdie." I turn at the sound of Lucy's voice and smile.

"Hey," I say.

"Liam has stopped at the nurse's desk at least five times looking for you." She glances over her shoulder and comes closer. "What did you do to that guy?"

"Did he say what he wanted?"

"The last time he stopped, he asked me to relay to you that there is a lot to discuss in the world of fundraising, and that he and your mom are going to meet at your house after work to continue the conversation."

I glance at my watch, and our shift is nearly up. "Do you have Gavin tonight? What do you say we go to that winery outside of town and have a couple of glasses?"

Lucy grabs my arm. "Gavin is at my parents' house tonight. You don't have to ask me twice. I just want to run home and change."

"No need," I say. "I'm wearing my scrubs. You may as well, too."

The winery is about a fifteen-minute drive, and we get situated at a table outside. Rolling hills surround us as we look out at the vines in perfect rows. We both opt for a crisp summer white.

"This is so fun," Lucy says, clapping her hands together. "You never initiate hangouts."

She leans forward. "Even if you did only ask me to hang out because you're avoiding a certain someone."

"Lu—"

"It's okay," she interrupts me. "If you let me, I could be your best friend. I get the sense that you choose to keep your circle pretty tight."

I stare across the table at Lucy. She's probably about ten years older than me, but age doesn't matter to me. She's a very pretty woman, with dark brown hair and olive skin. She's been nothing but a good friend to me.

"Tight inner circle," I say. "How about no inner circle at all?" I smile, and Lucy laughs.

"Well," she says, "I won't force anything, but I'm a good listener, have a million opinions on all sorts of things, and all you need to do is say the word."

My phone buzzes, and Liam's name appears. I turn it off.

"Should we get another glass?" I say, and Lucy smiles.

There is potential here.

Chapter Thirty

Lucy pulls up in front of my house, and I let out an audible breath because Liam's car is parked there.

"Do you want to come to my house?" she says. "Or I can drive you around town for a couple of hours with the hope that he leaves. I don't know what's going on with you two, but you've sure been avoiding him."

"No." I undo the seatbelt. "I stalled long enough. I probably need to face this."

"Call me later if you want," she says. "I'll be catching up on all of my reality TV shows."

I walk inside, and Liam stands in the entryway like he was about to leave. My mom pops her head around the corner.

"Birdie," she says. "Where have you been?"

"Sorry." I look between her and Liam. "I went out."

"Well." She puts her hands on her hips. "Liam and I figured a lot of stuff out that we can debrief you on. But it's getting late, so we can save it for another day."

"Here." Liam hands me a booklet.

I glance at it and flip through the pages. It's a timeline of all the next steps. Painting. Furniture. A bake sale and end of summer gala.

My mom studies me and then Liam. She takes a deep breath, like she's discovering something for the first time.

"I'm going to go to bed," she says. "Thanks for all of your time, Liam. Goodnight, Birdie."

We stay unmoved as she walks up the stairs. I watch her, and he keeps his eyes on me. When we hear her bedroom door shut, he turns to me. A few moments pass between us, studying each other. He narrows his eyes.

"Were you with him?"

"Him?" It takes me a moment to realize that he's talking about Will. "No."

He slowly nods his head. "Are you avoiding me, Birdie?"

"No," I say. "Why would I be avoiding you?"

"Okay." He nods toward the door. "Can we chat? Maybe go somewhere a little more private?"

"Sure," I say. "But I'm hot and need to get out of my scrubs. I'm going to change and be right back."

I put on my cutoff shorts and meet Liam downstairs. The sun has just set, but the sky remains lit up by orange hues. He watches me after I come down the winding stairs, and he follows me outside. We walk in silence toward the cemetery, the freshly cut grass beneath my bare feet. There's no sign of autumn, as the summer nights remain hot and humid. We pass the groundskeeper's shed, and Liam grabs my hand and pulls me around the corner of it.

"What are you—" I begin to say at the same time as Liam speaks.

"I can't stop thinking about you."

I press into the shed as Liam's arms anchor both sides of me. I push into his chest, creating distance.

"Hey." I shake my head.

He backs away from me, breathing heavily and looking confused. I walk toward my special bench. How can I want to kiss him while at the same time being resolute on our path forward? Liam sits next to me. I don't know what to say. I'm surprised I need to. I wasn't expecting Liam to want to see me so soon afterward.

"It's probably best if we don't, you know. . ."

My voice trails off. Hopefully, he'll understand what I mean without me having to say it.

Liam leans into my shoulder. "If we don't what, Birdie? Talk? Have lake days? Brainstorm fundraising ideas?"

"No." I shake my head. "The other thing."

Liam runs his tongue along the inside of his bottom lip and moves closer. "What other thing?"

My face heats. "You know what I'm saying."

"Sex?" he says.

"Exactly." I let out a breath. "We should go back to a couple of days ago when we were strictly friends."

"And not two people who have seen each other naked."

"Liam." I smack his arm. "I'm being serious."

"Okay." Liam studies me. "Will you at least talk to me? I'd ask you if it wasn't good for you, but well, I was there. I know how it was."

"Let's be honest," I say. "We knew it was going to happen at some point. We've been marching toward it since meeting. But—"

"But what, Birdie?" Liam says, cutting me off.

I close my eyes and breathe in the scent of grass. "I had a lapse in judgment. I wasn't thinking straight."

What I really want to say is I've never felt an attraction like the one I do with Liam, and I missed him when he was in New York and I allowed myself to get completely swept up in it.

"You're going to get the job in New York."

"That's a big if, Birdie, but—"

"If not this one, there will be another," I say, interrupting him. "And I'm not looking for anything right now, and I know you're not either. Yes, we could spend the rest of your time here having a lot of fun, but that's not who I am. I refuse to allow myself to like you. Or to listen to talks of a long-distance relationship because that would never happen."

"Okay." Liam says it slowly and lifts a leg to the other side of the bench so he's straddling it, and he turns me to him. "You're calling the shots here. If this is what you want."

"It is," I say. "I'm not good at intimacy."

My face heats, picturing the day before. "Yesterday was fun. But there are too many factors working against us. Against me. With everything going on, I need simple."

He presses his hands into the bench. "Do we still get to be friends?"

"Liam." I look up at the sky, and then to the hills on the horizon. The sun is still so bright, even as it gets lower in the sky. "Do you really think spending time together is a good idea?"

"I wouldn't have let anything happen between us if I meant I was going to lose you as a friend, too."

"I'm not good in any relationships, if you haven't noticed," I say.

Liam takes his cap off and wipes his brow with the back of his hand. He hits it against the bench but doesn't say anything. Silence envelopes us, and the only sound is the cicadas in the distance.

"Can I ask you something, Birdie?" Liam puts his cap back on, and I nod.

"Do you have any lifelong friends?"

"Kind of," I say. "A couple women I went to school with. We keep in touch. And a friend I often ended up at the same location with as a traveling nurse. We check in here and there. Not constantly or anything."

"Hmm." Liam stands and rubs his hands against his arms.

"Birdie," he says. "I realize I've only known you for a short amount of time. But you aren't going to convince me that we don't have a strong connection, and that you don't feel it too."

I press my lips together and nod.

The therapist I've been going to for the past few years' voice comes into my head. She diagnosed me with avoidant attachment style that stems from abandonment issues. Only I do sometimes let people get close to me, and I've gotten a lot better at letting people in. I've tried so hard to overcome some of the hurdles, and compared to my early twenties, I have made so much progress. But I still have a wall that comes up when I feel like I could get hurt.

Liam holds his hand out for me and helps me to my feet. "Let's get out of here before the ghosts come out."

"You didn't see that man behind the tree?" I point and laugh when I see Liam's look of fear. "I'm kidding. It was a joke."

"It wasn't funny." Liam puts his arm on my shoulder but then pulls back.

I walk him to his car, and he leans against it. "You never answered my question about friendship."

"We can try." I squeeze my eyes shut. "But I also don't see the point."

He looks down and kicks at the gravel. "Why?"

"Because neither one of us will keep it going after you leave. And that's the truth."

Liam leans back on the car and folds his hands over his chest.

"You seem really fixated on the fact that I'm leaving." His gaze hangs on me. "Why are you so quick to dismiss our current connection?"

"Fine," I say. "I'll try to be friends with you."

"That's all I'm asking." Liam stretches his hand up and squeezes his shoulder. "Goodnight, Birdie."

"See you," I say.

Liam glances over his shoulder, then hits the top of his car with his open hand, gets in his car, and drives away.

The binder is on the stair banister, and I grab it as I head upstairs to my room. I get comfortable under the covers, turn my light on, and open it. Each page is a different fundraiser idea, the purpose behind it, and the estimated amount of impact. Liam must have spent so much time on this. It details community outreach to donate furniture and paint for the nursing home. There are ideas of how to get sustainable donors instead of one time only. There are a couple of pages dedicated to hosting a gala, to highlight the stories of residents, as well as bringing the community together to get everyone bought into investment.

There are detailed projections on bringing in more residents so the nursing home operates more efficiently instead of being nearly half empty. Liam seems to really know his stuff, and all these ideas have the potential of having a huge impact on this place.

The lights flicker overhead. That's my signal to get some sleep. The day's been exhausting in so many ways, and I need to turn my brain off.

Chapter Thirty-One

"These chairs are ugly."

I turn to Joe and cross my arms. "They aren't ugly, Joe. They are brand new, and you're just used to the old chairs. These are better. Trust me."

Joe shakes his head. "They're ugly."

He stands by me and supervises as furniture is hauled into the nursing home, and the old furniture is brought out. While all this is happening, someone is painting the walls, and the residents sit around and watch. This is the most action that has happened in a long time.

The chairs are a walnut brown color with smooth upholstery, and they smell new. They'll be a much better fit than the ones with upholstery that always looked dingy and smelled of urine.

"Sit in one." I take Joe by the arm and lower him into one of the chairs. "It's comfortable, right?"

He wrinkles up his face, but I can tell he's comfortable. I poke him in the arm. "Come on, Joe. You know you like it."

"I'm too old for change, Birdie." He crosses his arms. "I liked the old ones."

I guide the workers bringing everything in. I can't believe how much Liam was able to get donated, and I'm not sure why no one thought of it before. We're all so focused on the residents that there isn't time for anything extra. But Liam is right. These small changes will make a difference, and we have too many empty rooms right now that should be filled. This lobby is the first thing prospective families will see. It's important we give them a good first impression.

"Not bad, right?" Liam brings in a corner table, and Lucy holds the door open. "I may move in here. It looks so nice."

"You're a miracle worker, Liam. Look at this place." Lucy puts her hands on her hips and glances around.

Liam puts the table down and grabs her shoulders. "All of your furniture had urine stains on it."

She laughs and throws a towel at him.

He nods his head in my direction but makes no attempt to talk to me.

I head to the nurse's station, and Lucy follows. My mom recently put offers out for two CNAs, and they should be starting soon, which means I can hopefully get off bath duty.

"So." I glance up, and Lucy is standing there, staring at me.

"Yes?"

"You. Liam. How'd things go last night? Did you talk?"

I press my lips together. "We're good."

"Birdie," Lucy says. "I can tell you like the guy. I can tell he likes you. Are you really not going to do anything with that?"

I like him too much to lose him.

"Birdie." Will comes to the nurse's station and beelines straight toward me. "Abigail isn't doing well. She asked for you."

"Thanks."

I inhale a sharp breath as I walk to her room. I've been dreading this day since the moment I met Abigail. It's dark, so I open the shades that look out at the courtyard. I roll a chair to her bedside and start taking her vitals.

"Hi, Abigail." Her heart is racing, and she has a low-grade fever. Her abdomen is distended, and her color is the worst I've seen.

"Birdie." She coughs, and a little blood comes up. I take a cloth and wipe it away. "Will you call my girls? It's time."

"I'll go call Samantha right now," I say.

I step into an office and dial. It rings a few times, and then she picks up.

"Yes?" she says.

"Hi, Samantha. It's Birdie, from the nursing home. Your mom's RN."

"I know who you are. What can I do for you?"

"Your mom is dying, and she asked me to call you and your sister."

There's breathing on the other end. "Please don't call Cara. It will only upset her."

"If you want to see her one last time, you should come quickly."

"I don't want to see her."

Now it's my heavy breaths that I hear. There was no hesitation on her part at all. She's probably been preparing for this day, too.

"Samantha," I say. "Is there anything you'd like me to say to your mom?"

"Tell her all of her 'I'm sorry's' won't reimburse me for the decades of therapy I've needed."

More deep breaths and then a loud sigh.

"Don't tell her that. Actually, don't tell her anything. Feel free to donate her stuff. I appreciate you letting me know, but you don't need to call again. I don't care what decisions you make from here on out, and you don't need to let me know when she's gone. I lost her a long time ago."

There's a pause, and then the phone goes dead.

Abigail is my patient and I do what she asks, but not one of the times she's asked me to call her daughters did either of them seem happy to hear from me. They never asked me to stop calling. Until now.

Abigail's eyes are closed when I get back to her room, and I grab her hand so she knows I'm here.

"Birdie," she says quietly. "Can I share my worst day with you?"

"I'd rather hear about one of your happy days," I say.

She shakes her head. "I need to say this out loud. It needs to be released."

"If you want to, Abigail. I'll listen."

"It was Mother's Day. The girls would have been about fourteen and twelve at the time. And Samantha, she always wanted to make me feel special. She made me this beautiful sign and hung it in the dining room. I decided to pour myself a glass of wine during lunch. After all, it was my day."

Abigail coughs, and I prop the pillow under her head. "One glass turned into two, then the bottle, and finally I opened the vodka. I don't even remember passing out. But I woke up, and the Mother's Day sign was ripped to shreds. I have no recollection of any of it. When I sobered up, I went up to Samantha's room, and she told me everything that had happened."

Abigail chokes out a sob. "Apparently, I got mad because I tripped over something she'd left on the floor and raged. I ripped up the sign and then told her that she's worthless. I don't remember any of it. Why would a mother do that to her child?"

"Abigail." My voice is weak, the sadness of it all heavy in my chest.

"That's the story I come back to," she says. "Every time I ask you to call my girls, and you come back without anything to relay, I remind myself of who I became to them. I deserve to die alone. I wouldn't forgive me either."

"You aren't alone. I'm here." I sit on the edge of her bed and stroke her shoulder. "You are also the person who danced in the snow with them, Abigail. That is you, too."

"You're too kind to me," she says. "But if you were my child, you wouldn't forgive me either."

"Have I ever told you about my dad?" I say, and Abigail shakes her head.

"Well." I clasp my fingers together. "He and my mom conceived me when they were seniors in high school. They married for a short time, but he couldn't handle the pressure and left us both and moved west to work in an oil field."

"Right before my fifth birthday," I say, "he started writing me letters. He said he'd come to see me on my birthday. I couldn't wait. I was in school now, and all of my friends had dads and I was so excited to show mine off."

"I asked my mom to buy me the fanciest dress. A twirl dress, I called it. My grandma curled my hair, and I'd never been happier. I just knew this was going to be my best birthday. I waited on the couch for him, and every time I heard a noise, I'd run to the window."

"Minutes turned into hours, but I refused to leave the couch. My mom, Grandpa, and Grandma tried to make me, but I sat there. That night, I went to bed in tears and refused to take my dress off. He never called or gave an explanation. I was seven when I heard from him again."

"I don't know," I say, grabbing Abigail's hand. "This world is full of imperfect beings. We bring all our ugly truths to the table. But what I've learned is my dad didn't show up because of his problems. You weren't the mom you wanted to be because of yours. All I know is the amazing person you are now, Abigail. I am so much better off because of knowing you. Thank you for sharing so much of your life with me."

"Will you stay with me?" she says. Her grip on my hand is weak.

"I'm not going anywhere. I promise."

Abigail's breathing gets shallow, soon followed by the death rattle. I used to think being at someone's bedside as they passed was the saddest part of my job. But now I see it as an honor.

Dying is one of the more intimate things that we do.

Abigail opens her eyes and smiles. She points to the corner, and I look over my shoulder.

"My mom's here."

The room is now dark, day turned to night.

"She's with an angel, Birdie. Maybe heaven will take me, after all."

"Of course it will," I say. "You're going to go somewhere beautiful."

I pick up her favorite book of poetry and read to her. The death rattle in her breathing settles in, but I keep reading. Poems about the grass. The trees. The evening breeze.

The moment life leaves Abigail's body, I can feel it. The energy shifts. The room is empty. It's just me left. I set the book down on the table and confirm what I already know. Abigail is gone.

Chapter Thirty-Two

The shower is so hot it scalds my back, but I don't move. I let the water rush over my body. I squeeze my eyes shut and replay my last conversation with Abigail in my head, then go through all my final actions—from calling the funeral home to logging the information for the state.

Sweet Abigail.

I lather myself in lotion and pull on shorts and a tank top. By the time all the steps were taken and the funeral home arrived, I had been up for more than twenty-four hours. My body needs rest. I go to shut the curtains so the morning light can't trickle in when there's a knock at the door.

"Yeah," I say. "It's open."

My mom usually gives me space when a resident dies. She knows me better than anyone and recognized early on that I prefer grieving alone.

"Hey."

Liam's deep voice rings out, and I snap my neck in his direction. His face is freshly shaven, and his hair still damp.

"Liam?" I blink, convinced I'm hallucinating.

He closes the gap between us, and before I can resist, his strong arms are around my waist. I bury my face in his shirt, getting intoxicated by the scent of him. I don't have the strength to pull away. I'm not sure I want to. So instead, I melt into the comfort of him.

"Sunny told me about Abigail." He moves a hand to the back of my head and presses me into him. "I'm so sorry, Birdie."

I pull away from Liam and shake my head. "It's unfortunately part of the job. I knew what I was signing up for."

Liam brushes back strands of my wet hair. "You don't have to do that. Not with me."

His hooded eyes, a piercing shade of deep blue, narrow as they lock onto mine. I find myself having to tilt my head back to fully take him in, my gaze tracing the sharp lines of his features. His nose, straight and flawlessly sculpted, could have been chiseled from marble. His lips, soft and pink, contrast with the firm set of his strong jawline. As he swallows, his Adam's apple bobs subtly.

"Why are you here?" I say softly as I move to sit on the edge of the bed. My feet feel unsteady, and Liam steps closer.

"Your mom let me in," he says. "She was on her way out when I got here. This is me being your friend."

No one ever checks on me. Not like this. But I've never really had a lot of friends either, and the ones I do have are colleagues who experience the same losses that I do.

"What I need is sleep."

I stretch my arms above my head and yawn. My eyes are heavy. If I can get a few hours, I'll feel better and more removed from everything once I'm awake.

"Can I stay with you?" Liam nods toward the bed.

"I'm just going to—"

"Let me stay." He stares at me.

I nod and pull down the covers. Liam closes the rest of the shades, and the bed dips when he gets in beside me. We face each other, but space remains between us. He rests his head on his hands. His eyes draw me in, and I can't look away. We study each other. His expression reveals little, but for me, I'm wondering why he came back. He's been a better friend to me than I have to him. Usually, when I so openly pull away from someone, they retreat.

"You're brave, you know." Liam takes my hand and folds his over mine. "To put yourself out there the way you do. To fully love the residents, even when you know your time with them is short."

"Do you want to know the ugly truth about me?"

Liam presses his lips together. "I think I want to know everything about you."

"Be careful what you wish for." I pull my legs into my chest. "I'm not brave at all."

Liam shakes his head and goes to say something, but I press a finger against his lips.

"It's easy for me to be myself and open up to people when I know it's temporary," I say. "I pour myself into them. That part is true. But I go into it knowing there's an expiration date."

Liam moves closer to me. He grips my lower back and drags me into his embrace. My face fits perfectly into the crook of his neck, and I take a deep breath. I don't know what aftershave Liam wears, but he smells like vanilla with hints of cinnamon. A little sweet and a little spicy.

"Abigail and I used to share our ugly truths with each other," I continue. "And it felt safe. I knew Abigail would take my secrets to her grave."

"There are no truths about you that I'd find ugly."

Liam tangles his leg with mine. Our embrace is intimate in a way that makes me feel exposed. Wide open. And if he sees me, then he knows.

"I'm broken," I say through a yawn. "You realize that, right?"

Liam grips me tighter. "We're all broken in one way or another."

"No," I say, pushing my hand into his chest. "I'm actually broken. I have an avoidant attachment style."

Liam continues to look at me, and something occurs to me.

"But you already knew that about me, didn't you?" I close my eyes.

"Only because I pay attention, Birdie."

"Most people think I'm just very self-sufficient. Independent. But the reality is, when something starts feeling too real, I put a wall up. And when someone calls me out on it, I'm very good at moving on without them. I think my dad messed me up more than I'd like to admit."

Silence engulfs the room. Our chests rise and fall against each other.

"Sleep deprivation must be affecting my brain," I say. "I can't believe I told you that. I've never told anyone that ugly truth before."

Liam tilts my head toward his and kisses my cheek. "We're all a little broken. I'm a people pleaser, and as I've been reflecting this summer, I don't think I've made one decision in a really long time that was for me. I take meds for anxiety. Turns out we all have things about us—"

"That needs fixing," I say, interrupting him.

Liam smiles but shakes his head. "I was going to say that needs accepting."

More silence between us, and my eyes grow heavy as his chest rises and falls against my face.

Liam brushes my hair with his fingers. "The way we've been living life, it doesn't mean we need to continue the cycle."

"I don't know if I'm capable of letting someone in," I admit.

"Don't underestimate yourself." Liam smiles against my forehead. "You've cracked the door open for me. Revealed bits and pieces about yourself."

I turn away from Liam, and he wraps an arm around me, cuddling into my back. He laughs into my neck.

"There's something you should know about me, Birdie." Liam takes my hair, moves it to the side, and presses his lips into my skin. "I'm scrappy. Persistent. And if you want to be my friend, and only my friend, I'll be the best fucking friend you've ever had."

"Liam." I smile and reach my hand around, patting his face. "You're probably the scrappiest person I've ever met."

Liam holds my hand tightly, and I squeeze it, then let myself fall into much-needed sleep. It's comforting feeling his presence behind me, which surprises me. My back presses into his chest, and he's firm and steady. An anchor that isn't going to let me drift out to sea.

I'm not sure how long I sleep, but when I turn over, Liam is propped against my headboard, a notebook in hand. He vigorously writes something, and I smile as I watch him.

I hate how handsome he is. I ponder why any part of him once wanted any part of me. Recently. I like being his friend. His soul is the best part of him, and I have a feeling he doesn't give that up easily.

"Are you checking me out?"

His voice brings me out of my fog, and my body heats. I glance up at him, and he's giving me a sideways smile.

"What are you doing?" I say.

"Invites went out for the gala," he says. "And it's coming up, so I'm working out the details."

I sit up, and he shows me the notebook. We already have all the food being donated, have been steadily collecting silent auction items, and have sold 150 tickets.

"I'm not sure why you're so stuck on getting back into finance." I grab the notebook from Liam. "I've never seen you look more excited about something."

"Yeah, well," Liam says. "I'm just excited to wear a tux. And to see you in a gown."

Liam jumps up and opens the curtains. Sun shines through the lace, and I glance at the clock on my nightstand. It's already late afternoon. I slept for six hours.

"Have you been sitting with me the entire time I slept?" I look around. I was dead to the world.

"Well." Liam drags his hand down his face. "I went downstairs and picked up a bit. You ladies are messy. And then ran to the store because you guys literally had no food in your fridge. And then yes, I watched you sleep for a while."

I toss a pillow at Liam, and he laughs.

"The day is still youngish. I say we go to the lake and lie out on the dock. What do you say?"

Liam stares back at me, and I want to say no. I should get things done. But he looks so hopeful.

"Fine." I hop out of bed. "Let's go."

Liam claps his hands together. He may be the closest friend I've ever had. Which is sad, scary, and a bit exciting.

Chapter Thirty-Three

After a resident dies, it's always quiet and melancholy at the nursing home. These people are brought together by circumstances, and whether they want to or not, everyone becomes family. Abigail may have struggled with her blood relatives, but these people loved her. She was one of them, and her loss is being felt profoundly.

Everyone loved her. I wish her daughters could have seen it—from her morning tea with Sis to her afternoon crocheting with Marilyn and evening baseball games in the main lobby.

I hate walking by her empty room. I avoid looking at the box with her name written on it in black marker. One box is the only physical reminder of Abigail's existence.

"How are you holding up?" Sunny comes down the hallway in my direction.

"I'm okay." I smile and put my hand on his arm. "How are you today?"

"It feels empty in here," he says. "I know how close you were to her."

"Will you come to the chapel later today for Abigail's celebration of life?"

Sunny nods. "Sis and some of the other women have planned an ice cream social for afterward as well. We're all going to share our favorite memories of Abigail. I hope you'll come."

"You know I wouldn't miss it."

"Hi, Sunny," Lucy says as she approaches us. "You're looking very handsome today in that blue shirt."

He shakes his head and laughs. "Oh, Lucy. You always know how to make a guy blush."

"We'll see you later," I say, and he continues heading down the hallway.

"Girl." Lucy grabs my arm and pulls me toward the bird sanctuary. "Where have you been? I've been looking all over for you."

"What's going on?"

Lucy looks to her left, then her right. She steps closer to me.

"Will and I were trying to get hold of you yesterday," she says, "which you probably noticed from all of your missed calls and texts."

"Yeah." I nod. "Sorry about that. I needed sleep after being up all night with Abigail."

Lucy sits in a chair, and I cross my arms and raise an eyebrow.

"So?"

She puts her face in her hands and shakes her head.

"I did something really stupid last night." She puts her face in her hands, then looks up at me. "Gavin went on a fishing trip with his dad, so he's gone all week. I thought, 'I'll see if Will and Birdie want to come over and have some drinks.' Innocent, right?"

"But you couldn't get hold of me, so..."

"So," she continues, "only Will came over."

"Go on," I say, biting back my smile.

"Birdie." Lucy covers her face again. "We made out like teenagers on my couch for hours. My lips physically hurt today."

I start laughing, and it feels so good to be having a light conversation. It's what my heart needed today more than anything.

"You aren't mad?" Lucy glances up at me, and I burst out laughing again.

"Umm, no," I say. "I kind of love this for you. And Will."

"But he was so into you." Lucy wrinkles up her face, then whispers, "And I'm a thirty-five-year-old woman. He, I found out last night, is twenty-seven."

"What's the problem?" I say. "First, he only thought he was into me. Nothing ever remotely happened between us. And second, who cares about age? You're not looking to marry the guy. You're a stunning, single woman. Have some fun. I bet he doesn't live in his mother's basement, so he's already an improvement from the last guy."

"Oh, man," she says, as if realizing something for the first time. "My guy is younger than your guy."

I push her arm. "I don't have a guy. But if you enter into some sort of situationship with Will, we should talk. Being with a guy in his twenties is exhausting with all the mental aerobics. You're going to love it."

Lucy grabs my arm. "We better get to Abigail's thing."

Abigail's celebration of life is attended by so many residents and people in the community who have grown to love Abigail. We all sit in the cafeteria. It's weird not having her here. She was one of the more social residents and loved being surrounded by people. But now the room is full, and her lack of presence is very noticeable.

"It's hard to say just one thing about Abigail," Marilyn says. "We would crochet for hours, and she'd tell me about her beautiful daughters and how proud she was of them."

"She knew baseball better than anyone in this hellhole," Joe says. "I'm going to miss watching the Twins with her."

"I'll miss her smile," Sis says, as she comes into the cafeteria, and Sunny pulls out a chair for her. "We'd have morning tea almost every day, and her smile lit up this place."

"And she always had a kind word," Sunny says, and Sis nods.

"How about you, Birdie?" Marilyn glances at me. "Anything you'd like to say about Abigail?"

I'm caught off guard, but I nod.

"What can I say about Abigail?" All the faces in the room stare at me. "Let's see. One of my favorite things to do with Abigail was to tell each other our favorite days. At times, they were things that had just happened, but more often, they were memories from a long time ago. We'd talk for hours when she couldn't sleep about these happy times."

"And I shouldn't be saying this." I make eye contact with Sunny, and he winks. "But sometimes I'd even sneak her ice cream."

"Boo," Joe says loudly, and everyone laughs. "And here I thought I was your favorite."

"Man," Sunny says, shaking his head. "We're all really going to miss her."

The bell above the main door rings, and I look over to see a man wheeling in another man, and my mom greets them.

Marilyn holds up a wrapped gift, and I walk over and grab it from her. "Abigail made this and thought it would look perfect in the lobby."

Leah Oman

I rip open the paper, and it's a beautiful, framed cross-stitching with the words *Tranquil Waters Nursing Home* written in thick, curvy blue letters, with the waves of a lake and rolling hills in the background. I blink away the emotions and hold it up for everyone to see.

"When did she have time to make this?" I say. "It's so beautiful and intricate."

"Every morning after tea, we'd sit by the birds and craft. Sometimes for hours."

"Wow, Abigail." I look up, picturing her spirit looking down on us. "This will be the perfect addition to the lobby."

"Birdie." I feel the breeze of his words on my neck at the same time I hear the whisper.

I spin to see Liam standing there.

"Can I steal you for a minute?" he says, and I nod.

He grabs my arm and pulls me out of the cafeteria and down an empty hallway. His smile spreads across his face and reaches his eyes.

"What's going on?"

Liam covers his mouth with his hands. "I just got a call. They want me in New York for a final interview."

Genuine joy spreads throughout me, and I wrap my arms around his neck, pulling him into a hug.

"Of course they do." I pull away and gently slug his arm.

"I called around to some people I know," he says. "It sounds like I'm the only candidate left. Unless I completely blow it with the CEO, I'm one step closer to landing my dream job."

He looks so happy.

"When is it?"

"All day Thursday, and I've booked a flight for Wednesday afternoon."

Monday is nearly gone, which means he's only here one more day before he goes.

"And don't worry," Liam says, "I've already booked my flight for Friday morning because I have a dinner Thursday night as part of the interviews. I should land and have time to drive here and get changed in plenty of time for Friday's gala."

"The gala." For the first time, I realize how close he'll be cutting it.

He puts his hands on my shoulders. "Everything is ready to go, Birdie. I know this is unexpected, but it's all going to work out."

"I'm so happy for you, Liam. Seriously."

He smiles and wraps his arms around me. "I'm going to get everything ready for New York, but let's connect tomorrow to go over the final gala details, okay?"

"Perfect." I hear laughter from the cafeteria and look back. "I'll see you tomorrow."

Liam grabs my face and kisses my cheek. "Thanks for being you, Birdie."

I wave as he walks away, very aware that I'm about to lose him.

Chapter Thirty-Four

For the fifth time in a row, Liam's phone goes directly to voicemail. I check my watch, and it's already six in the evening, and he leaves tomorrow morning for New York. I'm sure he's busy getting ready, but I can't imagine not seeing him before he goes.

"You seem anxious." My mom puts a bowl of fresh green salad in front of me. "Is it about the gala? Is anything else on your mind?"

"No." I send another text to Liam. "Did I tell you Dad is coming on Friday?"

My mom puts down her fork. "Your dad is coming to the gala?"

"That's what he says." I shrug. "We had lunch yesterday, and he was going to pick up a suit afterward."

"Birdie." My mom puts her hand over mine. "I don't want you to feel any sort of way when your dad once again doesn't come through for you."

My mom has spent her entire life trying to protect me from disappointment. As I've gotten older, I realize that she can't protect me from this. Not anymore. I'm either going to get hurt, or I'm not. Nothing that she does will change that.

"I'm not even sure if he has the ability to hurt me anymore." I stand and bring my bowl to the sink. "I have such low expectations for him. I expect him to mess up."

I call Liam once again. Now it's nearly seven. When I look up, my mom is staring back at me.

"Trying to get a hold of Liam, I'm guessing?"

"It keeps going right to voicemail." I blow out a breath. "He leaves tomorrow for his interview. I want to say good luck."

"Oh."

My mom wraps her strong arms around me and pulls me into a hug. "I wish I could protect you from everything in this world that could hurt you. And that everyone realized like I do how amazing you are."

"Mom," I say slowly. "Quit being weird."

"I hope he's worthy of you, Birdie."

"Mom." I say, annoyed. "Liam is my friend."

"Oh, Birdie." She grabs a bottle of wine from the counter and pours herself a glass. "You're almost twenty-six. It's okay to like a boy."

"Seriously, Mom." I roll my eyes as I look at my phone. "I'm going to run out for something. I won't be late."

I turn to leave, but my mom takes my arm and then grips my cheeks. "I love you, my Birdie girl."

"Love you." I grab the keys to my Jeep. "See you in a bit."

The drive to Liam's cottage is only about ten minutes, and I try not to talk myself out of coming. He's my friend. I want to wish him well. Maybe his phone isn't working? Or perhaps he doesn't want to talk to me. I start to lose my confidence and almost turn around when I reach the dirt driveway, but I press ahead.

His car is parked out front, so I know he's here. I inhale a deep breath, and before I have a chance to knock, the door flies open. Liam jumps back and puts his hand on his chest.

"Birdie," he says. "You scared me."

Liam holds the door open and lets me pass through.

"Hey," I say. "Your phone kept going to voicemail, and I wanted to see you before you leave tomorrow. Is this a bad time?"

He smiles, and it could light up a room. His hair is damp, like he just stepped out of the shower. His skin is bronzed from the late summer sun.

Liam holds his phone up. "I dropped it in the lake. It's completely dead. I was just leaving to come see you."

"Oh." Relief floods through my veins. "Good."

We stand in the doorway, both of us breathing heavier than normal, staring at each other. I crave closeness in a way that scares me. I want to drop my walls for him, or at least lower it to a safe height. Gravity pushes me toward him. I'm exhausted from the mind gymnastics that I play with myself, trying to convince myself that I can only be friends with this guy.

"You're staring at me, Birdie."

I bite into my bottom lip. "You're staring at me, Liam."

He nods. "I know. I can't help it."

I cup the nape of Liam's neck, lift myself onto my toes, and gently press my lips to his. He freezes, his hands at his side.

"Birdie," he says against my mouth. "Nothing's changed. I'm leaving."

"Yeah." I cup his face and move my hands through his hair.

"What are you doing?" His voice is quiet, but he leans into my touch. "What happened to just being friends?"

"I have no idea." I press myself against him.

Liam moves his hand to my waist. "It's not that I don't want to. But are you going to freak out again afterward and ice me out? Because I need you in my life."

I part his lips with mine, and he sucks in a breath. I move my other hand to his head and run my fingers through his hair. I kiss down his neck, and he tastes like vanilla and cinnamon.

"Do you want me to stop?"

"No," he says. His skin pebbles beneath my touch. "But you didn't answer my question."

I stop kissing him and look into his eyes. "The truth is, I never know how I'm going to react."

He nods, and I spread my fingers and run it down his chest, his stomach, and he holds his breath as I go below the belt.

Liam draws me close, lifting me effortlessly as my legs instinctively wrap around his waist. He carries me slowly toward his bedroom, our lips meeting in a deep, intoxicating kiss. I'm entranced by the overwhelming sensation of this man.

He lays me down on the bed, hovering above me. Liam gently lifts my shirt, his lips trailing soft kisses over the sensitive skin of my stomach. He pulls the shirt over his head, pressing his full weight into me—warm, heavy, comforting. His lips return to mine, kissing me slowly, as his knee presses against the heat between my thighs.

"Liam, please." I grab a fistful of his hair to bring him closer.

"The slower we go," he says, kissing a trail down my collarbone, "the longer I have you."

Liam pulls his shirt off and kisses my chest.

"This could actually take all night." He smiles against my skin. "I'm going to kiss all of your freckles. Every single one of them."

The heat between my legs intensifies, and I grind against Liam.

"Birdie," he moans. "You're not playing fair."

He unbuttons my jean shorts. "It's never a fair fight when you wear these little things."

He smiles as he pulls them off. He kneels above me, staring at me, his expression undecipherable.

"You're staring again, Liam," I say, moving to cover myself, suddenly feeling exposed.

He presses his lips together. "I like seeing you like this."

"Naked?" I draw a knee up.

"Well, yes," he says. "But I meant vulnerable."

I grab his hips, and he falls atop me. I push down his shorts, and both of us struggle to catch our breath. He reaches into his nightstand drawer. He pulls out a condom, opens it, and places it on his length. Liam cups my face, and we look into each other's eyes.

He moves with deliberate care, his body methodically gliding over mine. Our lips meet in a deep kiss as he takes my hand and places it over his heart. The friction against my sex is intense, building to a crescendo.

Liam hovers above me, his deep blue eyes locked on mine, never wavering. Is this what people call making love? It's the most intimate thing I've ever experienced. We truly see each other, with all our inhibitions stripped away.

"Liam." I cup his face as my body heats, and my lower belly reacts to the intensity of it all.

His mouth parts as if he's about to speak, but instead, he closes his eyes momentarily before flicking them open again.

Liam gently brushes the hair from my face, his lips trailing across every inch of my skin. My wall is filling with cracks and holes. I can't hold on any longer; an eruption builds within me. My back arches, and I moan into the crook of his neck.

He shortly follows as he murmurs something unintelligible against my face before collapsing onto me. He quickly realizes the weight of himself and rolls to his side, facing me. He takes my hand in his and kisses it. Neither of us says anything for a while. Only pausing our staring for me to kiss his cheek, and for him to reciprocate by kissing my nose.

"Birdie." Liam opens his mouth to say something else, but nothing comes out.

I'm uncertain about what being in love truly feels like, having never experienced it before. But this connection between us seems to be more than just friends with attraction. Best friends? That isn't enough either. As I delve deeper into my thoughts, I press a hand against my chest, feeling a sudden, intense ache.

"Hey, Birdie," Liam says again, kissing the top of my hand. "I need to say something. I—"

"Please." I press two fingers over Liam's lips before he's able to say anything else.

Liam shifts to his side, and I mirror his movement, pulling a sheet over myself. We lie there, gazing at each other, as I memorize every detail of his face. He seems to be doing the same, because he reaches out, his fingers gently tracing the contours of my face and jawline.

"You're beautiful," he says, and I shake my head.

"I'm not."

He leans forward and presses his lips to mine. "You're beautiful, Birdie."

There's no point in arguing with a man basking in the afterglow of a post-coitus high.

He takes my hand in his. "Spend the night with me."

I shake my head. "I shouldn't. I can't."

I sit and pull the sheet up with me, suddenly very self-conscious. Liam grips my wrist.

"Birdie," he says. "I feel like we should talk."

"Is that what you want to do?" I straddle my legs around him.

"Birdie, don't try to distract me."

"Liam." I move off of him and find my clothes that are scattered everywhere around the room. "This was perfect. Let's not ruin it with words."

"You really won't stay?" Liam sits, and I make the mistake of glancing at him over my shoulder, which nearly derails my plan of leaving.

"I don't really do sleepovers," I say.

Liam pulls on a pair of shorts and stands. "I've noticed that about you, except I did spend the night at your house once and nap with you another time."

"Sure." I shrug. "But there was no sex involved."

"Ahh." Liam nods. "I apologize that it's taking me a while to learn all of your rules."

Liam walks me to the door, but I pause and turn to him.

"I'm not running away, Liam," I say. "It's late, I work in the morning, and you need to be rested for New York. I'll see you Friday."

He grabs my hand. "Do you promise?"

"Yes," I say. "Are you going to get a new phone anytime soon?"

"Shit." Liam runs his hand down his face. "Hopefully, I'll have time to get one in the city tomorrow. If you don't hear from me, that's why."

"Good luck." I smile. "You're going to blow them away."

"You are going to love my tux. I'm picking it up in Minneapolis when I land Friday morning."

"You're going to love my dress. It's the most beautiful color blue."

Liam spreads his hand against my lower back and drags me toward him. I stick to the skin of his chest. It's so tempting to stay, but these feelings are new for me and I need to take baby steps.

"Two days," he says, pinching my chin and kissing me.

"What about two days?"

"Only two days apart, and I'll see you on the third."

But many, many days apart after that.

"Good night." I quickly kiss his cheek and walk out into the darkness.

Chapter Thirty-Five

Time stands still all day Wednesday and stretches into Thursday. Liam said he'd try to sort out the phone situation either in Minneapolis or when he arrived in New York, but I haven't heard anything from him. That either means he's busy, having fun, meeting up with the beautiful blonde Olivia, or hopefully, he just still doesn't have a phone. I haven't had the guts to call him. It's easier to believe he still doesn't have a usable phone than to wonder if he does and just doesn't want to talk to me.

The parking lot of the care center has been transformed. Tents are up, and the event company that volunteered their services from Rosso is setting everything up. We're going for a black-tie look but on almost no budget. Everything from the food to the tables has been donated.

"It's coming together." I jerk my head around to see my dad walking toward me. "You're going to pull this off."

"Hey." I put my hands on my hips as the tables are draped in black tablecloths. "What are you doing here?"

"I wanted to come by and see how things were progressing. Can't your old man check in?"

"Sure, but you can't wear that to the gala."

My dad runs a hand through his beard. "I'll obviously go home and change."

"So, you still plan on coming?"

"Seven, right?"

"No." I shake my head. "Remember, the residents get to bed by about eight, so we pushed the event up to six."

"That's right," he says. "Well, I'll be sure to iron my suit tonight so I can be there."

"I have to get back to work," I say. "But I'll see you later."

I smile as I watch Liam's vision come to life. The gala was entirely his idea, which is why it's my favorite of all the fundraising we've done. It wasn't Olivia's idea. When he suggested it, both my mom and I thought it was unnecessary. But he insisted it would help current and prospective families get excited about having such a great option right here in Wheaton. For the past few years, when people needed a nursing home, most went to neighboring, larger towns that could offer more.

Everything has improved here since Liam started offering his services. The building is shining with all the upgrades. I'm training two new RNs and four new CNAs, and we've gained six new residents in the past month. My mom offered Liam a job as her donor relations officer, but he told her she couldn't afford him. For now, I'm managing the physical donations. We have a room full of clothes, blankets, and bathroom supplies. The town has really stepped up for these residents who deserve it so much.

*****

My eyes look especially blue against my bright blue, floor-length dress. I glance at myself in the mirror in Sunny and Sis's room. The silk hangs elegantly on my body, and soft curls frame my face. I release a deep breath.

"It's going to be great," Sunny says as he walks into his room. "You're ready for this."

"Liam still isn't here." I glance at my watch. It's already five. "Have you talked to him? Has he called anyone?"

Sunny shakes his head. "He'll be here. He wouldn't miss this. It's all he's been talking about for the past month."

"He's the MC. He better not."

I head outside, and Lucy and Will are busy getting all the guests to their assigned seats. The residents will be ushered in by the staff promptly at six and will be scattered among all the attendees.

"Make sure everyone sees the silent auction table," I say, grabbing Lucy's arm.

She looks beautiful in her black cocktail dress.

"You've got it, Birdie," she says. "Deep breaths. Everything is going great. This event will practically run itself."

No matter how hard I try, though, I don't think I'll relax until I see Liam. Where is he? In fifteen minutes, he's supposed to be on stage, introducing tonight's program, including our first speaker, Sunny. It was my mom's and my idea to have him be the MC. He protested at first, but we convinced him. And now he's not even here.

"It's almost time," my mom says, coming up behind me.

"He's not here." I nervously bite my lip.

"Birdie girl." She shakes her head. "I wish you'd stop being surprised when your dad doesn't show up for things."

"Oh," I say, looking around. "Dad's not here."

His absence hadn't registered with me until this moment.

My mom narrows her brows. "Who were you talking about?"

"Liam," I say. "He's not here. What am I going to do? He was supposed to kick this off. Why isn't he here?"

She grabs my shoulders and smiles. "You've got this. It's not Liam who's turned this place around. It's you. Everything good that's happened this summer, and frankly, in my entire life, has been because of you."

At six sharp, all the guests are seated, and the staff brings out the residents who are well enough to participate in tonight's gala. Music plays and I try my best to focus, but I can't stop scanning the crowd, hoping that Liam will arrive.

I step onto the stage and look out at everyone. Public speaking is my nightmare. I wasn't supposed to be up here tonight, yet here I am. I'm not sure the words coming out of my mouth make sense. I'm dizzy, maybe partially blacked out, as I thank everyone for being here, mention the auction, and then hand it off to Sunny. I help him up the two stairs, and he stands at the microphone.

"Wow," he says, pausing as people clap and yell his name. His best friends are the loudest. He looks dapper in his black tux. He told me he's had it for thirty years. He glances at me, and I smile.

"Let's be honest," he says. "No one hopes the sunset of their life will take place in a nursing home. Sis and I spent almost our entire adult lives on Main Street, where we raised our two boys and had so many happy times, especially as we entertained our grandchildren."

I look at the people, and even Liam's parents are here, sitting at a table with Sis and other members of their family.

"Yet here we are," Sunny says. "And Sis and I could be sad about it, but it's hard to be when we're this well-taken care of. Not that long ago, we were at risk of being sent to another town, which would have taken us farther from family and the community we love. But thanks to everyone's generosity, the nursing home isn't going anywhere, anytime soon. And I get to go on almost daily visits out to the lake, which is my favorite place on earth. So, thank you for being here. Thank you for your support. Now let's eat."

Everyone stands when Sunny is done. As they eat, and between various speakers, a video plays of the residents and the different activities we offer at the nursing home. The entire gala lasts only an hour. We figured anything longer would be too hard on our people. All of that work, for only an hour. The auctioneer gets to work, and so many people bid. Almost every business in town donated something, and many of the people are here tonight. I spot the mayor, the owner of the grocery store, and the local bookstore. People really showed up for the residents, both physically and financially.

When the event finally ends and the residents are back in their rooms, I take a deep breath, but it does nothing to lift the heaviness weighing down my stomach. The worst part is how familiar this feeling is—the deep ache of disappointment from someone I love. It's a pain I haven't felt in years, yet it still lingers within me. I built thick armor around my heart long ago, refusing to let my dad make me feel this way anymore. But with Liam, I let my guard down. I allowed myself to love him.

"Birdie," Lucy says as she walks down the hall toward me. "I'm having people over to celebrate a great night. Join us?"

"People or Will?" I say.

She smacks my arm. "I invited quite a few people, thank you very much."

"Umm," I say. "I'll have to take a raincheck. I'm exhausted."

"Birdie," she says slowly. "Come on. You don't have to stay long. But stop by. Please." Lucy hugs my shoulder.

"I'll try," I say. "Let me wrap up things here, okay?"

I mask how I'm feeling. No one except my mom has any idea how much hope I had in Liam's presence. I get everything put away inside, and when I step out into the night, everything is nearly disassembled, but a couple of trucks still remain as they load tables and chairs into the back.

"Birdie." A figure comes out of the dark, and I don't need to look to know the voice. "I am so sorry."

I slowly turn. Liam is sweaty, a blazer slung over his shoulder, a roller bag at his feet.

"I don't know what to say," he says and then stops to look at me.

He drops his blazer onto his bag and rolls up the sleeves of his dress shirt, unbuttoning the cuffs and pushing them up his forearms. His hand rests on his chest as his eyes slowly take me in, lingering on every detail.

"You look beautiful," he says, his gaze never wavering.

"Don't." I hold my hand up, anger and disappointment bubbling to the surface.

"I'm sorry, Birdie. You have no idea how much. I missed my flight this morning and rebooked but had to fly through Detroit. I've been scrambling all day to get here."

"You didn't think to call?" My voice is steady and even.

"My phone is broken, you know that. I would have done anything to be here."

"How'd you miss your flight?"

Liam shakes his head and runs his fingers through his hair. He pats his chest with his hand. "That's totally on me. I set the hotel alarm clock and must have done it wrong. I was totally panicked. Birdie, you know me. You know I'd never miss this. I wouldn't do that to you."

He looks desperate for my forgiveness, his brow furrowed as he wipes away the sweat. But I can't give him what he wants. For the past few hours, I've felt physically ill from his absence.

"You know me," I say. "You knew how important tonight was. You could have borrowed a phone from someone, and if you didn't know my number by heart, you could have called information and reached the nursing home. You should have done about a hundred different things, but instead, you let me worry all day, with no regard for what that would do to me."

"I'm not your dad, Birdie," Liam says. "I know I messed up. I let you down. It won't happen again."

"You don't get to talk about my dad." My face heats. "Just because I've shared a thing or two with you, doesn't mean you know things."

"I'm sorry." Liam grabs my hand. "Don't ice me out again."

"This is all so stupid." I pull my hand away. "I don't know what this thing was between us, but it was going to end anyway when you left. All I know is that I hated how you made me feel tonight, and I don't want to go through that again. It has to be over. I'm done."

"You're done?" Liam steps closer to me as one of the event workers walks by. "Let me tell you something, Birdie. Sometimes people are a disappointment. And I'm sorry for all the shit you've gone through because no one deserves it less than you. But you can't cut people out like that. It's not fair. It hurts."

"You don't know—"

"Birdie," Liam says, cutting me off. He cups my face and presses his lips against mine. The force of it opens my mouth, but I push him back. "I love you."

All the blood rushes from my body, leaving me pale and speechless, my mouth agape.

Liam holds my shoulders. "I don't know when it happened exactly, but I'm man enough to admit it to you. It's been sneaking up on me all summer, and I've never been more sure of anything in my life. I love you, Birdie."

Silence surrounds me as Liam watches, waiting for my response. When I was growing up and my dad repeatedly broke my heart, my mom was always my safe haven. She would urge me to protect my heart, but it's only in this moment that I truly understand why. I hate this feeling—the emptiness—and I never want to feel it again.

"I can't do this." I slip my heels off and hold them in my hands, then turn away from Liam. "You don't love me. It's been a summer. It's too much for me. I don't think I can go there with you."

"Don't say that." Liam places his hand on my shoulder and spins me around. "You can't mean that."

"Yet I do."

I take a deep breath, my insides cold and numb. Liam's face contorts with emotion, his eyes glistening in the light. But my wall rises again, completely blocking out any feelings—my pain and his. Gone with the summer sky.

There's nothing left to say. We stand there, staring at each other, a skill we've perfected through our shared silence. His face is a mix of brokenness and confusion, a reflection of the turmoil I've created, but rarely stick around long enough to see. I give a slight nod, then turn and walk away, leaving behind the shards of what we once were.

Chapter Thirty-Six

"It's not my fault," my dad says, trailing behind me as I walk down Main Street, heading to the store. "I was at the blackjack table, winning big. Walking away would've been stupid."

I feel nothing. No disappointment. No sadness for the relationship that never was.

"I expect nothing from you," I say, not even glancing in his direction.

"And what's that supposed to mean?"

"Do you really want to have this conversation?" I stop at a bench and sit down.

"If you've got something to say, say it." He stands there, arms crossed, like he's challenging me.

"You're unreliable," I say flatly. "You always have been."

"That sounds like something your mom would say."

"It's not." I close my eyes and glance up at the sky, searching for calm. "You have no idea how much your absence hurt me growing up. It's like you didn't even care."

"You don't know how many times I sat on the couch, waiting for you. My birthday, holidays, or when you called out of the blue to make plans."

"I was messed up, Beatrice," he says, his voice almost pleading. "I was young and into bad things. Are you going to hold that against me forever?"

"But now you're a grown-ass man," I snap, my voice rising. "You promised me you'd be somewhere, and you didn't show up."

He nods slowly, like he's trying to absorb my words. "I had a tough upbringing, Birdie. It messed me up."

I sigh, the weight of his excuses pressing down on me. It's always the same with him.

"You need to work on yourself," I say quietly, "so you stop dumping your trauma on others."

"Just like your mother," he mutters under his breath.

"Thank gawd for that." I stand up from the bench, refusing to look at him. "Bye."

It's been two weeks since the gala, and this is his first attempt at explaining why he wasn't there. If only he realized—I don't care anymore. I've compartmentalized so much in the past few weeks that I'm on autopilot, numb, just going through the motions. I wake up, go to work, stay too long, and then come home to sleep.

After bringing the groceries home, I head into work for my evening shift. I stop by my mom's office as she's packing up to leave for the night.

"We've been two ships passing in the night," she says, looking up as I step inside. "All this extra staff is great, but now I feel like I need to hire an assistant administrator."

"Can you afford that?" I drop into the chair, feeling the fatigue in my bones.

"Actually, I think I can." My mom leans back against her desk, a smile tugging at her lips. "I can't believe how much we raised at the gala. I feel like I need an assistant administrator and a donor relations person. Also, a new resident came today. He's in Abigail's old room. Be extra nice to him. He's having a hard time adjusting."

"Birdie girl," she adds, "I may need your help with the new group of nursing home volunteers. Lucy filed the paperwork, and we've got five since the gala who've cleared the background checks and are ready to start contributing."

"There's plenty to do," I say, my voice distant. "We need someone to run bingo regularly, and the ladies love getting their hair and nails done. Maybe one of the volunteers could organize and distribute donations? The supply room is a mess."

"See?" My mom jumps up, putting a hand on my shoulder. "You're not just precious to me, but to this entire nursing home."

"You should get out of here while the night's still young," I say, pushing a smile onto my face.

I head to the main nurse's station and check my caseload for the night. Some of my favorites are on the list—Marilyn, Sunny, Sis, Joe—and a couple of new residents. We've grown by ten residents in the past month.

"Hi, Marilyn." I open her door, finding her lying in bed. I organize her medicine and help her sit up. "How are you feeling?"

"It won't be long now, Birdie," she says, her voice soft. "I've been feeling a lot of peace about it lately. I'm ready."

I sit at the edge of her bed, squeezing her hand. "You're not going anywhere tonight."

Marilyn smiles and takes her pills.

"We're doing a movie at seven. A romance. Will you come?"

"I never miss a romance." She pats the top of my hand, her smile warm.

I keep walking down the hallway and notice the light on in Abigail's old room. It's always hard to lose a resident and see someone else occupy the space. I step inside, and a man turns to me.

"You must be Bob," I say. He stares at me, clearly unhappy with his current situation.

"And you are?"

"Birdie." I point to myself. "I'm one of the RNs here. Welcome to Tranquil Waters Nursing Home."

"There's nothing tranquil about it," he grumbles.

It's not unusual for new residents to come in here kicking and screaming. Despite all the improvements, it's still a nursing home. I read through his chart: sixty-eight-year-old man, Type 1 Diabetes, double amputee below the knees.

"So, Bob," I say, glancing up, "what do you like to do for fun?"

His gaze is sharp. "I'm a writer."

"That's great. What do you write?"

Bob folds his hands over his chest, eyeing me. "Do you really care? Aren't you supposed to be asking how I feel?"

"I'll get to that," I say, my tone gentle. "But yes, I want to know what you write."

"I'm Bob Coster," he says, his voice tinged with pride. "Maybe you've read some of my supernatural fiction novels."

Bob Coster. I try to contain my excitement. "I have. I love them. I actually love everything about ghosts and the dead. I'm not sure if you're from around here, but I'm new to town and found out I'm living in the Hurst haunted house. You know, if you ever need fodder for future novels."

His eyes light up for the first time since I stepped into the room, and he actually looks at me directly. "I'm not from here, but I've been doing research for my next book and became fascinated with the stories about your house."

"Well"—I shrug—"if you're ever up for a field trip, I'd love for you to see it."

Bob seems too healthy for a nursing home. As if reading my mind, he says, "My husband died. He was my main caretaker. I'm hoping my time here is temporary until I can hire someone to live with me and take care of me."

"I see." I sit in the chair across from him, nodding. "This place isn't so bad once you get used to it. Some of the residents are non-communicative, but others are here for similar reasons as you."

I glance around at the stark, white walls. "I could help spruce this place up. You've got a beautiful view out the window, and the food's gotten a lot better. Tonight we're having Joe's favorite—spaghetti and meatballs."

Bob lets out a breath, and one corner of his lips turns up slightly. "Thank you. You have no idea how much I needed some reassurance tonight."

"Hey," I say as I get to my feet, "do you like romance movies?"

He raises an eyebrow.

"Movie night starts at seven. You should come. We're serving pie and ice cream."

"Maybe," Bob says as I continue my rounds.

Voices ring out from Sunny and Sis's room, so I peek inside and freeze—the room is full. I make eye contact with Camilla and Robby, and a blond man has his back to me. My chest tightens with hope. I'd love to see Liam. Maybe I'd tell him I was scared and wrong, and he'd be open to talking. But when he turns toward me, my chest sinks. It's not Liam. His eyes are a deep brown instead of blue, and his hair is a shade darker.

"This is our cousin, David," Camilla says. "Liam's younger brother."

"He's visiting from Florida," Robby adds.

"You must be Birdie." David stands and offers his hand. "I've heard a lot about you."

I study him closely. He and Liam share so many similarities—their height, the angularity of their jawlines, the same straight nose—but their eyes are entirely different.

"Yes." I finally smile. "Sunny and Sis have told me a lot about you. You're the artistic grandchild in Florida."

David laughs. "That's me. Liam tells me you're new to town and that your mom is the proud new owner of the nursing home."

Liam talked about me—to his younger brother. I wish I knew the context of that conversation. Was my name mentioned in passing, or did Liam go out of his way to bring me up?

"I'll come back later," I say, pulling my gaze away from David's to look at Sunny. "I didn't realize you had company."

"We're going out tonight," Camilla says. "Are you free to join us?"

"I just started my shift," I say, feeling a pang of regret. "I'm working overnight, but I appreciate the offer."

"Bummer," Robby says. "We're meeting a lot of people at the pool hall."

"Yes," Sunny adds. "You kids have so much to celebrate."

"Well," I say, backing out of the room, "you guys have a good night."

My disappointment at getting my hopes up, only to realize it's not Liam, is overwhelming. I continue down the hallway, slip into an empty room, and slide down the wall until I'm sitting with my knees pulled up to my chest. I'm the one who told Liam it was over. I'm the one who hasn't responded to his texts. I have no right to feel this much sadness that he's exactly where he said he would be.

No matter how hard I try, my mind is consumed with thoughts of Liam. I don't know how to navigate it because it's never happened before. I've never longed for someone after they left. Not since I was a child, longing for my dad.

It's been two weeks since that night in the parking lot with Liam—when he told me he loved me, and I told him it was over. Yet I still can't sleep. Instead, I lie awake, wondering what he's doing, who he's with. There have been moments where I've wanted to pick up the phone and call him.

But I haven't.

*****

Coming off a night shift feels like running a marathon with no sleep. My nights are spent organizing while the residents mostly sleep, and by daylight, a new energy fills the nursing home as the day staff takes over. I pull out my phone to check my reflection, noticing the dark circles under my eyes. I haven't slept well in days.

I reach the door just as David is walking up the sidewalk. He smiles when he sees me.

"Hey, Birdie."

David reminds me of a surfer—carefree, with longer hair than Liam's and a day's-old stubble.

"Coming to see your grandparents?"

"I am," he says. "And my parents arrive tomorrow. We all decided to spend the long weekend out at the cottage."

"Oh." I bite my bottom lip, resisting the urge to ask if Liam will be here. Of course, he won't be. He just got to New York. And it wouldn't matter if he was coming. Band-Aids were always meant to be ripped off quickly.

"Have you talked to Liam?" David asks, holding the door open. The alarm starts going off, so he quickly shuts it.

"Why would I talk to Liam?"

David narrows his eyes, tilting his head slightly. "Sorry. I thought…"

He smacks his lips together, cutting himself off.

"I'm going to say hi to my grandparents, but you have a great day, Birdie."

"You too."

David glances at me one last time before heading inside.

Chapter Thirty-Seven

I've always hated my birthday. First, because attention makes me uncomfortable, and second, because early September in South Dakota always meant back to school—and I hated school. I wanted to be home with my grandparents, my mom, and the horses. The weather would turn cool, and the melancholy would settle in. I hate my birthday, and I hate the end of summer.

"Joe, back away from the door." I gently hold his arm and turn him. "You're blocking people from coming in."

"No one in their right mind would want to come into this place," he says. "It's like a prison."

I laugh. "I've never been in a prison, but I have a feeling they don't have nearly as much fun as we do."

"You're full of shit, Birdie." He lowers himself onto a chair and turns his attention to the baseball game.

Bob wheels himself by, and I glance at him. "Care to watch the game?"

He shakes his head. "Going to the bird sanctuary to get some writing done. When are we going on a field trip to the Hurst haunted house?"

"Well," I say, "today's my birthday, but how about tomorrow? I can check you out for a couple of hours, and there's a ramp entrance at the back of the house so it's perfect."

"Tomorrow it is." Bob begins wheeling himself down the hallway. "And happy birthday."

Sunny and Sis's son Larry rounds the corner, followed by David. As long as I'm here, I won't be able to avoid memories of Liam. They're everywhere.

*****

My mom convinced me to go to the pool hall for my birthday and invite a few friends. The list is small. I sit on the wood floor in my bedroom and apply some makeup. The nights have turned cool, so I wear a pair of jeans and a sweater over my tank top.

This is twenty-six.

I get to the kitchen just as my mom pours two glasses of prosecco. I lean against the doorframe and watch her sway her hips as a song blares in the background. She's so beautiful and confident—so different from me.

"Birdie," she says when she sees me. She presses her hands together. "My gorgeous birthday girl."

"No embarrassing me today." I grab the glass of prosecco from the counter. "I agreed to go out, but no drawing attention to the fact that it's my birthday."

"Okay, fine," she says. "But I'm driving and you don't work tomorrow, so let loose and have some fun."

When we arrive at the pool hall, it's already packed. Cars line Main Street.

"Maybe we should go somewhere else." I bite my lip as I look around. "This place is nuts tonight."

"You already told people to meet you here," my mom says.

"Not people," I say. "Just Lucy and Will. That's all. I could tell them to meet us somewhere else."

"Nonsense," she says. "This is perfect."

We walk in, and it seems like the whole town is here. I quickly spot Dax and Carrie, and when they see me, they come over, and Carrie hugs me.

"Happy birthday, Birdie," she says. "Malik just called, and he's on his way."

"How'd you…?" I start to say but stop. "You guys just happened to be here tonight, right?"

"Or did a little birdie tell us?" Carrie says, and Dax smiles.

"I see what you did there," he says with a grin.

"We needed a night out," Carrie says. "Away from the kids. Camilla and Jake are here, too. And Robby and Jenna are in town. And David."

"Yeah, pretty much all of the Berglands," Dax adds.

Almost all of them.

I make my way over to my mom and grab her arm. "Is the entire town here tonight?"

"It seems so. I'm going to grab us drinks. See if Lucy and Will are here yet."

The bar is five people deep, so I move to the corner by the jukebox to be out of the way. David walks in, and I let out a breath, still not able to get over how much he resembles his brother. But then, two steps behind him, Liam walks into the bar.

I nearly do a double take when I see him. He's here, in his dark jeans and white sneakers, a simple black shirt. I duck around the corner so he doesn't spot me as he looks side to side. I'm not sure how it's possible to both want to see him and be happy he's here while also finding it painful that my plan to get over Liam has to start over and won't fully work until he's gone.

"Happy birthday!" Lucy throws her arms around me and pulls me into a hug. "Are you hiding back here or something?"

"Maybe," I say, peeking around the corner.

Will approaches. "Happy birthday, Birdie." He kisses my cheek.

"Did I see Liam walk in?" Lucy says into my ear, and I shrug.

"Seems so."

He must be here for the long weekend, like the rest of his family. I knew I'd have to face him at some point since he has family in Wheaton, but I wasn't expecting it to be this soon.

"I thought I saw his name come across my desk for a background check," Lucy says, looking over her shoulder, and I grab her and pull her back.

"What do you mean?"

"Your mom put me in charge of the volunteers. I could have sworn I saw his name as one of the approved background checks that came through."

That makes no sense. I narrow my eyes and then lock gazes with my mom as she holds two glasses in her hand.

My mom comes back with a shot and a drink. I'd usually protest, but being a little foggy might suit me tonight. Music blares from the jukebox, and I focus on my mom, Lucy, and Will as we try to find a table that isn't occupied. To my left, Liam stands in the corner, saying something to a woman, and she laughs. He looks over his shoulder, and our gazes meet. He says something to her, and she looks my way as well, and they both walk in my direction.

Liam is coming directly toward me.

He smiles warmly at me and puts his arm around the woman.

"Birdie," he says, "I'd like you to meet Jenna, my cousin Robby's wife."

Recognition spreads across my face. I saw her from afar at Asher's birthday party earlier in the summer, but we never officially met.

"Birdie," she says. "Can I give you a hug? I feel like I know you already."

I nod, and Jenna wraps her arms around me.

"I'll be right back," Liam says, holding up a finger.

Jenna grips my shoulders. "It is so good to finally meet you."

"Me?" I raise my eyebrows. "It's so good to finally meet you. I don't even know where to begin to thank you for bringing awareness to our little nursing home in Wheaton."

Jenna squeezes my hand. There's a warmth about her, and I feel like I know her from all she's shared about her story. She's been through so much, yet she looks so confident and breathtakingly beautiful.

"Liam is not the kind of guy to ask for favors." She takes my other hand in hers. "So when he reached out about this project, I knew you must be someone very special to him."

A song comes on, and people start singing along, making it hard to hear anything.

"It's not like that." I get closer to Jenna and speak into her ear. "He's just a helpful person."

Jenna tilts her head and smiles. "If it's not like that for you, that's okay. But it's like that for him."

"Well." It's too loud to have this conversation now.

"I'm here for a few days for the long weekend," Jenna says. "Would you be up for grabbing coffee or something?"

"Yeah, yes," I stammer. "I'd love that."

I like her already.

Liam approaches us. Jenna gives me another hug and then excuses herself.

His mouth moves, but the noise in the bar gets louder. I shake my head.

"What?" I point to my ears. "I can't hear a thing you're saying."

Liam nods toward the door, and I freeze at first but then nod.

Liam cuts through the crowd, and I follow. We reach the door, and he holds it open for me, and I slip past him. We step into the dark night, and there's a coolness in the air, signaling the next season's arrival.

We stand there, locked in this unbearable silence, each of us trying to decipher the other, like a riddle we're desperate to crack. He's never looked better, and it twists something dark inside me. I wish I could glance at him and feel nothing, let the attraction dissolve into the void, but it clings to me relentlessly. My heart is lodged painfully in my throat, suffocating me with every beat.

"Happy birthday, Birdie."

"How'd you—"

"Grandpa Sunny," he says before I can finish. "It was on the board at the nursing home. He thought maybe I'd want to know."

Liam chuckles and puts his hands in his pockets.

"Why are you here?"

"The pool hall or Wheaton?" He presses his lips together.

"Both, actually," I say.

Liam looks at the ground, and then his gaze flicks to me. "I'm at the pool hall because I called your mom and asked what you were doing for your birthday."

"Hmm."

My mom knew. That's why she insisted we stick to the plan of coming here. Perhaps that's why Liam has brought almost his entire family.

"I'm in Wheaton because I didn't feel done with this place. New York no longer seemed like where I wanted to be."

"You didn't get the job?" I wrap my arms around my body as a shiver runs through me.

"I got the job," he says. "Turns out it's not what I wanted."

We continue to gaze at each other. Thoughts swirl in my mind before I can articulate them, so I say nothing.

"Anyway." Liam reaches into his back pocket. He takes my hand, opens it, and then puts a small square box wrapped in gold in my palm. I look at it. "For you."

"Liam." I take a deep breath. "You shouldn't have gotten me anything."

"Birdie," he says, his voice low, convincing. "I wanted to get you this."

"Do you want me to open it?" I hold it out and then shake it against my ear.

Liam laughs. "Only if you want to. Or open it when you're alone. Your choice."

Curiosity gets the best of me. I take a long sip of my drink and then hand the glass to Liam. I loosen the string around the box and open it. A beautiful blue velvet jewelry box is the only thing between me and the surprise inside. I pull it open and nearly gasp.

It's a white gold, oval-shaped pendant, just like the one my grandma gave me when I was young. The one I lost on the very day I lost her. It's almost identical—ornate, shaped like a teardrop, with an intricate pattern etched delicately across its surface.

I open the locket, and I rapidly blink back tears at the words inside. It's the same quote from the book my grandma would read to me every birthday. I couldn't remember it when I told Liam about the pendant my grandma gave me, but here are the famous words from Dr. Seuss, the very ones my grandma had etched on the locket.

"How'd you know exactly what it looked like?"

"You were wearing it in so many of the pictures from that album in your bedroom," he says.

"Liam." I look up at him, and he wipes away my tears with his thumb. I hadn't realized one had escaped. "Why are you doing this? Why are you making things so difficult?"

He leans forward and kisses my cheek. "I once told someone I love that I'm scrappy and persistent. I want to prove that to her."

"Liam." I shake my head. "Why are you here? Why did Lucy say she saw your name as a nursing home volunteer? You said you wanted to be in New York."

"Turns out, I want to be where you are." Liam reaches for my hand, but I pull back.

"I can't accept this." I close the box and push it toward him. "It's too much. You're too much."

He wraps his hand around mine. "And I can't take it back. Happy birthday, Birdie."

Liam turns and walks inside, and I'm left standing there with the nicest gift anyone has ever gotten me.

Chapter Thirty-Eight

The sun shines through my lace curtains, and I roll onto my side with a groan. My head pounds like a steady drum. I was never the kind of girl who looked ahead at her life and wanted to be in certain places by a certain age. If I had thought about it, I probably wouldn't have imagined myself living with my mom at twenty-six. But there are many things about my life I wouldn't have anticipated.

I throw a robe over my pajamas, my feet heavy as I head downstairs toward the smell of coffee. I remember Liam walking in after we spoke, the gift he gave me and refused to take back, my mom driving me home and tucking me in. Some of the other details are a bit foggy, and I was too overwhelmed to put everything together.

My mom glances at me, concern etched into the delicate lines around her eyes. She holds up the pendant Liam gave me last night, her fingers gently tracing the intricate design.

"This locket, Birdie." She opens it up and presses it closed. "Where did it come from? It looks exactly like the one…"

Her voice trails off, but her worry is clear. We don't often talk about that day—the one where everything changed. I was never the same after that. None of us were.

My mom spent hours with me in that pasture searching for the necklace. I'd come home from school, we'd visit my grandma at the hospital, and then we'd get our tall boots on and head outside to search until nightfall. She wanted to stop well before I did, but I thought if we could find that locket, maybe I'd get a piece of my grandma back. My mom knew it was illogical, but she still came out with me every day to search. I didn't give up for months, but when the first snowfall came, I knew it was gone forever.

"I know," I say, resting my elbows on the kitchen island. "It's exactly how I remember it."

"But it can't be the one my…"

Her voice trails off.

"That Grandma gave you. Can it?"

"No." I squeeze my eyes shut. "It was Liam's birthday gift to me. He gave it to me last night."

"Oh, Birdie girl."

My mom narrows her eyebrows and hands it to me. I put it back in the box.

"How did he know?" She presses her hands into the counter until they turn white.

"I must have mentioned something to him." I shrug.

I downplay it all, but I remember the night I opened up to Liam about my grandma's accident and the locket that I was never able to get out of my mind. He's the first person I shared any of this with.

"You told him about the accident? About your beautiful grandma?"

"It's no big deal, Mom. We talked about a lot of things." I fix my eyes downward on the mug in front of me.

"Oh, honey." She grabs a cup of coffee and sits at the circular table in the corner by the large bay window. "It is a big deal."

"Birdie," she continues, tracing her finger along the rim of her mug. "You are the very best thing that's ever happened to me. But I worry about you. We're so close that you don't often let other people into that beautiful soul of yours. You wear your pain like a shield. So the fact that you told a boy about the worst day of your life is a very big deal—in all the best ways."

"You're being dramatic." I hop up onto the counter, crossing my feet at the ankles. "It's you and me against the world, Mom. I don't need anyone else."

She shakes her head. "That's what worries me, Birdie. Maybe we are too close. I spent my entire life trying to protect you, and I should have spent more time letting you go."

"Mom." I press my palms into my eyes, rubbing in a circular motion. "You've been my safe place. All those times that Dad would disappoint me and never follow through, you were there. You're the one who told me I needed to protect my heart."

Her face falls, and it's then I realize she's crying. She pats her hand against her wet cheek.

"Birdie," she says slowly, as if the sound of my name pains her. "Your dad was the worst. He never had it in him to live up to what you deserved in a parent."

She grabs a tissue and dabs the corners of her eyes. "Sometimes I think about what Liam does for a living. What he did for the nursing home. He calculates risk. He thought of all the different scenarios, all the roads we could travel down. And based on those data points, we came together to make a decision—risk versus reward."

My mom looks out the kitchen window and lets out a heavy sigh.

"If your dad had let you down once or twice," she continues, "I'd say, open up your heart. He'll figure it out. No one is perfect, and everyone is capable of letting someone else down. But it was hundreds of times, Birdie. So yes, I did want you to protect your heart from someone who was never going to be enough for you, never what you deserved. But I never wanted you to close yourself off to getting close to anyone."

I hop down from the counter. My head is fuzzy, and I wasn't prepared for this conversation, especially so early in the morning.

"Birdie." I glance over my shoulder as my mom pushes away from the window. "You get to make the decisions in your life. You're an adult, and at this point, I'm just as much your friend as I am your mom."

"But honey," she continues, "if you're going to write off every person who's disappointed you once or twice, you're going to live a very lonely life. That boy… well." She points at the box with the locket.

"If that isn't love, I don't know what is," she says. "And not just because it's beautiful, but because he clearly listens to you and understands what's important. Please don't block everyone out of your life because I chose the world's worst dad for you."

I turn away from my mom and wipe a tear. When our eyes meet, she stares at me.

"What am I supposed to do?" I ask.

She wraps her arms around me and whispers into my ear, "I can't answer that for you."

The cemetery remains my peaceful place. Maybe there's something wrong with me that I'd rather be among the dead than the living, but after talking to my mom, this is where I know I need to be. I can't stop thinking of Liam.

I told him things I never shared with friends I've known much longer or boys I've dated.

When he didn't show up at the gala, I completely wrote him off. I've always had a zero threshold for error. I blame my life for that. But it's never been about Liam.

It's always been about me. Broken, scared me.

I slip off my shoes, letting the long grass gently massage the soles of my feet. My fingers trace the cool surface of a headstone, and I glance at the name engraved: Beatrice Bergland.

"Hey there, Beatrice," I say aloud, the only person in the entire cemetery. "It appears we share a name. Maybe you're a relative of this man I can't stop thinking about. Liam. His dad's a jerk, but his grandparents, Sunny and Sis, are the most amazing people."

I sit next to the headstone and study the details of the stone and the etched words. "If you are related, you'd be proud of him. He's a pretty decent human."

A huge gust of wind comes out of nowhere.

"Hi, Beatrice," I say. "Thanks for visiting me."

The large oak trees cast cool shadows over me, shielding me from the sun. I lie back and gaze up at the billowy white clouds drifting across the sky.

"Okay," I finally say after lying there for much too long. "Enough."

By the time I get back to the house, it's well after dinnertime, and I've already blown off Bob's visit to the Hurst haunted house. Hopefully, he'll understand. I shower and decide to go to the nursing home to explain to Bob why I didn't show up for him today and maybe start organizing the donation room. When I was there yesterday, boxes were everywhere, and it needed some serious attention.

I walk into the main lobby but avoid seeing the staff by slipping through the chapel and down the long, deserted hallway. I reach the supply room at the end and quietly slip inside, unnoticed. The donations are a reminder of the love that surrounds this place. I gently close the door behind me.

"Birdie?" Liam's low voice rings out, and I cover my mouth to stifle a scream. My heart races.

He's in the corner, sitting on the floor, leaning against the wall. A box is open beside him, with piles of clothes separated—one for men, one for women.

"You nearly gave me a heart attack," I say, taking a deep breath. "What are you doing here?"

"Volunteering," he says, raising an eyebrow. "My first task. What are you doing here?"

I move a box aside and sit against the wall, positioned perpendicular to him. He hands me a box cutter, and I slice it open, spilling the clothes onto the floor.

"Same as you, I guess," I say. "I came in here yesterday and couldn't deal with the mess. We've caught the attention of the entire community, and donations are pouring in. But we don't have the time or resources to deal with it."

Liam nods and continues making neat piles. We work in silence for a few moments, sorting clothes, our breathing the only sound between us.

"I have to ask." I turn to face Liam, and he pauses. "If you turned down the New York job, what do you plan to do for a living?"

"It's still in the works," he says. "I filed the paperwork and am waiting to hear back from the state. But I'm starting my own consulting firm, something like an actuary. Very similar to what I did here at the nursing home. But instead of just laying out different risks, I want to help businesses like this one survive."

"There aren't enough businesses locally," I say, narrowing my eyes. "How will you make a living off that?"

Liam leans back and presses his head against the wall. "I've thought of that. I plan to stick to the Midwest initially. I've been doing research all summer. You'd be surprised at how many companies need someone like me."

"And to think you helped us for free," I say. "The services you provided for the nursing home—how much would that normally cost?"

Liam chuckles. "More than your mom could have afforded. Good thing this place is special to me."

I stare down at the barely worn women's clothes on my lap. Some of them still have tags on them. We could set up an entire room here where residents could come in and pick out their wardrobe.

"What does your dad think about this idea of yours?"

Liam presses his lips together. "Larry and I aren't talking at the moment, which is awkward because he and my mom are here for the holiday weekend and staying at the cottage with me. He's cut me off financially, which I fully expected."

"Ouch," I say. "But this is what you want? You're at peace with your decision?"

Liam nods. "I feel like I woke up at some point this summer, took stock of my life, and wondered who the hell I was making decisions for—because they weren't for me."

I look down at the pile, then move it out of my way. I cross my legs and face Liam.

"But New York…"

"It was my dream." He stretches his long legs out. "But dreams change. People change. The interview went great. I clicked with the CEO, and by the time dinner had finished that Thursday evening, he'd offered me the job. It would have been more money than I'd ever dreamed of making."

"Yet you're here," I say, avoiding his gaze.

"Millions of people live there, yet it felt empty," he says, running his fingers along the fabric of a blouse in his hand. "You weren't there."

"Liam." I hold my breath for a moment before exhaling. "You can't go from making decisions for your dad to making them for me."

Liam runs his tongue against the inside of his lip. "Trust me, Birdie. This decision was solely for me."

All the reasons I've kept pushing him away this summer swirl in my mind. He's leaving, and I've been afraid to get attached. He missed an event that meant a lot to me. But now, those reasons seem insignificant, almost nonexistent. The only thing left is my stubbornness—my reluctance to admit I've been wrong about so much and to finally allow myself to feel what I truly feel.

"Good," I finally say.

"Birdie." Liam presses his lips together. "I was being honest when I said I was scrappy. My feelings for you—they haven't changed. I don't think they ever will. But if you want me to back off, I will. Just say the word."

The moment has arrived—the one where I must choose whether to put myself out there and take the risk, or keep dancing around this uncertainty, fearing that I might eventually get hurt.

I push a pile of clothes between us out of the way and crawl toward him. Liam helps lift me until I'm straddling his lap. He wraps his arms around my waist, and I nuzzle my face into the perfect space between his neck and shoulder. My body melts into the solid warmth of Liam beneath me.

"There you are," he whispers, pressing his lips tenderly to my temple. "I've missed you."

We hold each other, our chests moving together, our breaths slowing as I sink farther into his embrace. His hand trails down my back, holding me close.

"I love you," I whisper into his soft skin.

Liam pulls back and cups my face. "You love me like you want to be my friend and have days at the lake? Or like you love me, love me?"

I laugh and cup his face, too. His eyes searching mine make me feel exposed, so I lean in and press my lips to his.

"Both."

Liam runs his hands down my arms until he grips my hips. I stretch back to reach the door of the small storage room and hit the lock button. A smile tugs at the corner of his mouth, and our lips meet in a passionate kiss. He lifts my shirt, then pauses, his hand brushing against the pendant he gave me.

"You're wearing it," he says softly. "Beautiful."

"I don't think I ever said thank you." I hold my hand over his. "My grandma would love you, too."

"I love you like I'll do everything in my power to never hurt or disappoint you," he says, kissing my neck.

"I love you like I will work to build trust with you every single day so you'll know I'm going to be a constant for you, and never someone who will let you down," he continues, kissing the other side of my neck.

"I love you in ways that I hope you'll never again feel alone in your experiences or traumas because I'll help carry the burden of them." Liam kisses my lips, and my heart swells with something foreign and heavy.

Hope.

Epilogue

9 Months Later

The nursing home is buzzing with activities today. Bob has agreed to do a reading from his newest novel during coffee. He's settled in nicely here, and we love chatting about all things paranormal whenever we're together. After that, the bus will take residents to a few stores, followed by bingo, and then the local high schoolers will stop by in their tuxedos and gowns on their way to prom.

There are only five empty rooms now, and it's hard to believe that just a year ago, when I started, half the building was vacant. I glance at my watch—it's nearly five, and I told Liam I'd meet him at the cottage by then. I shoot him a quick text that I'm heading home to change and might be a few minutes late. I slip into a summer dress, and before running out of my room, I catch my reflection in the mirror, rubbing my thumb along the ridge of my pendant.

"You off to Liam's?" my mom's voice calls from the kitchen, and I pop in.

"Oh." I pause in the doorway when I see him. "Hey, Bodhi. Hey, Mom. Yeah, I was supposed to meet him a while ago, but work ran late."

Bodhi is new in town, having moved from the cities to become a general surgeon at the hospital. My mom insists they're just friends, but I believe that about as much as she believed me when I said the same about Liam and me all last summer.

"Hi, Birdie," Bodhi says, pointing to a bag on the counter. "I was at the farmer's market and ended up buying way too much, so I brought some produce over."

I raise my eyebrows and smile. "That was nice of you."

"I thought I'd make my famous summer salad and sit out on the deck with a glass of wine," my mom says.

"Okay." I press my lips together to hide my grin. "Well, you two have a good night. I'll probably stay at Liam's tonight."

"I figured," she says. "Love you, honey."

The summer is already off to a hot start. I open the sunroof of my Jeep, letting my hair blow in the wind all the way out to the lake. When I pull into Liam's driveway, he's already outside, pacing. True to form, I'm running late, but he never told me why he needed me there at a specific time.

When he sees me, the worry etched on his face disappears, replaced by a wide smile. We have that calming effect on each other.

"You're late," he says, holding out his hand and pressing his body against mine as he kisses me.

"Work was crazy today," I reply, glancing at my watch. "And I'm not that late."

He opens the car door for me and then gets in on the driver's side.

"Where are we going?" I ask as he pulls out and drives down the gravel road.

"I want to show you something." He reaches across the middle console and takes my hand.

We drive south from the cottage, passing Camilla and Jake's house, then Dax and Carrie's bed and breakfast, and keep going.

"I've seen this lake a million times, you know?" I squeeze Liam's hand, sensing his nervousness.

"But you've never seen this spot," he says. "We're almost there."

Liam turns down a gravel road, taking a right, and suddenly, there are no other homes or cottages in view—just an opening on the lake.

He goes to the trunk and pulls out a blanket and a basket. He lays it down and then takes out a bottle of champagne. I don't ask questions. Instead, I lean back on my elbows and look out at the pristine, still lake, with only a couple of boats in view.

Liam hands me a glass and then leans back, too. "When I decided to stay in Wheaton, my dad and uncle said I had until May to figure things out since I was staying in a shared cottage. Now that summer is here, out-of-town relatives have signed up for their weeks. No one comes in the winter, so it was fine then."

"It's May," I say, and Liam nods. "You're out of time."

He stands and points. "Imagine standing at the sink, looking out at the south end of the lake. Or cuddling up with a book, looking north. Or sitting in a gazebo with a glass of wine, watching the sunset over the South Dakota hills."

Liam gestures to a stake in the ground that I hadn't noticed before. "I'm thinking three bedrooms on the main floor, and then in the loft, a primary bedroom with huge windows overlooking the lake. And back here, a large pole barn to store a plow, a boat—you know, lake stuff."

I stand and look around. "Wait, are you talking about this for yourself? I know you've loved being at the cottage, but if you build here, it will be hard to leave. You'll be tied to this place."

Liam inhales deeply, his chest rising. He presses his lips together. "Once I met you, I was never going to leave."

Most of me knows this, but there's still a small part of me that needs to hear it now and then.

"So, you're going to build a house here?"

He nods. "My grandparents bought this land when they first moved to the area. I've been in talks with Grandpa Sunny for a while now, and I just bought two-and-a-half acres. The land is mine."

"And," Liam says, taking my hand and intertwining his fingers with mine, "I know you have your reasons for taking things slow, but—"

"I always thought I'd wait until I was thirty before getting serious, you know?"

Liam laughs. "You didn't let me finish. I—"

"Wait." I place a finger over his lips, and he smiles. "Before you say anything, I don't need to wait until I'm thirty anymore. Because by then, you'll be nearly thirty-eight, and it wouldn't be fair to make you wait. And I don't want you to be an old dad."

Liam takes my finger and kisses it. "Can I finish, Birdie?"

"Yeah. Sorry."

"What I was going to say is that I want this house to be ours, but you can move in at your own pace. It can start with just a drawer full of essentials and grow from there. It's completely up to you."

Liam understands me.

He pulls me closer, resting his hand against the small of my back. "But this house will be ours. I want your opinions on the floor plan and design throughout the entire process. And…"

Liam's voice trails off. He gently lifts my chin and presses his lips to mine. "Unless your feelings change—because mine won't—we'll spend our lives together."

Liam reaches into his back pocket and pulls out a ring box. My breath catches in my throat, and I find it difficult to inhale. We've had many conversations over the past year, and I've admitted that I'm not sure I want a traditional marriage. I'm more interested in partnership and commitment.

But now he has a box. I panic.

Our eyes meet, and Liam chuckles.

"You can relax," he says. "I'll never ask you to marry me without your permission first. It won't be a surprise, and I won't put you on the spot."

He opens the box slowly, revealing a ring. It's a thick band, and I narrow my eyes to get a closer look. Liam holds it up.

"It's a promise—nothing more, nothing less." Liam holds up his hand, revealing a similar band on his pinky finger that I hadn't noticed. "I have one, too."

He takes my hand and places the ring in my palm. It's silver, with different birds etched around it. The curvy letters of B and L are woven throughout the design.

It's the perfect baby step—something only someone who knows me as well as Liam does would understand. I take the ring and slip it onto my ring finger, but it's too big, so I move it to my middle finger, where it fits perfectly. I continue to study it.

"It's beautiful."

He hooks his pinky with my finger so our rings touch. "Never underestimate a scrappy man in love."

It's perfect.

"Now, about the house," he says, looking out at the lake. "Does it scare you to death? Or not so much?"

I drape my arm around his waist and glance up at him. "Not so much."

"Good," he says. "I promised Grandpa and Grandma we'd be back for root beer floats and to see the prom kids."

"Plus"—Liam leans in and whispers in my ear—"I showed them the promise ring I planned to give you, and I'm sure they'll want to see it."

"Of course, they already know." I shake my head, laughing.

I feel like a high school girl receiving a promise ring from a boyfriend as we both prepare to go off to different colleges. But I also feel seen.

Liam drives us back to town. I hold his hand, looking out the window as we pass miles of cornfields with rolling hills behind them. It's been a busy year, and I barely recognize where my life was a year ago. My mom owns a nursing home that's thriving, and I'm in love.

Never say never.

When we arrive, Liam opens the car door for me and takes my hand. We walk through the doors, and a huge group is gathered in the lobby.

"Congratulations," Sunny says, getting up from a chair to shake Liam's hand. "You're going to love that spot on the lake. It's one of my favorites."

Sunny glances at me. "And you walked through the door with my grandson, which means you're not entirely opposed."

I laugh. "I'm not. I'm very excited for him."

"For us," Liam says.

I glance at him and kiss his cheek.

My mom rounds the corner with Lucy, and when she sees me, a smile spreads across her entire face.

"You're still here, so that's good." She winks at me. "Does this mean I'll be in that big, old house all by myself?"

"We'll see." I shrug. "We're starting with a drawer and working our way up from there."

"You basically sleep at the cottage every night already," my mom says. "This isn't that big of a change. You know that, right?"

"Yes," I say slowly. "But that's very different from sharing a home with someone."

Lucy has been standing back, but when our eyes meet, she claps her hands. "Did I miss something? What's everyone talking about?"

"Liam is putting down roots and building a house on the lake. I'll move in—slowly, very slowly."

"Well, that is exciting," Lucy says. "As long as you still do girls' nights with me in town."

"You know I will." I glance down at my ring.

I look across the room to where Liam is still talking to his grandparents, and I spot Joe trying to leave as people walk in. I rush over to him.

"Joe," I say, grabbing his arm. "You can't go out. Stay here. We're going to have root beer floats."

"I hate this place," he grumbles.

"Yeah, I know." I help him into a chair. "But it would be so boring here without you."

"Well, I won't argue with you there."

Joe sits on the couch, and I join him. I look around the room as the residents are handed their floats. Liam stands in the corner talking to Bob, and when our eyes meet, I smile. The wall behind him is full of plaques from all the donors, and next to that, it's covered with photos of residents we've lost. When Marilyn passed away a few months ago, I hung her photo right next to Abigail's.

Liam disappears down the hallway just as some of the prom kids arrive. Joe and I turn to watch the teenagers walk in, adorned in beautiful gowns and tuxedos.

"Okay, Joe," I say. "I'm going to go find that boyfriend of mine."

"Looks like you won't have to." Joe points, and I gasp.

Liam comes down the hallway in a tux. I cover my mouth to hide my smile and surprise. He holds out his hand to me.

"Since I missed the gala last year, I know you've been dying to see me in a tux."

"Okay," I say slowly.

He spins and he does look very handsome, but I suddenly feel extremely underdressed.

"I've signed us up to be prom chaperones," he says. "There's a beautiful gown waiting for you at home. Will you go to prom with me?"

My mouth drops open, but I'm too stunned to speak. "You're serious, aren't you?"

"What do you say, Birdie?" He takes my hand and spins me.

"Okay." I kiss his cheek. "Let's do it."

About the Author

When she isn't writing novels featuring strong female leads on a path to self-discovery, Leah Omar makes her career at a global medical device company. From Eyota, Minnesota, she holds bachelor's degrees in communications and English literature and a master's in business administration from Augsburg University in Minneapolis.

As a writer, Leah is devoted to giving her readers contemporary love stories that make us remember that we have more similarities than differences, and that love can conquer all. When Leah's not busy writing women's fiction and romance, she can be found watching a basketball game on TV, traveling somewhere far away, eating something spicy, or trying to shape the lives of her two amazing kids.

Leah now calls Minneapolis home, which she shares with her husband and two kids.

Check out more from Leah at: www.leahomarbooks.com

www.ingramcontent.com/pod-product-compliance
Lightning Source LLC
LaVergne TN
LVHW091704070526
838199LV00050B/2272